EXODUS FROM TREACHERY

Gwen Richardson

EXODUS FROM TREACHERY

Gwen Richardson

EXODUS FROM TREACHERY.

For information: Cushcity Communications, 14300 Cornerstone Village Dr., Suite 370, Houston, TX 77014.

FIRST EDITION

Cover design by Fran Krailo and Sergius

ISBN: 978-1-7374496-5-2
ISBN-10: 173744965X

10 9 8 7 6 5 4 3 2 1

To all who understand what it means to watch, fight, and pray

PROLOGUE

The members of the group of twelve were seated around a large, oval-shaped, mahogany conference table, waiting for the dossiers of the potential political candidates to be uploaded to their individual tablets for review. The group, known within their limited circle as "The Committee," met only a few times a year but never in the same location on two consecutive occasions. Meeting face to face was risky, but every conceivable precaution was taken to ensure the Committee's secrecy.

They were an extremely cautious bunch. There was no paper or digital trail connecting the twelve to each other nor to the unsavory, but necessary, deeds they often set in motion. They had underlings, or henchmen thrice removed, to perform the actual dirty work while they awaited the outcomes via twenty-four-hour news outlets or social media platforms.

There was no limit to what they would do to achieve their goals; they were self-appointed masters of the universe and did not believe in or answer to a higher authority. As far as they were concerned, their power was only limited by their ability to bend others to their will.

The more squeamish among them—and there were a few—experienced frequent bouts of ulcer-producing stomach cramps that endured for several days preceding and after their meetings occurred. Yet their abdominal discomfort did not dissuade them from casting an affirmative vote when an action was deemed necessary.

Among the ranks of the Committee were two attorneys, one physician, two real estate tycoons, one retired architect, a book publisher, a media mogul, two heads of Silicon Valley corporations, and two oil barons. There were at least three billionaires among them with the remainder not far behind in terms of net worth. They were all financially secure enough that salaries were no longer needed to sustain their opulent lifestyles. They lived off the accrued interest and dividends on their substantial investments, as well as the kickbacks from the multi-billion dollar contracts they secured with government entities around the world. Their kickbacks were usually buried within trillion-dollar legislation passed by Congress that had been strategically positioned to fill the coffers of the well-heeled members of the Committee.

Their leader, attorney Michael Goldberg, commenced the meeting by pounding a wooden gavel against its base, the sound of which broke the hum of low-decibel murmurs that hovered around the room.

"This meeting is now called to order," he said in his authoritative baritone. Michael's voice had always commanded respect but was also useful in the romance department. He'd charmed the panties off more than his share of women, including his current—and third—wife, Heather.

"We're here to review the list we've compiled of potential candidates for the upcoming election cycle," announced Michael. "The ten individuals shown on your screens represent the most promising prospective Senate candidates that we'll support in the primaries. We need to narrow down the list to the best three people in both political parties and then approach them one by one with our usual offer package of fame, funding, and personnel. Once we get one of them elected, he'll be ours for life."

"He or she," chimed in Sarah Reiner. "It could be a woman." The retired architect among them, Sarah was also a die-hard feminist. Michael didn't know her back then because she was more than twenty years his senior, but according to legend, in the 1970s, she had marched in the streets with Betty Friedan and Pauli Murray as they all burned their bras for the cause of gender equality. She still wore her hair in the same straight, stringy style she had worn back then, along with her oversized round eyeglasses. Like she had in her twenties, Sarah wore no makeup and little jewelry. What would have been considered natural beauty in the 1970s was now reduced to mostly wrinkles, age spots, and crow's feet. Now well into her eighties, her mind was still sharp, but in conversations, she had a tendency to dwell on the past.

Michael smiled. He'd learned to expect these sorts of outbursts from Sarah, and he usually took care to couch his pronouncements about their targets in gender-neutral terms. This time he forgot.

"You're right, of course, Sarah. When we make the final decision, as always, we'll select the candidate who most closely matches the qualities we are seeking—one who best suits our purposes."

The others nodded in agreement. Seats in the U. S. Senate and House of Representatives, governorships—and even the presidency—were not beyond the Committee's reach. Over the past ten years, they'd backed nearly thirty Senate and congressional candidates to election victory, making sure they were strategically placed on the most powerful legislative committees. And there were several presidential candidates they were eyeing for the next national election cycle. The candidate's political party made no difference as the Committee was decidedly non-partisan. The smart money always plays both sides. Their strategy was all about power.

Michael preferred that their final choice not be a woman. His world view hadn't changed much since the 1990s when he first got involved in behind-the-scenes politics. His views would be considered antiquated if publicly known, but he kept his opinions close to the vest. His personal technique of analyzing behavioral patterns and trends to draw his own conclusions hadn't failed him yet.

Michael was well aware of the women's movement, the Me Too movement, and the "woke" crowd, but he refused to be politically correct—at least not in public. Men and women were different, and that was all there was to it.

Based on his observations, women tended to be schemers, plotters, and long-term planners. In fact, women were often two steps ahead of the traps the Committee set for them and were less easily manipulated by the tactics the Committee utilized. But women's emotions often got in the way. Between the two sexes, men had the most outsized egos by far, and their egos were fragile and easily bruised.

The bigger one's ego, the more easily one could be manipulated. Bigger egos also meant bigger skeletons in their closets. The skeletal bones could be mangled remains from past indiscretions, or the potential target's lapses in judgment could be ongoing, making them ripe for present surveillance so they could be caught in nefarious acts. But candidates' skeletons were the key ingredient to the Committee's success. The clandestine group of twelve had myriad seductive tricks in its arsenal, and its members were looking for potential candidates that were as pliable—and easy to manipulate—as possible. And they were also very, very patient.

CHAPTER 1

Lloyd Palmer sat at his desk and stared at his news division's quarterly budget report that had just landed in his email in box. He blinked—just to make sure he wasn't seeing things—and then stared again. Despite refocusing his vision, the numbers on the spreadsheet were still there; they hadn't changed. The publishing executives whose offices were on the top floor of the Houston *Ledger* headquarters were cutting his budget—again.

Years ago, when he accepted the news editor's job at the *Ledger*, the largest daily newspaper in Texas, he knew that the news business was in a tumultuous state. Every newspaper editor in the country had been cutting their budgets year after year, engaged in a perpetual rat race to stay ahead of the constantly decreasing circulation as fewer and fewer readers under the age of fifty received their news in paper form.

Some daily newspapers had taken dramatic steps to survive, like publishing print editions only three days per week or foregoing a print edition altogether. But all of them had, long ago, lost most of their younger readers; the Internet, social media platforms, and twenty-four-hour cable news stations had claimed them for good. The *Ledger*, like so many other papers, had a readership of mostly senior citizens, and even they were getting tougher and tougher to retain. Its base market of readers was literally dying year by year.

The framed *Time* magazine cover hanging in Lloyd's office behind his desk was a constant reminder of the high standard he sought to meet. The cover featured his image and the headline, "Can Lloyd Palmer Change the Face of Journalism?" The article portrayed him as a modern-day crusader willing to do whatever it took to uncover the truth.

None of this dissuaded Lloyd from pursuing his original plan to refashion the newspaper's content so the *Ledger* would actually report stories on matters of substance instead of elevating the most bizarre human behavior of the day to heroic proportions. He'd save that for the tabloids.

He knew he would be going against the existing grain within the news industry, but so what? Yet events seemed to be in control of his decision making. He knew they were competing for eyeballs with social media and YouTube, but he also knew there were instances when the interests of reporting jaw-dropping events and newsworthy developments coincided. That was the sweet spot he constantly sought.

Lloyd had recommended the *Ledger* use "click bait" to increase eyeballs and boost advertising revenue on their website, and the tech department had revamped their site to try to make it more appealing. Featuring celebrity gossip, fashion tips, and funny cell phone videos seemed to be working, but his efforts to keep pace with online trends made him feel like a hamster panting for breath on a wheel.

And it was nearly impossible to stay ahead of the enormous wave of TikTok and Instagram videos. Thank God for obits—people didn't seem to mind the high prices the *Ledger* charged for posting a one-day announcement about the death of a loved one. If not for the obits and clickbait,

Lloyd would have had to reduce his staff down to a skeleton crew.

He'd pushed back hard against the hefty budget cuts his news department received each quarter. After each one of these financial "realignments," as his bosses called them, Lloyd would go into their offices and argue for more funds. Sometimes he would win, sometimes he would lose, but he was determined not to go down without a fight.

While assessing his budgetary decisions, he reflected on the question his dear African friend, Rudo Hamisi, had asked him years ago while Lloyd was still a reporter: *You do not tell readers what they need to know?* Keeping that question at his core kept Lloyd from falling into the ever-present morass of the news business: reporting mostly about sleaze and scandal. That was because Hamisi was more than a friend.

Lloyd always thought that the African's deep ebony skin tone belied his actual age. Hamisi seemed to be simultaneously ancient and futuristic, wise beyond measure. As a member of the ancient Lemba tribe, Hamisi existed in a world of certainty built on a blood line and traditions that spanned five hundred generations. In Lloyd's reality, when it came to what was considered newsworthy, the ground beneath him was constantly shifting toward fluidity and inevitable uncertainty. But Hamisi was a touchstone for Lloyd's ideals as a journalist, reminding him of the naïve young reporter he was when he received his first news assignment decades ago.

On that fateful day when Wilson Cox, the *Ledger*'s executive vice president, had called Lloyd into his office and informed him about his promotion to editor, it had taken some convincing for him to accept. But Cox had really laid it on thick.

"Lloyd, you're exactly what this paper needs to be competitive in the future," said Cox. "We need to be able to appeal to a younger, more diverse demographic. Besides, with your boosted national profile, you've given the *Ledger* the kind of credibility newspaper publishers would die for. New readers will flock to the paper in droves once we announce that you're taking over the reins."

While he was still a reporter, Lloyd had become a household name when he uncovered a mother's complicity in the murder and kidnapping of her infant son, Hunter. The mother, Christina Pauley, a local wealthy socialite, actually murdered her own child and falsely accused a fictitious Black man of the crime. To get the actual facts about the murder, Lloyd had to go to great lengths far beyond his role as a reporter and actually do some detective work. Once he uncovered the crime, his advice to the newspaper's executive team had also saved the *Ledger* from what could have been a devastating legal entanglement.

The previous editor, Ed Jackson, was not only a bigot but was sent to prison for conspiracy to commit murder—with Lloyd as his target. Jackson had fifteen years to go on the twenty-year sentence he had received. After the negative publicity the paper received from Jackson's actions, Cox believed the *Ledger's* only viable option to resolve its public relations nightmare was to appoint Lloyd as the paper's savior. Lloyd had the upper hand, which gave him leverage when presenting his demands before he had signed the multi-year contract.

"Mr. Cox, I appreciate the offer and the confidence you're showing by promoting me to editor, but before I accept the position, I have a few non-negotiables."

"Okay, I'm listening." Cox folded his arms and replied with marked anticipation.

"First, I would need to have the final say-so regarding the news that goes into the paper. That includes reporting assignments, headlines, front page placement above and below the fold, and what goes on the inside."

"No problem. All of our editors have that."

Lloyd wanted to make sure Cox was clear about this request. "But I'm serious about not being challenged by the executives about what the *Ledger* should be reporting."

"I assure you that you'll have no challenges whatsoever."

"Second, I need full authority over all hiring and firing decisions in my department. I only want reporters and staff working for me who are highly skilled and can get on board with the paper's new direction. If I meet some resistance, I want to be able to eliminate whoever is standing in the way of progress. And I don't want to be undermined by the executives upstairs."

"Done. Anything else?"

This was going a lot smoother than Lloyd had expected, but Cox was obviously willing to bend over backward to repair the paper's reputation and keep the *Ledger* afloat. Lloyd continued with his list of demands.

"My salary needs to be at least $80,000 a year with comprehensive family health insurance fully paid for by the *Ledger*, plus an additional week's vacation."

Cox was less eager to agree with this condition on Lloyd's list. The paper had only so many resources. But he was between a rock and a hard place since Lloyd was the best hope for the paper's future success. Cox shrugged his shoulders and exhaled. "That's a little steep, but we can make it work. As long as the *Ledger*'s circulation remains steady, you have complete control over the expenditures in your department, including salaries. Do we have a deal?" Cox said, extending his hand to Lloyd for a handshake.

"As long as all of my terms are put in writing, then you've got a deal."

Cox had the *Ledger*'s in-house counsel draw up the employment contract and presented it to Lloyd the next day. He'd started his job as editor a month later, and he'd been in the position now for five years.

But how did they expect him to cover the constant flow of newsworthy events in the Houston area and throughout the state with the dwindling resources he had at his disposal to spend on personnel? This quarter, the head honchos had cut his budget by nearly twenty thousand dollars compared to the quarter before.

Fortunately, he had been able to retain most of the top reporters in his department, even with the budget cuts. But eventually he was going to have to make some tough personnel decisions. Lloyd's reputation as a straight shooter, in addition to his national prominence, had gained him the respect of nearly every journalist in the country. He regularly made the rounds on all of the cable news stations as a go-to source for news about the Bayou City and the Lone Star State. That helped keep the *Ledger*'s name in the public's consciousness.

And because of the paper's reputation, lots of reporters—both new and experienced—wanted to work at the *Ledger*.

There wasn't a week that went by when Lloyd didn't receive at least a dozen resumés from potential reporters looking to join the *Ledger*'s staff. But hiring from outside the *Ledger* was a non-starter. Most of the reporters who worked for him were willing to at least meet him halfway in terms of salary demands until, hopefully, the paper's revenues stabilized. Lloyd couldn't hire anyone new unless one of the existing reporters made their exit.

There were a couple of holdouts who had been at the *Ledger* long before Lloyd joined the staff and didn't like the idea that they had been passed over for promotion when Lloyd became editor. Warren Blackstone and Jane Paulsen both had been with the *Ledger* for over twenty years and had made it clear they wanted the editor's job. They both considered it a personal affront that they were passed over for Lloyd to take the position.

Lloyd had to constantly look over his shoulder so he wouldn't be a victim of their backstabbing machinations. They never passed up the opportunity to undermine his authority and his new initiatives. Blackstone was a perpetual thorn in Lloyd's side, and he had mouthed off during one of their recent exchanges. Blackstone had presented a story to Lloyd for publication in which he attributed the underlying facts to only one unnamed source; in other words, the reporting was sloppy.

"You do realize you work for me and not the other way around, don't you?" Lloyd asked Blackstone pointedly.

Blackstone fumed. "What do you mean?"

"As your editor, I have an expectation of professionalism in your work product. Also, I can terminate your employment with the *Ledger,* and I won't hesitate to do it if you refuse to follow my directives. Is that clear?" Lloyd said emphatically.

Blackstone was not pleased and stood up to leave Lloyd's office. "Yes. Is that all, sir?"

"As long as you understand my expectations, then, yes, that is all for now."

Blackstone's posture was one of defiance, and Lloyd knew that wouldn't be the last time the two of them would butt heads. Lloyd would be glad when both Blackstone and Paulsen finally retired because the prospect of firing them created a whole other set of problems.

Neither Blackstone nor Paulsen hesitated to send Cox pointed emails about what they believed were Lloyd's obvious shortcomings. They were flustered by the most mundane of perceived slights and were always complaining that their stories weren't prominent enough on the paper's website or the printed edition. Fortunately, Cox kept Lloyd in the loop regarding the shenanigans that occurred behind the scenes.

"I just got another email from Paulsen," said Cox, during a recent phone conversation. "Is there something I need to handle?"

"No, Wilson, I have it under control," replied Lloyd, knowing that involving Cox would only make matters worse. If he had learned anything from his years as a reporter, it was that respect had to be earned; it couldn't be commanded from a higher authority. Having Cox serve as a referee to settle news division squabbles would only make Lloyd look weak.

In many ways, luck had been on Lloyd's side since he'd taken over as editor. Some of the nation's more recent misfortunes had translated into increased circulation for the

Ledger's print edition and an arc in traffic to the paper's website. Police brutality against unarmed African-American men had sparked national outrage resulting in worldwide demonstrations. This had allowed Lloyd to justify sending half a dozen reporters into the field for on-the-scene interviews and reactions.

A global pandemic and a contentious presidential election—following which, even two years later, millions questioned the outcome—had also heightened reader interest. Yet events seemed to control Lloyd's decision making rather than the other way around. For all of his high ideals, the newspaper was still essentially the purveyor of bad news; in other words, if it bleeds, it leads.

He remembered one of the last things Hamisi had said to him before he left town years ago. "Lloyd, as the *Ledger*'s editor, you could be in the position to determine what readers believe is truth and what isn't."

Hamisi believed Lloyd could not only better inform the public but also perhaps help lower the political and social temperature with an even-handed approach. In an era where consumers were constantly bombarded with misinformation, Lloyd's decision making could result in a more enlightened readership. The idea that Lloyd could wield that kind of power was scary but also humbling.

But the news competition was fierce, and the *Ledger* had to keep up with the proverbial Joneses in the media universe. Every year he felt like he was treading water, hoping that the decisions he made would keep his department afloat without betraying his principles.

Lloyd was disturbed by the constant focus on high-speed car chases that ended in multi-car explosions; a missing toddler whose lifeless body was later found in a wooded area; and women brutally pummeled in acts of domestic violence or shot in front of their children. He really wanted the paper to do more than report on the most tragic things that happened in Houston every day. If only things were that simple.

CHAPTER 2

There was a knock on Lloyd's office door, and Charles Scott poked his head in. Charles was one of the *Ledger*'s top reporters, a close friend, and Lloyd's strongest ally at the paper. Lloyd could hear the familiar sounds of newsroom chatter among the reporters and support staff behind the slightly opened door even as he continued to study the spreadsheet before him.

"Got a minute, Lloyd?"

"Sure, Charles. Come on in and have a seat," Lloyd responded as Charles sat in the leather-backed armchair across from his desk. "I'm just going over these latest budget figures," lamented Lloyd with his eyes still on his computer screen. "They've cut our budget again. If they keep shrinking our personnel allocations, I'm going to have to eliminate one of our administrative aides or, even worse, a reporter. I don't know how many more of these cuts we can take."

"I know you'll work it out, Lloyd. But if you have to lay me off, just let me know a couple of weeks in advance so I can use all my vacation time first," Charles said with a jovial laugh.

Charles's laugh was infectious, and his humor was a welcome distraction. "I doubt it will come to that, but I'm glad to see you have a sense of humor about it. But I know you didn't come in to talk about the budget. What's up?"

"Well, I discovered something that seems to be a little suspicious with one of the Texas senatorial campaigns, but I need some time to dig deeper."

"What's suspicious about it?"

"I was checking the Federal Election Commission filing reports for the list of the contributors to each of the campaigns and noticed the name of a political action committee that I've never heard of before. It's a super PAC, and they call themselves Americans for True Freedom. They use the moniker AmFree on their social media pages. They've already contributed a boatload of money—over $20 million in fact—to incumbent members of the Congress and Senate throughout the state.

"And the contributions don't appear to favor one party over the other," Charles added. "They're hedging their bets by contributing to candidates in both parties."

"There's nothing unusual about that, Charles. Most of the lobbying outfits make donations to multiple candidates so they can have a seat at the table no matter who wins. We both know they really don't care who wins as long as their interests are protected."

"Plus, look at the story click count," Lloyd said as he nodded in the direction of the flat screen behind his desk that showed which stories on the *Ledger* website were getting the most traction. "The police chase on I-45, the NBA forward caught on a pleasure boat with his side chick, and the lost child wandering in a south-side apartment complex—those are the top stories of interest, in that order. The political stories we publish rarely get even a hundred clicks, unless a scandal is involved." Clicks translated into advertising revenue, which the *Ledger* sorely needed.

"But there's more," Charles persisted. "Other than the names of their president and legal counsel, I can't seem to find much else about them, and I wanted to investigate further to identify the PAC's key contributors. I know there's a major story here. I can feel it."

Lloyd folded his arms, indicating indifference. He loathed being captive to the paper's story click count and felt like he was betraying his profession when he constantly checked its status throughout the day. But he was already having to justify every penny in his department's budget, and having Charles go on what could turn out to be a wild goose chase seemed like a waste of their limited resources.

"Charles, you know there are literally hundreds of PACs. The floodgates opened after the Supreme Court's Citizens United decision that essentially made political contributions unlimited and private. There's more money in the system than ever before, and it's only going to get worse."

"The efforts by Congress to reform the system have been symbolic at best," Lloyd continued. "The lawmakers always leave themselves a loop hole so the cash can keep pouring into their coffers. You can't put the fox in charge of the henhouse. Why should we care about yet another PAC?"

"A couple of the candidates that AmFree backed won their seats as a result of competitors' scandals reported in the press at the eleventh hour only a few days before the election."

"That's nothing unusual, simply one of the tricks of the political trade," Lloyd said, half-listening and quickly losing interest as he focused on his computer screen and scrolled across the spreadsheet's rows, hoping somehow that the totals would change.

Charles persisted. "One guy's opponent was caught in bed with a nine-year-old boy, and the pictures were posted on social media a few days before the primary vote."

"I hope they didn't show the boy's face." Lloyd's response was an anxiety-filled half-question.

"No. Fortunately, whoever posted the photo obscured the boy's face to protect his identity, but the face of the guy running for office was clear and unmistakable. What's not so clear is who videotaped the sordid scene and how they knew enough about the candidate's lifestyle to start filming his bedroom activities."

That got Lloyd's attention, and he leaned back in his seat, musing. "You may have a point, Charles. You said there were two campaigns. What happened in the other one?"

"Well, for the other race, the guy's challenger was an attorney. The lawyer was running about six points ahead in the polls a week before the runoff, but then one of the investigative reporters at Channel 7 showed up at the attorney's house accusing him of bribing a judge."

"I remember hearing something about that situation," Lloyd interjected, trying to jog his memory. "I can't recall the details. Exactly what happened?"

"When the reporter asked him to respond, the unexpected presence of the television cameras clearly caught the attorney off guard. His expression was like a deer in the headlights. First he stammered incoherently, then he quickly collected his wits and claimed his innocence before abruptly closing the door. But the damage had already been done, and he lost by about four percentage points. The timing couldn't have been better—or worse, from the attorney's perspective. The judge the Channel 7 reporter referred to had already been suspected of taking bribes from other attorneys, so that gave the accusation some credibility."

"Now it's coming back to me," Lloyd reflected. "That attorney probably would have won the runoff too if that story hadn't blown up all over the news. But you know how these things go, Charles. Politics is a blood sport. Political campaigns collect opposition research for the distinct purpose of leaking it to the press at the last minute before the challenger has a chance to craft a reasonable response or to recover his campaign's momentum."

Charles was undeterred. "Lloyd, I have a feeling this is really important. Just give me a few days to look into it more thoroughly," he said, hoping his persistence would pay off.

Lloyd understood a reporter's instinctive need to follow up on a hunch. His own inquisitive nature was what had led him to go the extra mile in investigating the murder that had propelled him into the national spotlight. Charles's story had potential, but it was also tied to government corruption. The *Ledger*'s readers seemed to have become not only jaded but weary of the political machinations that seemed to now be so commonplace. Still, he had learned to trust Charles's instincts.

Lloyd thought for a moment and was willing to give Charles some leeway. After all, when Lloyd was a reporter, he had experienced an adrenaline rush whenever he could sense a major story was unfolding. A gut feeling—the nagging, nervous sense that there was more to a situation than meets the eye—often had more impact than the initial facts that a journalist uncovered.

That was one of the many things Lloyd missed about being in the field as a reporter. That's where the action was.

Plus, Charles had been the one person Lloyd could depend on—even if the situation might be dangerous.

"Do you think this group, AmFree, had a hand in what happened or that their involvement as a contributor to the eventual winner is simply a coincidence?" asked Lloyd.

"I just want to take a closer look. It could be nothing, but I have a hunch—and you of all people should know that hunches can lead to clues that can lead to breaking news stories."

Lloyd knew that all too well. As a result of following his hunch in the Pauley kidnapping, he was catapulted to national stardom. After he single-handedly solved the kidnapping scheme, he was on the cover of *Time* magazine. That feature story led to interviews by nearly every major newspaper and cable news outlet in America.

Lloyd relented. "Well, you can look into it, but don't let it consume all of your time. This sounds like the sort of project that could take months of research time and then end up being one big nothing burger. I still need you to be available to work on some of the hard news stories that surface throughout the week."

Lloyd could not believe how much he sounded like his old boss and nemesis, Ed Jackson, who would chip away at Lloyd's self-confidence with constant micro-aggressions. In classic Jackson bullying style, he would also thwart Lloyd's career advancement by discouraging him from pursuing leads about potential stories that didn't fit the if-it-bleeds-it-leads mold. The necessity of having to rein in any of his reporters' enthusiasm was one of the things Lloyd hated about being an editor.

Charles's impassioned response helped redirect Lloyd's thoughts to the here and now. "I'm on it, Lloyd, you know that," he said. Then he added, "I may incur some travel expenses," almost as an aside.

"Oh boy, here we go" Lloyd sighed. "Charles, you know how tight our budget is. How much money are we talking about?"

"I'm not sure, but most of my travel should be within the state or at least the region."

"You'll need to do most of your travel by car, stay in low-budget motels, and limit your per diem for meals to forty dollars a day. Does that seem doable?" Lloyd hoped the meager travel budget would dissuade him.

"I'm willing to be flexible. A few bed bug bites shouldn't be too painful," Charles joked. "But seriously, I usually only eat breakfast and dinner, so the per diem is manageable. So it's a go?" Charles asked, keeping his fingers crossed behind him.

Lloyd exhaled, shrugged, then made his decision. "I'll give you two weeks to come up with something concrete. After that, you're moving on. Understood?"

This was music to Charles's ears. "I love you, man. I'll get out of your hair and let you get back to your budgets," Charles said and winked at Lloyd as he opened the office door to leave.

"Ha, ha, very funny," replied Lloyd. Charles closed the door, and Lloyd reluctantly went back to tweaking the numbers on the spreadsheet for the upcoming quarter's expenses.

Lloyd's parents had come from meager beginnings in the small, rural town of Navasota, Texas. They were both laborers whose parents sharecropped cotton for most of their lives. They'd taught him the fine art of stretching a dollar until it hollered, but he would need to apply all of his parents' penny-pinching skills and then some to keep the *Ledger*'s news division afloat.

CHAPTER 3

Michael Goldberg strummed the fingers of his well-manicured right hand on his Dutch cedar desk as he reviewed a private placement memorandum for one of his multinational clients. The high-rise view from his thirtieth floor corner office in downtown Houston displayed the sprawling urban skyline in all its panoramic splendor. From his window, he had a bird's eye view of all the city's major landmarks—Buffalo Bayou, the historic Emancipation Park, the world-renowned Texas Medical Center, Minute Maid Park where the Houston Astros played in three World Series, and the NRG Stadium where the Houston Texans played their National Football League home games.

As a sought-after attorney and managing partner of Goldberg, Landon & Schein, Michael spent most of his days reviewing documents for multi-billion dollar business deals. He spent very little time in courtrooms; he had staff attorneys who took care of those types of routine tasks. Although his parents were wealthy, he had taken the Goldberg wealth chest to another level. He had become wealthy beyond even his wildest imagination, and he made a very good living representing well-heeled clients worldwide. Michael enjoyed the finer things in life and was accustomed to being chauffeured in a private car, and entering through a private entrance, and on a private elevator to a private floor.

Michael was always meticulously dressed and wore only the finest Italian, custom-designed suits and ties. Tom Ford and Gucci were among his favorite designers. With his six-foot, two-inch muscular physique, he was an imposing figure when he walked into a room. His dark hair with just a little gray at the temples added character to his face. Michael was a man of uber self-awareness. He realized his good looks were an asset and used them to his advantage.

The antique writing desk in Michael's office was a gift from his grandfather, Abraham Goldberg, a Hungarian immigrant who had started the law firm more than fifty years ago. After working his way through law school, Abraham had started the firm with five attorneys and only a handful of clients. Goldberg, Landon & Schein was now one of the fastest growing and most respected law firms in the country with offices in Houston, San Francisco, New York, and Hong Kong.

Michael's father, Jonah, was a workaholic and was only at home for brief periods of time. His travels worldwide servicing their international client list left little time for child-rearing, and he left that task to Michael's mother, Deborah. As a result, Michael spent an inordinate amount of time with his grandfather, and their bond was forged during Michael's formative years. Out of all five of Abraham's grandchildren, Michael was the one most likely to follow in his footsteps.

The two of them would go for car rides during his visits to his grandparents' summer home in Lake Jackson, Texas. They had frequent outings to Houston Astros baseball games, the library, the theater, and the ballet. He once traveled with his grandfather to New York City, where they visited the New York Stock Exchange and witnessed the ringing of the opening bell.

"If you're the smartest person in the room, you'll always come out ahead," Michael's grandfather used to tell him from the time he was only ten years old. Michael internalized that nugget of wisdom, among others, and embraced his grandfather's high expectations, graduating as valedictorian of his class at Harvard and near the top of his class at Harvard Law.

"There are some things you have to keep secret from your partners at the firm and even from your wife" was another one of his grandfather's axioms. That was the primary rule of thumb Michael used in his work with the Committee. Neither his wife, Heather, nor any of the partners at the firm knew about his clandestine activities, and he wanted to keep it that way. Conversely, the members of the Committee knew very little about his legal work or his clients. The best way to keep a secret was to tell no one. That adage didn't come from Michael's grandfather; he had developed it himself.

The identities of the Committee's members, its candidate selection process, nor its manipulation of elections could ever see the light of day—not ever. Such revelations would produce a scandal and trigger federal investigations that would ruin everything he had worked for. He had promised his father that the family's reputation and legacy would be safe in his hands—a promise he planned to keep.

His greatest challenge was keeping the egos of the Committee members in check. Any time a group of highly successful people convened, those around the table were confident about their IQs. Michael's balancing act was to keep them thinking they were steering things when, all the while, Michael was engineering the entire process and made sure the outcome of their efforts was the one he preordained.

He took extreme precautions to ensure the Committee's invisibility. Whenever there was a need for a meeting of the Committee to be called, Michael sent a coded text message to the other members of the group a few days before the gathering was to take place. He kept a well-hidden supply of burner phones and SIM cards underneath the false bottom of his office desk for this purpose. He never used his personal cell phone for Committee business, no matter the circumstance. And every morning he swept both his private office and his study at home for electronic listening and video devices.

Today was Tuesday, and the next Committee meeting was scheduled for Friday of next week—ten days from now. The Committee had four different meeting locations, so the text messages used the four seasons of the year to designate the location. They always met in the evening, so the text message Michael sent—*Summer 8*—alerted the members to meet at the home of the physician in the group on Friday night at eight o'clock.

Their meetings normally lasted about two hours, and outsiders were never allowed. The host of each meeting was required to conduct a sweep for electronic listening or video devices at the meeting location on the morning of the meeting day. The coded messages ensured secrecy, and the recipients' phone numbers were encrypted. Even if one of the members' phones was compromised or hacked, neither their plans nor the Committee's existence would be divulged.

The purpose of their gatherings was usually to review a slate of potential candidates for office. During their last meeting, Sarah Reiner had pitched a former professional athlete as a prospect.

"His name recognition is phenomenally high," Sarah enthusiastically asserted regarding Darrius Wayne Weaver, a former tight end for the Cleveland Browns. "He's made all the right moves in terms of his public profile since his retirement from the League, and he's been doing lots of work with well-respected non-profit organizations," she added. "Handsome with an incredible physique and a picture-perfect family—just the attributes we're looking for. He would also be a hell of a fundraiser, and donors would be lining up to contribute to his campaign." She was certain she'd given her strongest pitch yet at a Committee meeting.

Sarah had a confident exterior, but her confidence could be easily shaken if she was challenged. That was exactly what happened. She was abruptly interrupted by one of the real estate developers, who was clearly not impressed. "Our success rate with athletes has been well below fifty percent," he interjected. "Athletes have a tendency to crash and burn," continued the developer, who had built several strip malls in the ever-expanding high-income areas in the Houston metro area known as Tomball, Kingwood, and Sugar Land.

"They relish throngs of adoring fans and receive little media scrutiny during their athletic careers. Once they're off the field or the basketball court, they have difficulty making the adjustment to a political lifestyle, where they need to have coherent and logical answers to actual public policy questions."

The real estate developer didn't stop there. "Don't you remember what happened with the last two former NFL players we were grooming? The community townhall events that we organized because we thought the attendees would act like fawning groupies turned into fiascos."

Then he said the quiet part out loud. "And frankly, some of the athletes aren't very bright—and that's an understatement. They make arcane statements that are impossible to correct or clean up after the fact."

The Committee members held their collective breath and then exhaled. The real estate developer had expressed their feelings to a T. Then the book publisher, the media mogul, and the two oil barons around the table nodded in agreement.

The real estate developer, like other members of the Committee, was risk averse. The members liked to bet on sure things—as sure as things could be in the unpredictable realm of politics. Sarah, feeling defeated, acquiesced. For now, athletes represented a risk not worth taking.

Michael and members of the Committee all knew something that was unbeknownst to the voting public: By the time the candidates' names appeared on the ballot on primary or general election voting day, most of the political decisions had already been made. The deck had already been stacked. Voters' choices were inconsequential from the start.

The voters' routine exercise of going to the local precinct to cast a vote had a limited effect on the process or the outcome. In actuality, the candidates were selected by the rich and powerful—like members of the Committee—long before the campaigns even began.

Only those candidates backed by the powerful, largely unseen political kingmakers had any chance of mounting viable campaigns or winning. This axiom applied to both incumbents and challengers; it made no difference, although challengers had a much more difficult mountain to climb. But that was more a function of finances than fitness for office.

"We can't leave the prospects for our financial future to chance" was an oft-repeated phrase used by the Committee's lone physician. She was the member most mindful of the status of the Committee's sizeable war chest as it was her job to keep tabs on all of the Committee's various accounts.

She also administered and dispersed money transfers to specific politicians' coffers through their political action committee, Americans for True Freedom, whose name was patriotic and ambiguous enough not to draw much attention. The registered agent's office was located in Brookshire, a little Texas town far from media scrutiny, but the money transfers were funneled through a labyrinth of LLCs and shell companies, rendering the transactions essentially untraceable.

Although she held the title of physician, she hadn't practiced medicine in several years and was able to live lavishly on the investments she'd made through her contacts with the Committee. Their scheme was brilliant. Before an IPO was announced to the public, a broker who cut deals for Committee members would let them know the timeline for the deal. The members were among the early shareholders who purchased stocks just as the new shares were issued. Once the stock exchanges opened all the members—at a minimum—quadrupled their initial investment in a matter of hours.

The physician identified other money schemes for the Committee to employ. Its funds were invested into financial instruments that were used to fund high-interest loans for financially strapped consumers. Payday loans, high-interest credit cards or lines of credit, and cash for auto title loans were gravy trains for the entities that fronted the funds. By investing in these instruments, the Committee usually doubled its money within two years.

A woman who believed she deserved the very best things life had to offer, the physician wore clothes and shoes by the top fashion designers. She owned more than a million dollars of jewelry from designers like Tiffany, Dior, and Harry Winston. She often graced these eye-catching pieces on her forays to cocktail parties, the ballet, and the theater.

Her home base was in The Woodlands, Texas, a planned development north of Houston, but she also owned plush condos in Vail, Honolulu, and Santorini, Greece. She had chosen the profession and used the title in front of her name for the sake of prestige, but as a lifelong germaphobe, she had no interest in actually touching, treating, or examining patients.

Michael had given her carte blanche to manage the funds as she saw fit. "Just make sure none of it can be traced back to any of us," he'd told her last month during one of their periodic trysts at Houston's downtown Four Seasons Hotel. The hotel was close to Michael's office and convenient for a mid-afternoon rendezvous. Their relationship, if one could call it that, was on-again off-again. Michael had made it clear there were no strings attached and there was no chance of him leaving his third wife, Heather. Still, the physician was hopeful he'd eventually commit to her being his exclusive side chick in the future.

Breathless and sweaty after an hour of vigorous lovemaking, she'd asked him if he had any preferences about where the Committee's funds were distributed. "I'll leave it to your discretion," he'd replied.

The physician kept track of the Committee's funds—which totaled more than $500 million—offshore in a number of different countries, like the Caymen Islands, Switzerland, Singapore, and Belize. When funds were needed, the money was transferred using a complex web of LLC accounts and a minimum of five different financial institutions.

The Committee had also stashed duffle bags filled with cash and had them strategically placed in airport and train station lockers around the world for situations where ready cash was the preferred form of payment. This reservoir of riches was available to them at any given time to pay the numerous contractors they hired to tip the electoral scales in their favor. They had a team of couriers, none of whom knew each other, whenever a cash exchange was required. Utilizing the same methods as a group of terrorist cells, they made sure that none of the dozens of operatives within their vast web of clandestine treachery would ever be able to connect the dots.

The Committee was able to amass its wealth chest through carefully crafted earmarks strategically inserted within massive pieces of legislation. Over the ten years of the Committee's existence, they had funded or contributed substantially to the campaigns of eighty-four Congressmembers and Senators—enough to tilt almost any legislation in their favor.

With bills often exceeding two thousand pages that members of Congress were required to vote on within forty-eight hours after receipt, even the congressional staffers couldn't read the legislation fast enough to zero in on all the details. When these bills quickly came to the congressional floor for a vote, the Committee's henchmen and women voted as they were instructed to do.

If any questions were asked about the earmarks, which rarely happened, the job of the Committee's cohorts was to steer the media and their fellow legislators in a different direction. Like small children, most media operatives suffered from short attention spans. By the time they were done chasing their tails looking for and tweeting about this or that, the bills had already been passed.

Ten million dollars here, fifty million there—sometimes the Committee was even able to sneak through one hundred million or more—and it had taken them less than ten years to reach the magic mark of five hundred million. These payments went largely undetected by the public and easily distracted reporters who were lost in the fog of the ubiquitous social media bubble.

Trillion-dollar crisis bills were the best vehicles of all to siphon millions of dollars with little to no scrutiny. In the midst of a crisis, the entire nation was largely driven by fear. Military engagements, wars on terror, natural disasters, extreme weather events, global pandemics—the nature of the crisis did not matter.

"Fear is one of the easiest emotions to manipulate," Michael's grandfather had once told him. "Fear makes people hide in a metaphorical cave," his grandfather had elaborated, "refusing to look at what is happening while, at the same time, hoping not to become one of the victims of the crisis at hand." Michael adored his papa's sage wisdom, which was a lot more prescient than any of the modern-day predictions espoused by so-called experts.

The Committee had invested wisely in terms of their candidate selections. For the chosen few among the candidates, the wheels had already been greased. But the average citizen still believed they held the power. Blinded by emotion, they became intensely invested in the outcomes of each election cycle. That was the beauty of the system and the Committee used it to their advantage.

CHAPTER 4

Charles Scott loved being a reporter; it was his lifelong dream. His inspiration began in childhood as he watched nightly news broadcasts, the contents of which he would share at school during times designated for current events. He admired network news anchors like Dan Rather, Peter Jennings, and Tom Brokaw but was also inspired by the *Superman* movies of the 1980s starring Christopher Reeve. By age ten, Charles had watched this series of movies multiple times. He thought that Clark Kent using the disguise of being a reporter to camouflage his true identity as Superman was the coolest thing he'd ever seen.

Charles even bought a pair of the same horn-rimmed, book-nerd eyeglasses Kent used to wear and wore them to his elementary school. His teachers got the wrong idea and thought he was sight-impaired. But he thought the eyeglasses made him look smart—as if he knew secrets the other kids didn't know. That certainly suited his ambitions, since reporters always seemed to know things that other people didn't.

He quickly followed his dream and became the editor of his school newspapers, both in high school and college. And he attended every journalism conference his meager budget could afford. Sometimes he got lucky; there were a couple of times when the dean of the School of Journalism included him in the department's travel budget as a representative of the university.

After being in his chosen profession for the past seventeen years, one of the best benefits to being a reporter was the independence. He had no ambitions to be promoted to the ranks of editor or even associate editor. He saw how hard Lloyd had to work to try to appease those whose offices were on the top floors of the building in the executive suite and those below in the news room. He'd rather be water-boarded than have to deal with those headaches. After spending so many years in the industry, Charles was at the top of the journalistic food chain as a reporter and now had his pick of assignments.

Charles also liked solving riddles. He got a kick out of starting with one small fact about a potential story and following wherever it led. That small fact became a thread, and after researching it for days, weeks, or even months, he was able to piece the threads together until the riddle was finally solved. Solving riddles gave him an immense sense of satisfaction.

Most of today's journalists sought the limelight, choosing the profession in hopes of landing a regular gig as a go-to analyst on one of the cable news networks or a lucrative book deal with a hefty advance. Instead of treating journalism with the objectivity it required, they became political commentators, partisans who chose sides rather than remaining neutral.

But not Charles. He preferred to be low key in his profession, saving the excitement for his personal life. As a confirmed bachelor and a ladies' man, he had his pick of many desirable women. During his adult years there were a couple of women who had almost gotten him to the altar, but he always got cold feet as the wedding day approached. None of those women had been able to seal the deal. He just wasn't ready to sleep with the same woman night after night into infinity.

Yet, his chosen profession didn't offer many dating options in the workplace. The exception could be Chelsea Bannon, a new reporter Lloyd had recently hired who was a real looker. She was thin with bounteous locks of auburn hair and had an amazing body. Charles didn't know whether she had a regular workout routine or was simply blessed with good genes, but she filled out her clothes perfectly in all the right places.

So far Charles had only engaged her in idle office chitchat, but he hadn't ruled her out entirely for a possible hookup. When she was in the newsroom, she created quite a distraction—not only for him but also for the other male reporters at the *Ledger*. Heads turned when Chelsea strolled into the newsroom, and the perfume she wore left a lingering scent for several minutes after her departure.

Charles had to shake himself out of his daydreaming about Chelsea and focus on this latest political puzzle for the moment. After his discussion with Lloyd, he was determined to piece together what appeared to be a number of disparate events; he was certain they were all connected. He could feel it. Over the years, he had learned to trust his instincts, which had led him in the right direction regarding breaking news. His instincts had garnered him dozens of front-page news story bylines. When he followed his internal antenna, he was generally on the right track.

The PAC that he had recently discovered, AmFree, presented a new challenge. So far the information he'd found on the group was scant, but he was sure if he kept digging, he'd find out more about the key players involved.

He tried googling the name for the umpteenth time, and the same listings appeared as before. He clicked over several pages and then, on page six of the search results, he saw something he hadn't noticed previously. There was a link that included the name of the registered agent of the group, Joseph T. Wallace. The address listed was a post office box in Brookshire, Texas. Hiding behind a post office box was one of the best places for a nefarious organization to remain largely invisible.

Charles jotted down the information in the notes section of his cell phone. Then he tried searching Federal Election Commission filings for names of candidates who had received contributions from AmFree. There were dozens of them in different election cycles, living in multiple states, and dating back to the 2010s. He wrote down some of the names so he could research how they had fared during their campaigns.

Most of the names didn't sound familiar but three of them caught his attention: Margaret Hancock, Robert McCracken, and Jarrod Bronson. Each of them had won their congressional seats in the last election. AmFree seemed to have a good track record of betting on winning candidates, or if one looked at it through a conspiratorial lens, the PAC had a method of putting their thumb on the scale to benefit their favorites.

Just as he began writing down their names, Chelsea Bannon walked into the office. She wore a button-down cotton shirt that would be considered conservative attire on most women, but she had opened the top three buttons, just enough to make her boobs look like they'd bust loose at any minute.

Her red hair was pinned up in a loose bun on top of her head, as if it was a last-minute fix as she rushed to leave home for the office. Wisps of soft, curly strands gently draped her face on both sides. She smiled briefly at Charles and then sashayed to her desk. Chelsea wasn't the chatty type and seemed to zero in on her passion, which was reporting on intriguing, jaw-dropping stories. She had only been on the reporting staff for six months, and he made a mental note to ask her out for drinks soon...very soon.

Casting the distraction aside, Charles searched for information on the first name on his list, Margaret Hancock. She had impressive credentials—graduating from Yale with a law degree from Princeton—and was relatively new to politics. She was elected in Oklahoma and had never run for office before but seemed to have no problem raising money. Her coffers filled to more than ten million dollars for the primary campaign, which scared off most of the potential competitors and cleared the field for her in the general election.

Her opponents seemed to drop out one by one for some reason or other. One primary contender was literally caught with his pants down during a prostitution sting operation set up by the county sheriff's department. Another had to withdraw his candidacy due to a mysterious illness that kept him bedridden for weeks.

A third candidate was actually killed during a skiing accident in Vail, Colorado, a month before the primary. Clearly, Lady Luck seemed to be on Hancock's side. But Charles had learned that not all luck was random and could often be manufactured. He was going to keep digging because this pattern of misfortunate for Hancock's competition seemed too good to be true. It just didn't feel right.

Charles googled the distance between Houston and Brookshire, and the exurb was only thirty-two miles away. He could make a day trip of it and be back by nightfall. If he had to stay overnight, Lloyd had already said yes to a limited travel budget. Tomorrow morning he'd head to Brookshire.

CHAPTER 5

Charles was from the old school of journalism: research facts; look for discrepancies, unusual patterns, or red flags; chase down leads; and interview as many relevant sources as it took to write a credible news story. He loathed the new brand of lazy journalism fueled by social media platforms, especially Twitter, now rebranded X.

Most reporters spent their days monitoring Twitter for tweets and retweets then engaging in breathless reporting on whatever was trending on social media. They tracked responses to the tweets and the responses to the responses and thought that mundane exercise could replace actual hard-nosed journalism. Leaving their newsroom desks or laptops at home to get in their cars or take public transportation to meet real people face to face was becoming more and more uncommon and, for some reporters, even loathsome.

Charles knew that most of his Gen Z colleagues didn't select journalism as their college major because they wanted to write news articles and do actual legwork. They saw the field as a launching pad to bigger and better things. Legwork required them to occasionally get their hands dirty, venture into seedy parts of town, and spend hours conducting research without relying exclusively on Google. God forbid, they might even have to venture into a library, check microfiche of old newspapers and magazines, or leaf through an actual book.

For most of them, becoming the next social media sensation—the next influencer—to amass a million followers on Twitter or Instagram was their ultimate goal. Millions of followers led to almost certain financial rewards. A book deal from one of the large, New York-based publishers would be even better. For those with political activism in their blood, a high-powered lobbying position with a K Street consulting firm or a well-funded non-profit group was on their vision board. Journalism was merely a stepping stone to fame and fortune.

Charles's method took much more time, but he loved it. His method also achieved much better results. He put in the hard work to get the facts right and didn't have to constantly submit corrections and retractions for Lloyd's review. His method also kept the newspaper out of legal hot water for charges of libel and saved the newspaper thousands of dollars annually in attorney's fees. The icing on the cake was that Charles could sleep at night with the assurance that he hadn't smeared someone and ruined their life based on completely false information or half-truths. If consumers of the news realized how much misinformation they were getting from the media, they would lose faith in the journalism profession altogether. Many already had.

That's why Charles had decided to go straight to the source to track down the players behind AmFree. He knew from previous experience that he'd probably have to peel back layers and layers of hidden entities to get to the truth. It was possible that he never would. But he'd visit Brookshire, Texas, and try to interview Joseph Wallace or at least some of the townspeople to find out what they knew. Talking to some of the local townspeople might give him a better sense of who, exactly, Wallace was.

Brookshire's population was fewer than six thousand and was about thirty-five miles west of Houston. He turned on his pop rock playlist for the short drive which gave him time to collect his thoughts and come up with a game plan. Immersing himself in the sounds of Adele, Bruno Mars, and Bon Jovi helped relax him for the day's activities.

He had already done a Google search of Joseph Wallace's name, but there wasn't much information; Wallace's office address, the year he earned his Harvard degree, the year he passed the Texas bar exam, and a few other extraneous tidbits were about it.

As Charles left the Greater Houston area, he left the high-rise scenery behind. Buildings over ten stories high faded into the distance, and open fields dominated the landscape on both sides of the highway. Along his route on I-10 West, Charles passed the Katy Mills Mall, one of the largest malls in the region, with over one million square feet and located about ten miles east of Brookshire.

A light drizzle started falling as Charles took the Brookshire exit off of I-10. He made a left turn at the traffic light and noticed how unremarkable the town looked. The hamlet was named after a captain in the Texas Army, Nathen Brookshire, and was similar to thousands of other tiny Texas towns. As he arrived at the town's outskirts, he was greeted by a message—*Welcome to Brookshire*—carved on a large granite boulder positioned adjacent to the set of railroad tracks that divided the small city.

Before making his way toward Wallace's law office, Charles wanted to first get the lay of the land. The residential areas looked like pre-1950s construction, and as in many Southern towns, there was an abundance of Protestant churches. A forlorn-looking First Baptist Church was the first house of worship he encountered as he traveled through the town's narrow streets, and he mused that every town in America must have a church bearing that name. He was sure there was a reason for that, but the source of the reason had likely died with previous generations.

If Brookshire were a person, it would be described as having a sleepy demeanor. But there were also signs of looming prosperity in this tiny Texas hamlet. Charles crossed the town's railroad tracks and traveled on the four-lane road that was the town's artery, driving slowly so he could look on both sides of the road for signs of life. Other than a flock of vultures that had begun feasting on a dead armadillo's carcass, he didn't see much at first.

Then he noticed three major companies with distribution warehouses within the city limits or nearby. There were large facilities for ecommerce behemoth Amazon, cooler manufacturer Igloo, and the food giant Goya. Those three companies were likely responsible for employing most of the town's people and, indirectly, providing revenue for the dozens of mom-and-pop enterprises that peppered the town's main thoroughfare.

Charles checked his cell phone's GPS, which showed he was two miles and five minutes from Wallace's law office. Joseph T. Wallace & Associates was located in the town's primary business area...if one could call it that. It was even less impressive than the street view he had seen when he searched for the location via GoogleMaps.

The office was in the middle of a poorly maintained strip mall, anchored on one side by a nail salon and on the other by a sandwich shop. The structure was badly in need of a new coat of paint as well as a power wash. In the parking lot, there were large potholes that could easily lead to tire damage if a driver wasn't paying close attention.

Wallace's storefront office window bore gold lettering that was faded and had clearly been there for years. There were lights on in the office, but the mini-blinds on the windows were closed so he couldn't see inside. There was a sign that read "Ring for Entry." He rang the bell and a buzzer sounded, allowing him entry. Charles hesitated to go inside, but his curiosity got the better of him. He wondered why whoever buzzed him in felt comfortable enough to do so, but his question was answered as soon as he walked in.

In the office's reception area, there was a bank of multiple video monitors affixed high on the walls showing images of all sides of the building from a variety of angles. The office furnishings were simple—the standard desk, file cabinet, copy machine, and sofa, none of which looked new.

The receptionist was a middle-aged woman who was slightly overweight. Her face was flushed, with minimal makeup. She wore an ill-fitting, light blue poly-blend pantsuit with a simple white cotton blouse. On her head was a brunette wig that needed to be either adjusted or replaced—soon. Clearly, neither fashion nor style were her strong suits. She remained seated as Charles walked in.

"Hello. May I help you?" she greeted Charles as she peered over the top of her tortoise-shell reading glasses.

"Hello, ma'am. I'm looking for Mr. Wallace. Is he in?"

"Do you have an appointment?"

"No. I thought I'd drop in and take a chance that he'd be here."

"Are you an existing client, or are you seeking his legal services?"

"Neither. My name is Charles Scott, and I'm a reporter for the Houston *Ledger*. I wanted to speak with him about another matter, not seek legal advice."

"Can you be more specific?"

"He's listed as the registered agent for a political action committee called Americans for True Freedom. The PAC seems to have been around for several years and has backed dozens of candidates. I'm considering writing a story about their success. I wanted to know how long he's worked with them and if he could provide the names of some of the officers."

"Any work Mr. Wallace does with his clients is protected by attorney-client privilege, so he wouldn't be able to release that information to you," she responded, clearly digging in her heels.

"With all due respect, Miss--?"

"My name is Ms. Swanson. Can you tell me your name again?"

"It's Charles Scott. As I was about to say, Ms. Swanson, the names of the officers of any political action committee are a matter of public record. I was just hoping Mr. Wallace could give me some insight into the PAC's objectives as far as candidate contributions are concerned."

"I'm sorry, but I'm not authorized to give you any client information whatsoever. At any rate, Mr. Wallace keeps limited office hours and won't be in until later in the week.

I'd be happy to take your business card," she said as she extended her open palm.

Charles could take a hint. Any additional information he discovered would likely not come from Ms. Swanson. He handed her his business card.

"Will you tell him I stopped by and that he can call me anytime? My cell number is also on the card."

Ms. Swanson examined the card suspiciously. "I'll put the card on his desk and bring it to his attention when he comes in, but I can't guarantee you'll hear from him."

Charles left Wallace's office with one overwhelming thought: Something about Joseph Wallace just didn't add up.

CHAPTER 6

It seemed that Joseph Wallace had lived in Michael Goldberg's shadow his entire professional career. He hated it but couldn't escape it. Things hadn't started out that way when they met in college, but since then, Michael had all but dominated Joseph's life.

Joseph and Michael had met in college and quickly bonded as fellow Texans from the Houston area, although from vastly different neighborhoods. Michael grew up in the Memorial Villages section of Houston, one of the city's wealthiest areas, known for its stately mansions with large white columns. Joseph was from an area southwest of downtown whose main artery was Bissonnet Street. The area would later become known as a hub for human trafficking and the subject of a docudrama.

The two young men were both handsome enough that women were always receptive to their advances. In fact, most of the women at Harvard were not bashful; they had no reservations about being the aggressors when it came to the dating game. Joseph and Michael dated two freshmen—Hillary and Jennifer—who happened to be cousins from legacy families. Their parents were Harvard alumni, and their families spent their summers in vacation spots like Aruba and their winters in ski towns like Aspen.

Joseph and Michael weren't dating the cousins because of their mental acuity; in fact, the cousins were intellectually shallow. But they were Barbie doll types with the right sort of breeding that made them acceptable companions for family outings and Harvard alumni cocktail parties. Attending Harvard parties was essential for making the all-important connections for career advancement. The cousins sported perpetual tans, probably a combination of weekly visits to tanning salons and vacations to tropical climates during spring and summer breaks.

Michael's intellect bordered on brilliance. He got all As and graduated at the top of their class at Harvard. His family had money and lots of it. Michael didn't have a problem flaunting his wealth and was always driving the latest sports car—a red Alfa Romeo sophomore year and a turquoise blue BMW Z1 sportster when they were seniors. But Michael had a very, very high opinion of himself, which could be a big turnoff in social settings and made him exceedingly unpopular.

As a result, he rarely got invited to parties, and when he did go, it was usually because he tagged along with Joseph. Michael also wasn't much of a conversationalist. His outsized ego ensured that his conversations with others were largely about himself. He honestly believed that he was intellectually superior to just about everyone he encountered. Michael's lack of interest in the person he was speaking with was noticeable and quite genuine.

Michael and Joseph had opposite personalities. Joseph was a party animal and always knew where the next beer bash was being held and how many kegs the sponsors had trucked in. He had dozens of friends and was well-liked, but his grades suffered as a result of his late-night partying and early morning hangovers.

At Harvard, their relationship was mutually beneficial. Michael helped Joseph with his coursework, although Joseph still graduated in the bottom half of their class. But Michael was clearly going places, and after graduation, Joseph made sure he hitched his wagon to what he knew would be a full-fledged star.

With marginal grades in college and an even more marginal LSAT score, Joseph could only gain admission to an undistinguished law school. He limped through three years of legal studies and barely passed the Texas bar exam on his third try. He didn't really have any passion for the law but was determined to follow the same career path Michael had chosen. Michael, being the star that he was, sailed through law school, was the editor of the *Harvard Law Review*, and was among the top three graduates in his class.

Joseph had married Hillary soon after college graduation and the marriage remained strong. They had three beautiful children—two boys and a girl—and led a quiet life in an affluent Houston exurb. Michael married Jennifer a few months after Joseph's nuptials, but Jennifer quickly bored him. She showed little interest in his career, she had few career ambitions of her own, and shopping seemed to be her only hobby. Their marriage lasted only five years, it produced no children, and a few years later, Michael moved on to wife number two, Jessica.

Michael thought perhaps he'd married beneath his station when he married Jennifer. Jessica, on the other hand, was also an attorney representing corporate clients. With Jessica, he thought he'd found his intellectual equal, someone like-minded with whom he was compatible. As it turned out, Jessica had few interests outside of the legal cases she defended. Her ability to socialize was nil. Even worse, her sexual appetite was less than zero. She lacked imagination in the bedroom and seemed to hold her breath while the deed was done until Michael climaxed.

Jessica was attractive enough, but as a mate, she offered nothing beyond her ability to discuss jurisprudence. Since Michael worked long hours, when he left the office and headed for home, he wanted to leave all things legal behind. His marriage to Jessica was even shorter than his union with Jennifer. After two years, he and Jessica called it quits.

Despite Michael's lackluster marriage track record, as the years progressed, he represented several multinational corporate clients and won some high-profile cases that received international media coverage. His career's trajectory appeared to be limitless. He became a partner in his law firm within five years, a rare accomplishment.

Meanwhile, Joseph's legal career languished as one of ten associate attorneys at Beck, Miller & Beck, a personal injury law firm with offices in Houston, Austin, Dallas, and San Antonio. The first named Beck in the firm's trio was Jeffrey Beck, the patriarch of the Beck family. The second was his son-in-law, Ralph Miller, who had married Beck's daughter primarily as an inroad to joining the firm. The third was his oldest son, Stanley, who was a proverbial legal midget when compared to the giant shadow cast by his father. But sons must do what sons must do. The firm's lawyers were essentially ambulance chasers, but the elder Beck had crafted a moniker for himself that few who heard could forget.

He called himself the "Annihilator" and claimed to extinguish tight-fisted defendants with his fiery legal advocacy. Those who refused to pay his clients what he considered to be the money they deserved for the pain and suffering they endured in car crashes became the object of his legal wrath. His firm had purchased huge billboards on almost every major Houston freeway. His television commercials were legend and were shown on every local network affiliate at least once an hour every single day. They featured Beck looking directly into the camera with a detonator in his right hand, his left poised to depress it.

"I'm Jeffrey Beck, and I'm the attorney known as the Annihilator," the elder Beck said emphatically. "I'll annihilate the greedy insurance companies that are trying to low ball your car accident settlement. You need that money for your medical bills, your hours missed from work, your physical therapy to recover from your injuries, and your pain and suffering."

The elder Beck didn't stop there. "These insurance companies are stingy. They want to pay you nickels and dimes when you deserve big, big dollars. Hire Beck, Miller & Beck, and watch us annihilate their grip on the money you rightly deserve."

After that, the elder Beck would depress the detonator, and a series of mock explosions would occur in the background, replete with sky-high flames. The commercials also included on-camera client testimonials about the amounts Beck, Miller & Beck got them for their car crash settlements.

"When an 18-wheeler rear ended me and put me and my wife in the hospital for weeks," said one client, "the insurance company told us they would only pay me for two weeks' salary because of the liability limits of the truck owner's policy. But after we hired Beck, Miller & Beck and they threatened to take them to court, they suddenly changed their tune. They offered us a six-figure settlement that covered our medical bills, physical therapy, back pay, and more. The Annihilator gets it done."

It wasn't clear whether the "clients" were actors or actual plaintiffs, but the effect was powerful. At the end of each commercial, Beck, Miller & Beck's number and website were shown on the screen. The "Annihilator" ads were unforgettable, left an indelible mark on the viewers' minds, and kept the firm's phones ringing day and night with calls from potential plaintiffs.

But for Joseph, the ads were a source of embarrassment. After graduating from law school and finally passing the bar, he had shopped his resumé around to top law firms in the Houston area, but the competition was fierce with so many newly minted lawyers seeking employment. He had imagined himself enjoying a much more illustrious, respectable legal career.

When he envisioned his future as an attorney, he never pictured chasing ambulances—not once. In fact, he and Michael used to joke about ambulance-chasing lawyers being bottom feeders, at the lower rungs of the attorney status ladder. And even though he and Michael didn't see each other often during the first several years they were lawyers, Joseph felt as though he was always in Michael's shadow.

When Joseph attended legal soirees and conventions, he shied away from telling his colleagues his place of employment because doing so always elicited pitiable laughter and whispered snickers. Beck, Miller & Beck compensated Joseph well enough. They paid him a six-figure salary that afforded him and his family a two-story home in a well-manicured neighborhood. He, Jennifer, and the kids took one-week vacations every summer to the typical family vacation spots: Disneyland, Universal Studios, and Pennsylvania's Pocono Mountains. They'd even been to Hawaii once. Hillary worked part-time at a high-end fashion boutique and never complained. But since he possessed a Harvard undergraduate degree, Joseph always felt like his career was one big disappointment.

Joseph's career contrasted dramatically with Michael's, who wasn't satisfied with simply being a successful attorney. It had been nearly ten years since they both graduated from law school, and Michael's ambitions extended far beyond being a mere law firm partner. He wanted power—the kind one achieved by controlling those that made decisions about the trillions of dollars in the public's purse. That's when he got the idea to form the Committee.

Michael decided to use a political action committee, commonly known as a super PAC, as the vehicle for the Committee's clandestine activities. With a PAC, he could hide his activities under the cloak of loose restrictions and limited oversight. The PAC was the perfect camouflage for the millions of dollars that would need to be procured, amassed, and transferred to untraceable financial institutions and instruments so he could wield the power he sought.

All he needed was another attorney that could manage the paperwork and periodically file the required financial disclosure forms. He didn't have to think long before deciding which attorney he would select. He knew he could count on his old friend, Joseph, to serve as the PAC's registered agent. He could depend on Joseph's discretion and utter devotion. Plus, he would offer his friend a handsome sum for his efforts.

After he had sufficiently mulled over the idea to launch the PAC, Michael decided to give Joseph a call. Joseph was at his law office and had just finished taking the deposition of the driver of a minivan that was T-boned by a Ford F-150 when he saw Michael's incoming call on his cell phone. The van's driver had suffered whiplash and a broken pelvis. Automobile accident victims were Joseph's stock-in-trade in the mundane business of personal injury law. When he saw the call coming in from Michael, his spirits lifted.

"Hi, Michael. Long time no see...or hear from."

"You're right. I should do better about staying in touch more often. How's the personal injury business treating you? Have you chased any ambulances lately?" Michael asked as he smirked.

Joseph winced. "Ha—ha, very funny. Chasing ambulances pays the bills, so I can't complain. Any chance you can send some of your top-tier clients my way?"

"Our corporate clients would be more likely to be defendants in personal injury cases like the ones your firm represents. They see firms like yours as the enemy. Since you're a plaintiff's' lawyer, I doubt there'd be any opportunities with them."

"Just thought I'd ask," Joseph said, crestfallen.

"Don't sound so dejected. I actually do have a new client for you, one that will probably surprise you."

Joseph's mood perked up. "I'm all ears. What kind of case is it?"

"It's not actually a case. It's a long-term project that I think would be perfect for you. And you'd be paid a monthly retainer."

"How much of a retainer?"

"How does thirty thousand dollars a month sound?"

"Don't kid around like that, Michael. You don't have to rub my nose in your success. What's your net worth now? Ten million dollars...or is it more?"

"My financial position has become strong over the years. I won't deny that. But I'm not kidding about the retainer amount. The assignment pays thirty thousand dollars a month and doesn't require you to do a huge amount of work."

"Why so much, and for how long?"

"It could be years, but I know it will be for at least twenty-four months to start."

Joseph was dubious. "This isn't one of your practical jokes, is it? I mean, I don't have to do anything illegal, do I?" He knew there was a thin line between what was unethical and what was illegal. Lawyers were masters at toeing the line and knowing the difference. The latter could potentially land him in jail.

"Of course not. We're both attorneys. I have no interest in being disbarred for committing crimes of moral turpitude. I assure you it's completely legit."

"Then what's the catch?"

"Why do you think there's a catch?"

"Because I know you, Michael. You're tightfisted with money and you wouldn't spend that much unless it was something really important. Plus, you've never been all that confident in my legal abilities."

"You know me all too well, my friend." Michael laughed lightly, the haughty laughter he'd perfected for when he wanted to set his adversaries at ease...the laughter that masked the depths of his treachery. "But you're wrong about my confidence in you. When this opportunity came across my desk, you were the first person I thought of."

Joseph was slightly perturbed. "Your fake flattery is unnecessary. The facts will suffice."

"There is one slight catch."

"I knew it. Go ahead. Spill it. What's the catch?" Joseph was waiting with bated breath. Since he'd graduated from law school, he'd never been paid a monthly retainer by a client. And he'd been waiting his entire legal career for Michael to invite him into his substantial web of influence. Even though he wanted Michael to believe he might say no, he was more than ready to take him up on his offer if it was anything reasonable.

"You'll need to resign from your firm immediately and not take on any other clients."

"How soon would I need to resign? I have open cases on my desk."

"You can give Beck, Miller & Beck the usual two weeks' notice."

"I need to hear every detail before I consider making a change after so many years at my firm. A bird in the hand is worth two in the bush, wouldn't you agree?"

"This will be an exclusive assignment, and you'll only have one client, a new political action committee I've formed. Also, you wouldn't be able to tell anyone about this assignment, including no mention of the entity you're representing."

"Attorney-client privilege covers that."

"But when I say nothing, I mean nothing—nothing on a resumé, nothing on social media, nothing on LinkedIn or any headhunter websites, no media interviews. Your digital footprint needs to be all but nonexistent. Your name would be listed as the registered agent for the PAC, but the mailing address would be a post office box. We'll establish a physical office, but it would be at a nondescript location and purely to fulfill government requirements."

Joseph was wary. "Why so much secrecy?"

There was no need for Joseph to know anything about the Committee, and Michael would make sure he didn't. "I'd prefer not to have my persona directly connected to the entity so it's not easily traced back to me. It might create some conflict of interest challenges for me with some of my corporate clients, and I'd prefer to avoid them." Michael had already thought through an explanation for the need for secrecy that Joseph would find reasonable.

"I know you don't think much of my position at Beck, Miller & Beck, but I have established a solid career there and the company has been extremely stable. They're even considering making me a partner." Joseph decided to lay it on thick by telling a bald-faced lie. There had been absolutely zero discussions with the elder Beck about the firm making Joseph a partner. But Michael didn't know that, and he didn't need to know that.

Joseph's mind was whirling as he thought about the stipulations he could insist be included. He wanted to up the ante to see how much Michael was willing to give up. "For me to seriously consider your offer, I'd need to have a guarantee of at least five years at the retainer of thirty thousand dollars a month, with a ten percent increase every year starting in year number two."

If Michael wanted him for his PAC as badly as it appeared, Joseph needed to extract as much as he could. He'd also begun thinking ahead and calculating what he'd be able to do with the extra money he'd be getting. His current yearly salary was only $125,000, so Michael's offer represented almost triple what he was making. Private school for all three of his children would be first on the agenda. He'd also have enough to contribute substantially to each of their college funds.

Meanwhile, Michael exhaled a confident sigh. He had been willing to go as high as fifty thousand dollars a month if Joseph had put up strong resistance. As it turned out, Joseph was true to form, always undervaluing his worth. He had never learned the fine art of negotiating and had folded like a house of cards. Michael feigned an effort at soul-searching, pretending to contemplate Joseph's counter.

"Ten percent a year? Hmmm...I think we can make that work."

Joseph was trying to cover all the bases he could think of at the moment. "If I can't put the assignment on my resumé, what happens when the assignment ends? How will I explain the lapse in employment when I apply for other positions?"

"For that time period, just indicate on your resumé that you managed a private legal practice during that time. I will write you a glowing recommendation letter that will open doors to any law firm in the country. Getting hired by another law firm will not be a problem. In fact, with the experience and recommendation you'll get, a law firm will probably put you on the fast track to becoming partner."

Joseph wanted to play hard to get but not too hard. He was itching to take the deal Michael was offering him. Under normal circumstances, he would consult with Hillary before making a final decision, but there was no way Hillary would want him to turn down over $300,000 a year. Most likely, she would immediately start looking at real estate listings so they could upgrade to a much larger house, and change her shopping destinations from Marshall's and T.J. Maxx to Macy's and Nordstrom.

"So all I have to do is keep the PAC's records and file the necessary documents. There has to be more to it than that."

"Nothing you haven't done before. We'll need you to create several LLCs in the states with the most favorable corporate registration laws. For starters, Delaware and Nevada are the best two. You'll also be creating LLCs in countries where federal authorities cannot easily seize assets. Start with the Virgin Islands, the Cayman Islands, and Panama."

"We'll need the certificates of formation to open bank accounts. Then you'll need to file whatever annual paperwork is required for each corporation and the PAC's financial disclosure statements. You'll also need to respond to any correspondence the PAC receives. We'll provide you with an assistant that will take care of letter-writing, answering phones, and other routine administrative tasks."

"That all sounds doable. Most of it I've done before, except creating the overseas LLCs. But that should be simple enough."

"So do we have a deal?"

"I think so, Michael. No, I know so." The smile on Joseph's face was magnetic and he could hardly contain his glee.

"I knew I could count on you. I'll get the agreement over to you in the next couple of days. Meanwhile, you can give Beck, Miller & Beck your two weeks' notice."

Then Michael decided to sweeten the pot. "I'll also give you a twenty-five thousand dollar signing bonus for your trouble. That's the least I can do since you're giving up a sure thing for something new and unknown."

"That's awfully generous, Michael. I'll await receipt of the agreement, and I can't wait to tell Hillary."

"Give her my love, and tell her Jessica and I hope to see her soon."

When they had entered their arrangement, Michael had still been married to Jessica, wife number two.

Joseph ended the conversation and could hardly contain himself. It almost sounded too good to be true. Deep down, he hoped he wouldn't live to regret this decision. Michael had a dark side that few people knew about...except him.

CHAPTER 7

The five years that Michael had originally proposed for Joseph's assignment had now become ten. During those years, their arrangement had gone smoothly with few, if any, glitches. Joseph had set up a total of twenty-two LLCs for AmFree that, unbeknownst to him, were used to shuffle millions of dollars every year among the many moving parts that encompassed the Committee's network.

Joseph knew nothing about the mountains of money the Committee actually controlled. Michael provided him with bogus financial reports meticulously generated by the physician. The figures included in the reports represented less than ten percent of the actual money the members controlled and were included strictly for government paperwork requirements. Still, the sums AmFree reported in terms of campaign contributions were impressive when compared to PACs across the board. The millions they reported were more than enough to finance the campaigns of their candidates, both existing and new.

For the most part, Joseph was kept in the dark regarding the Committee's true purpose, a situation he didn't seem to mind at all. In fact, he preferred knowing no more than necessary. His workload was minimal; he worked barely thirty hours a week. He and Hillary were able to upgrade their lifestyle, purchasing a five thousand-square-foot home in Kingwood, Texas, a wealthy Houston suburb. The house included a spacious home office where he did all of his legal work.

Due to the nature of his AmFree assignment, client meetings were no longer needed, so having an office at home worked perfectly. Incoming mail came to the PAC's post office box. Other than an annual state tax bill, official financial forms to be completed, and some occasional junk mail, the post office box received little mail or attention. Wallace mailed a money order on January first every year to pay the box fee. He checked mail at the post office box only at night and made sure his face was obscured so his image wouldn't be captured by the surveillance cameras mounted on the inside walls.

The office Michael had set up for him in Brookshire was necessary but was an embarrassment. Although he understood why Michael wanted the office to be understated, he had a sneaking suspicion the rundown location was a symbol of Michael's low opinion of him as a lawyer. He rarely went there, and his communication with Ms. Swanson was mostly done by phone and email. On the few occasions he visited the office, he usually wore a hoodie and sweat pants so he wouldn't be recognized.

His children were all enrolled at a private high school and would soon be heading to college. Because of Michael's generosity, he was living the good life. Sometimes he actually pinched himself.

Meanwhile, Michael was more committed to his quest for power than ever. The day of the next Committee meeting was approaching, and Michael worked after hours at his office making his final preparations. After the usual office activity subsided and his assistant had left for the day, he could work without interruption. He could lean back in his Evan luxury leather chair, relax a little, and strategize about the Committee's next moves. This meeting was an important one.

The Committee members planned to select three potential candidates to run for the U.S. Senate from among the list of individuals they had scrutinized during their previous session. Michael would preside while the members discussed the merits and weaknesses of each candidate. The discussions could be raucous.

At one prior meeting, the two oil barons almost exchanged blows about which one of two candidates' wives was better looking as they believed the candidate whose wife was more attractive had better odds of winning. Statistically, they were probably right.

At another meeting, the Committee's book publisher insisted he be guaranteed the first option to sign a candidate for a book contract if they won the primary. But any actions that would bring Committee members out of the shadows and into the public light were strongly discouraged. Michael would make sure it never happened. The book publisher's greed would have to be squelched; he'd have to make his extra millions with a different client. At meetings, Michael's gesture of elevating both his hands about six inches above the cherry wood conference table as a sign of restraint helped calm the raised voices. He had an eerie, uncanny effect on most people.

Michael was not distracted by the rancor and kept his focus on the ultimate goal. He ruled the Committee with an iron grip. Any semblance of democracy was merely a façade.

When he formed the Committee, he made sure their vetting and winnowing processes were thorough. They'd devised a system that would produce the best possible result—or at least close to it. The target's positives must outweigh the skeletons that would ultimately be found in their closets. Everybody had skeletons. Everybody.

Personal skeletons tended to be somewhat ordinary in nature. For men, it could be adolescent sexual mischief, an out-of-control temper, drug abuse, alcoholism, an adulterous affair, a second (or even third) family in a different geographic area, financial malfeasance, or an arrest record. For women, the list was similar but could also include a teenage pregnancy they preferred to hide, multiple abortions, or promiscuous behavior evidenced by videos and photos.

Over time the Committee had perfected the process to increase the odds of success with their first pick. Mistakes could be costly, not only in terms of finances but also in terms of the time lost and the missed opportunity for victory.

Michael established a rule that the candidates must be telegenic, with the ability to think on their feet. During the Committee's last meeting one of the Silicon Valley billionaires reminded them that in terms of a candidate being able to respond to questions from both the public and the media: "Being a politician can often be like dancing on the head of a pin or walking a tightrope."

Of course politicians changed their issue positions all the time, but there was a fine art to perfecting political rhetoric. It required the ability to be able to answer a question in vague terms without providing a definitive answer. In other words, the candidate needed to seem like he was answering the question asked without answering it at all.

When an issue position had to be adjusted, the seasoned ones knew how to make it appear that a change in position was the result of thoughtful consideration, not from putting a proverbial finger in the air to see which way the winds of public opinion were blowing. They knew how to appear to be genuine when they were anything but.

"Voters don't expect politicians to be saints, but they detest liars and phonies," Michael emphasized at the Committee's initial meeting. "They dislike candidates who seem to be hiding something most of all." The description offered most often in focus groups was that the candidate had "shifty eyes."

For candidates who suffered from shifty-eye syndrome, the Committee hired top-notch image consultants to work with the prospects on making constant, direct eye contact with the camera or the interviewer. But their advice didn't stop there. The consultants decided which colors were best to wear, which hairstyle was most flattering, which accessories symbolized power and prestige, and which shoes personified practicality and stature.

Michael hired focus groups to assess everything from campaign slogans to a candidate's pet's name. Besides the polling firms Michael hired to collect public opinion data, focus groups represented one of the Committee's biggest expenses. Both were well worth the cost.

But one of its priorities was also to either eliminate or discredit competition without raising suspicion, especially from reporters. Most reporters used their positions as stepping stones, but there were still some nerdy reporters that thought nothing of spending hours in the library scanning digital copies of newspapers that were decades old. They were the ones that knew Google had its limits. They were the most dangerous to the Committee's ultimate mission: to amass fortunes for each of its members so they would be among the wealthiest and most powerful people in the world.

Michael had already done his homework and had reviewed the digital dossiers for all of the prospects they'd discuss at the meeting. He already had a candidate in mind as his favorite. Individuals who had been anointed as either martyrs or heroes by the media and the community at large were the easiest to pitch to voters. His preferred candidate was a little bit of both. The candidate's name was Ron Singleton.

CHAPTER 8

For the past five years, Ron Singleton's life had been like a whirlwind. He considered his previous job as the chief engineer for the City of Houston to be fairly mundane—routine, repetitious work with little to no excitement. That all changed five years ago when he was on his way home from work one evening and was pulled over by overzealous cops.

According to the officers, they'd stopped Ron because his car had a nonworking tail light, but things quickly spiraled out of control. The entire Houston police department had been on high alert that day, and officers were stopping virtually any Black man they encountered that was driving a black SUV—the general description of the man who had kidnapped Hunter Pauley, the infant son of a prominent Houston family.

Fearful that his name could be added to the long list of victims of police misconduct, Ron went out of his way to comply with the officers' directives. He immediately put his hands on the steering wheel so they would be in plain sight and responded to the officers' commands to the letter in as quiet a tone as he could muster.

But Ron made the unfortunate mistake of reaching for his wallet to retrieve his driver's license without first asking permission to remove his hands from the steering wheel. The moment he did, the officers drew their weapons, pointing them directly at Ron's head, and ordering him to show his hands and get out of the car. Ron opened his car door with care, moving at a snail's pace so as not to give the officers any excuse to pull their triggers.

They handcuffed him and roughly tossed him into the backseat of the police cruiser. A small crowd that had gathered nearby took cell phone videos of the entire incident. At least there was video evidence if anything happened on the way to the station. Ron had never been so humiliated in his entire life.

Ron was transported to the downtown Houston city jail along with dozens of other Black men who were driving black SUVs that night. His best friend, Lloyd Palmer, bailed him out of jail within a few hours and all charges were dropped, so the scars he sustained were more mental than physical.

The general description provided by Hunter's mother, Christina Pauley, was vague enough to imperil Black men throughout the city of Houston. Had it not been for Lloyd, many innocent Black men could have been indicted on specious charges, resulting in criminal records.

Lloyd was suspicious of Mrs. Pauley's account from the very beginning. During his interview with her, her answers were vague and incongruous. Despite the strong objections of his editor, Ed Jackson, Lloyd followed the evidence until he got to the bottom of what really happened. Mrs. Pauley murdered her own son to collect the insurance proceeds in order to pay close to a million dollars she owed in gambling debts. She buried Hunter's body beneath a tree in a neighborhood park and then claimed he was kidnapped by a Black man.

Lloyd's innate curiosity as a reporter led to Mrs. Pauley's arrest and his meteoric rise to national stardom. Jackson couldn't stomach Lloyd having the upper hand and later tried to engineer Lloyd's murder, but his plan was foiled, he was arrested and later imprisoned. With Jackson no longer at the *Ledger*'s helm as editor, the executives at the paper offered the job to Lloyd and he accepted.

For the next few months, Ron had recurring nightmares about a police officer pointing his gun at his head and pulling the trigger. During his dream, the gunshot being fired would cause him to wake up abruptly. He would be sweating from head to toe, breathing heavily, and sometimes even screaming. It would take him a few seconds to reorient himself and remember exactly where he was.

These episodes alarmed his wife, Shirley, as Ron's screams would awaken her. "Babe, did you have another nightmare?" she'd asked, and then she would comfort him with a slow, gentle, and steady circular back rub.

"Yeah. I'll be glad when they stop."

"Well, your therapist said they were getting less frequent. That's a good sign that you've turned the corner."

"I suppose so. But I know I'll never forget that night as long as I live."

Shirley's reassuring words helped him finally settle down enough to relax and eventually fall asleep, but the next day at work, he'd be exhausted from sleep deprivation. Ron had sought counseling to figure out how to grapple with his new reality—the before and after imbalance that was created by law enforcement overreach.

His therapist said he was suffering from night terrors, a form of post-traumatic stress disorder, common for people who went through traumatic experiences. She prescribed sleeping pills to help him sleep through the night, which did help some. But he'd heard about people becoming addicted to sleeping pills and didn't want to add that to the challenges he had to overcome. He tried to use them as sparingly as he could until the nightmares eventually stopped occurring.

One positive outcome of Ron's horrific experience was that it lit a social justice fire in his belly. Before his arrest, Ron had never considered getting involved in politics. He performed his civic duty by voting in elections but largely sat on the sidelines when political and social issues arose. Before his arrest, he steered clear of any active participation in politics. To him, most politicians were not only dishonest but dishonorable, constantly blaming the opposing party for societal problems while offering no solutions of their own. Politicians from both major parties were guilty of the same shameful behavior, with little to no accountability.

But his pivotal encounter with the police awakened the activist that had apparently been buried deep within his psyche. That seed had been sown by his parents, who were active in the 1960s civil rights movement. They'd shared some of their harrowing brushes with local sheriffs as they demonstrated for voting and civil rights. They'd also described some of their near-death experiences with bands of racist marauders that took the law into their own hands.

On the night he was arrested, Ron realized he had been lucky. Other than an occasional traffic stop, he'd never experienced any direct run-ins with law enforcement—at least none where he felt his life might be in danger. That night, it was clear that whatever luck he had had run out.

As he sat in the back of the police cruiser on his way to what he hoped and prayed was the precinct, he had flashbacks of what had happened to the three civil rights workers—Andrew Goodman, Michael Schwerner, and James Chaney—who were murdered in Philadelphia, Mississippi, on the fateful night of June 21, 1964. All three were shot multiple times by members of the Ku Klux Klan, their bodies buried at an earthen dam and discovered seven weeks later.

Ron was born more than a decade after those horrific slayings occurred, but the incident had become a tragic milestone of African-American history and a catalyst for equal justice for Blacks nationwide, particularly in the South. On the night Ron was arrested, he wasn't sure if he would emerge unscathed...or if he would even make it to the police station alive.

That experience was life altering. After that, Ron spent several months working with other community leaders to enact measures to reform the Houston Police Department. He advocated for extensive training for both rookies and veteran officers as well as for a citizen review board in cases where charges of police misconduct were alleged.

Ron became a regular guest commentator on local news and public affairs programs and, as a result, was encouraged by community leaders to run for office. The following year, he decided to run for state representative.

His opponent in that race was the embodiment of everything people hated about politicians. She had been in the state legislature for decades, with a lackluster record of accomplishments, and had been re-elected mostly because of her familiar family name. Ron's status as a political neophyte gave him the advantage of being underestimated by his challenger. Ron's fundraising strategy of receiving small donations from hundreds of contributors allowed him to wage a competitive campaign, and he handily won the election.

Once he took office, although he was among one hundred fifty lawmakers in Austin, the state capital, he really felt like he was making a difference. He quickly sponsored legislation that was passed and brought attention to his top issue: education. He knew that without a solid educational foundation, children in disadvantaged neighborhoods had little chance of success. Since the position of legislator paid only six hundred dollars per month—less than most part-time fast food jobs—Ron maintained his engineering position with the city.

His election as a legislator raised his profile, and he often received inquiries and invitations to dine with movers and shakers within Houston's business community. So it was not surprising when he received a call at his office from one of the city's most successful attorneys, Michael Goldberg. While Ron was eating a light breakfast at his desk, his assistant, Lisa, informed him that a call from Goldberg was on hold. For most of his incoming calls, he'd have Lisa take a message so he could mull over when or whether a callback was warranted, but this time he washed down his bagel with coffee and answered the phone, mostly out of curiosity.

"Mr. Singleton, this is Michael Goldberg, and I'm a Houston attorney. How's your day going?"

"Good so far. What can I do for you Mr. Goldberg?"

"Call me Michael please. Our law firm's client roster includes some of your financial supporters. I've noticed the yeoman's work you're doing in Austin and called to congratulate you."

"Thank you for the compliment, Michael," Ron responded as he took another sip of his lukewarm coffee. "I'm familiar with you and your law firm. With the prominent legal victories your firm has racked up in recent years, your reputation precedes you. What can I do for you?" Ron repeated his question, anticipating that Goldberg would get to the point quickly.

"I was wondering if you had time in your schedule to have lunch with me next week."

"Is there anything in particular you need to talk to me about?" Ron asked, hoping to dissuade him. "Perhaps it's something that can be handled over the phone or in a brief meeting at my office." Ron emphasized the word *brief* and awaited Goldberg's response. He'd found it necessary to limit the number of lunch invitations he accepted. They had grown in number, and if Lisa didn't screen his calls carefully, he could spend all of his weekday lunch hours listening to constituent complaints or meeting with those seeking legislative favors—the least favorite part of his job as a politician.

"It's a bit too detailed to discuss over the phone," Michael replied, believing this would pique Ron's curiosity and convince him to meet face to face. "I promise it will be worth your while."

Michael's approach had been carefully focus group tested by the Committee and this entire process was considered to be more of a science than an art, comparable to creating a math formula for success. Eating over a meal—whether breakfast, lunch, or dinner—created a relaxed atmosphere for putting potential candidates at ease, thereby giving the Committee the advantage. It was a key element in their plan.

An office meeting, especially at the intended target's office, gave the prospect the upper hand and Michael always kept the advantages in the Committee's corner.

Ron was reluctant to accept Goldberg's invitation, but his instincts nudged him in that direction. He recognized Goldberg's prominent role in city politics, and Ron thought it best to hear him out. He started looking through his cell phone's calendar and noticed that on Wednesday of next week, his lunch hour was free. "Depending on where we'll be going for lunch, I can meet you next Wednesday for an hour. But we'll have to stay strictly within that one-hour timeframe because I have a meeting at one o'clock that afternoon."

"Excellent! You pick the place and the time," Michael replied, feeling triumphant.

Ron thought for a moment about a lunch location that wasn't too far away from the office and had good food, where they could still have a bit of privacy. "Are you familiar with Lucille's Restaurant on LaBranch Street?"

"Yes, I've heard their food is amazing, and I've been hoping for an opportunity to eat there. What time?"

"Let's meet at eleven thirty to beat some of the lunch crowd and so we'll have our pick of the tables. I'll see you then."

"I'm looking forward to it," said Michael as he ended the call.

Ron sat at his desk for a moment with his chin propped in his right hand, wondering what Goldberg wanted from him. Calls requesting meetings might be couched as casual get-togethers, but they never were all that casual. Most were requests of some kind, either for favors or access to influencers. But Ron's moment of contemplation was interrupted by the ringing of his phone and, according to Lisa, a call from a constituent. He'd have to think about Goldberg's motives later.

CHAPTER 9

When Michael Goldberg settled on a candidate whose political career could be jump-started by the Committee's efforts, his first move was to create an extensive, detailed digital dossier on them. The dossier included copies of birth certificates, driver's licenses, marriage licenses, divorce decrees, birth records of offspring, credit reports, travel records, criminal records, legal filings, property deeds, bank accounts, retirement funds, feature stories, commentaries they'd penned, books they'd written, dating apps, TikTok and YouTube reels, social media posts, photos, and videos—basically everything about them the Committee could find. Sometimes they even used one of their designated hackers to obtain the target's online search history or cell phone usage. This was where they might find clues about an obsession with porn or sexual vices if they thought it might add to what they'd already uncovered.

So far the Committee's data gathering operation on Ron Singleton hadn't unearthed anything that raised red flags—no unusually large bank deposits or withdrawals, no money hidden in offshore accounts, no side chicks, no love children, no nefarious vices. Compared to other candidates, Ron had led a fairly straight-laced life.

But no matter how much background information the Committee collected on their prospects, Michael still believed one had to look into a person's eyes to assess the person's true character, especially regarding vulnerabilities and shortcomings. Learning which emotional buttons to push to meet the Committee's ends could be achieved most efficiently one on one. Then he initiated a face-to-face meeting over a meal.

He preferred dinners because there were fewer time constraints—no job to return to. But he'd settle for lunch or breakfast if preferred by the targeted candidate. Every move the Committee made was based on a well-studied calculation. Nothing was left to chance.

Michael had zeroed in on Ron Singleton, who had all of the characteristics they were looking for, as a possible contender for the U.S. Senate. Attractive, articulate, accomplished, and African-American, Ron had received a spate of good publicity during the past few years because of his false arrest by the police and for taking principled positions as a member of the Texas legislature.

Candidates with principles got voters' attention because they went against the grain of the prevailing image of most politicians: corrupt, dishonest, and deceitful. A public perception of a candidate's honesty and integrity was something money could not buy. And in the Committee's favor, candidates that had principles also tended to be among the most naïve, blinded by their idealism.

Despite decades of evidence to the contrary, these idealist candidates sincerely believed their presence and influence could change the political system. They suffered from *Mr. Smith Goes to Washington* syndrome—the classic 1939 James Stewart movie where a guy from the boonies gets elected as a senator only to have his reputation smeared by the politically powerful. In the end, Mr. Smith triumphs when a long-time senator finds his conscience. But Mr. Smith was a fictitious character; finding a conscience among federal officeholders was like searching for the Loch Ness Monster.

The idealistic candidates didn't seem to understand that the nature of the system was corrupt and it didn't matter whether or not a candidate had pure motives. Once they were elected and entered the system, if they stayed there long enough, they would be corrupted by the experience. To the Committee's advantage, these optimists were also easier to manipulate than those that were pure politicians who would say anything they thought the public would swallow.

In legal and political circles, Michael was known as a well-connected political operative with top-tier connections. He was usually the one who met prospects face to face, although occasionally the Committee's book publisher or media mogul were assigned this task. When he invited potential candidates to lunch, their acceptance rate to the invite was nearly one hundred percent. An invitation from the distinguished Michael Goldberg was hard to turn down. Ron Singleton didn't break the pattern. After some brief hesitation, he accepted Michael's lunch invitation.

Michael left his office an hour early to meet Singleton at the restaurant he had selected, Lucille's. He usually allowed the target to select their restaurant of choice because this was a move the Committee's research showed set the target's mind at ease. In doing so, he ran the risk that he'd run into some of the Committee's other prospects by accident. That had happened once before and he took great pains to make sure it never happened again. If the target selected a familiar restaurant that he'd been to fairly recently, he steered them in a different direction. It was simply too dangerous to let any of the prospects know any others existed. Secrecy was an absolute necessity.

Michael always liked to arrive early to his meal meetings, select the table, and be seated before the target arrived. He always chose a table at the rear of the restaurant to ensure privacy and sat facing the front door so he could see everyone that entered.

Lucille's, located in Houston's Museum District, had a small hometown feel to it. The quaint restaurant had a bar area near the entrance and a section in the back that was two stairs up from the floor. Michael requested the table farthest back in the elevated section because from that position, he could see every patron that entered. The multicultural crowd was sparse since it was eleven o'clock and the heavy lunch crowd had not yet arrived.

Ron arrived right on time at eleven thirty and checked in with the hostess, who directed him to Michael's table. As Ron approached, Michael stood and extended his hand for a handshake.

"It's good to meet you, Ron. You look just like you do on television," said Michael, knowing that starting things with a bit of humor combined with flattery would have the desired disarming effect.

"Well, I can't say the same thing about you since the only photos I've seen of you were ones I googled before leaving my office," replied Ron. "My curiosity got the best of me, and I wondered if our paths had crossed before. I've certainly heard your name mentioned numerous times when political influencers are the topic of conversation."

"Since I represent well-known corporate clients, I try to maintain a low public profile," Michael offered as a response. "That way I don't become a distraction when I'm sitting across the negotiating table from their opposition."

"Have you eaten here before?" asked Michael.

"Yes, and their food is delicious. In fact, Lucille's was recently named on Oprah Daily's list of nine Black-owned businesses to support when folks visit Texas. The list was created in honor of the Juneteenth holiday. Would you like a recommendation from the menu?"

"Absolutely! What's good?"

"Their grilled octopus is the talk of the town. Have you ever eaten octopus, or would you like to pick something else?"

Michael had traveled all over the world and had eaten octopus prepared a number of different ways—fried, grilled, boiled, sautéed. He'd even had octopus sushi. "Yes, but I've never eaten octopus the way Lucille's prepares it, so I'd love to try it."

After Michael gave the waiter their orders, he was the first to speak. "I'm sure you're wondering why I invited you to lunch."

"Quite frankly, yes, since your invitation was somewhat cryptic."

"I've been talking with some of the members of Houston's business community, and they've been eyeing you as a possible candidate for the upcoming Senate election."

"You mean the U.S. Senate?" Ron had entertained thoughts of running for the Texas Senate a few times, but had never contemplated running for statewide office. The U.S. Senate was a big deal and well beyond his reach.

"Yes, the U.S. Senate. You're already a leader at the local level, but we'd like to make you a national leader. As divisive as national politics have been in recent years, voters are hungry for politicians who are driven by something greater than their own self-interest," said Michael, adding to the previous plaudits he'd showered upon Ron.

"Your passion and selfless commitment to integrity within government is just what's needed on Capitol Hill." Michael could see that his thick layer of compliments was having the desired effect. Ron's body language showed that he was about halfway there in terms of saying yes.

But there was still more convincing for Michael to do. "A campaign for the U.S. Senate would require a huge fundraising effort," Ron countered. "I don't have the resources or the connections to raise the millions of dollars I'd need to wage a credible campaign. During the last Senate race, both candidates raised well over ten million dollars. Plus I would need an experienced staff to run things."

"Fundraising will be no problem. We'll make sure you'll have all the money you'll need," Michael responded. He noticed Ron's reaction—incredulous in nature—so he elaborated.

"The political donor class is very supportive of any candidates we endorse," he continued. "They don't open their wallets unless they are sure a candidate has been fully vetted, which is one of the main roles we play."

"We would also make sure you had an experienced campaign staff to manage your office and help you with your policy platform and messaging," he added. "In other words, you won't be starting from scratch. It will all be seamless. You'll see."

The waiter arrived and brought them their meals, interrupting their conversation. This allowed Ron to spend a few seconds contemplating Michael's offer. The wafting aroma of the octopus he'd ordered reminded him that he had long since digested the bagel he had eaten earlier that morning.

Ron restarted their exchange. "This almost sounds too good to be true. What about my positions on the issues?" asked Ron. "Don't you want to know where I stand on major public policy matters? And I have zero foreign policy experience. In fact, I've never been outside the United States. My wife, Shirley, and I have always wanted to travel internationally, but we haven't gotten around to it yet."

Michael was always amused when politicians actually thought their issue positions mattered. Voters responded more to soundbites than to details, more to headlines than to specifics. Most of the time, the back-and-forth banter between senators that happened during legislative sessions was just for the television cameras. The real maneuvers occurred behind closed doors and outside of the public's view.

That's why campaigns hired pollsters whose primary mission was to find out which issues were popular among voters and where the majority of likely voters stood. That way candidates could craft their public statements accordingly. In other words, the politicians were following, not leading, the masses. Ultimately, the only issues that would really matter for Ron's campaign and his role in the Senate, if he were elected, were the ones the Committee deemed important.

"From what I've seen," replied Michael, "your principles are of the highest caliber, which means your issue positions would be based on what is in the voters' best interests." This was his canned response to this often posed question as he knew that most so-called principles were poll tested. Those that weren't were few and far between.

"Why me?" asked Ron. "Why make me this offer as opposed to someone else? I'm sure there are potential candidates with more experience in government. I've only been in the Texas legislature for two years."

The "why me" question was also common among candidates that still had a modicum of modesty and humility. But sometimes candidates asked the question just to have their egos stroked, just to be told that they were, indeed, a cut above the rest. Either way, Michael had developed scripted responses.

"As you know, we're in a period of heightened political division and tension, and voters are looking for principles over experience," said Michael as he smiled. "They distrust career politicians and are eager to inject new blood into the political system with the hopes for more integrity and consensus in decision making. People like you are just what's needed to turn things around and make the system work for everyone."

Michael knew that the general public, as well as political neophytes, were all clueless about the way politics really worked. They still held out false hope that adding new faces to a corrupt system would somehow have a cleansing effect. That would be like staying pristine during a mud wrestling match. This misguided belief made Michael's assignment easier to execute.

"If I agree to do this, it's a very big step. I'd need to discuss this with my wife, Shirley, in terms of how it would affect our family. To move forward, my wife and entire family would need to be on board."

Referring to future discussions with family members was a sure sign that Michael's message had gotten through and that a yes from Ron was all but assured. If a potential candidate's answer was no, the response would be immediate. The Committee's research data had shown this to be a consistent pattern.

When candidates played the wife or husband card, it was a clear signal they were all in. Their time would be spent crafting a persuasive argument to present to their spouse while on the way home from the meeting—maybe even sooner. Spouses were usually reluctant to have their personal lives so intensely scrutinized in the political arena and rightly so. But in the end most wanted to be supportive and just required a bit of persuasion to get them onboard.

"How much time do you think you'll need before you make a decision?" Michael asked in an effort to show that time was of the essence. Truthfully, the Committee had months to find the ideal candidate but preferred the process to be completed speedily. "We're looking at a number of potential candidates and were hoping to settle on one within the next two weeks. Of course, you are our first choice."

"I should be able to give you a definitive answer, one way or the other, by Monday. Is that soon enough?"

A short decision window spelled victory as far as Michael was concerned. "Monday would be fine, and I look forward to hearing from you then. Now let's finish eating."

CHAPTER 10

After his lunch meeting with Ron Singleton, Michael returned to his office and was all but certain Ron would say yes to his offer. The picture he'd painted for Ron's campaign laid out a clear path to victory, one that was unobstructed by pitfalls and giving the promise of future political power. Michael has focused only on the upside, not the downside. People tended to hear what they wanted to hear, with their egos at the forefront.

Michael had seen this scenario play out many times before and his instincts were usually spot on. He proceeded as though Ron had already given him the green light to proceed. The infrastructure for the way forward was already in place. All that remained were Michael's instructions to the Committee's key operatives to set the wheels for Ron's campaign in motion.

Providing the financing and staff for the Committee's select few was not only the key to success but also essential to total behind-the-scenes control. "He who has the gold rules" was an axiom Michael's grandfather had lived by. His vast experience showed him that despite the situation or circumstances, the person that held the purse strings was ultimately in control. The trick was to let the targets think they were in control for as long as possible.

Idealists might want to believe that finances had no impact on decision making, but who were they kidding? Themselves perhaps. But once the money faucet was turned on, no one wanted to lose their cash cow, because they'd already adjusted their lifestyles based on regular infusions of large sums of money. They'd long ago gotten used to dining at tony restaurants while hobnobbing with celebrities; they'd enjoyed jetting off to hot vacation spots at the drop of a hat. They'd gotten comfortable; they'd gotten a little lazy. Money did indeed matter.

Michael also knew that control had to be managed and exerted at the proper times; it wasn't necessarily automatic. The Committee had no problem taking the gloves off when necessary, when those under their umbrella had to be nudged to do their bidding. When the dust settled, those that had the money—the gold—were still in charge. As far as the Committee was concerned, Michael intended to be the only man in charge—period.

He'd wait to hear from Ron by Monday but was confident he'd get a yes. The fact that Ron's best friend, Lloyd Palmer, was the editor of the Houston *Ledger* was an added bonus. Because of their long relationship, the Committee was confident it could count on favorable news coverage regarding Ron's campaign. At the very least, there wouldn't be a barrage of negative stories. But to hedge their bets, the Committee had someone on the inside at the *Ledger*—someone who could feed them information on what stories the paper was covering or, when necessary, plant news articles that would inure to their benefit.

Michael was already making mental notes on which team players to pull in to run Ron's campaign. They had all managed campaigns before, and with their turnkey system, they could have the entire operation up and running within a few days. They were well paid for their efforts...and for their prudence. Not only had they all signed non-disclosure agreements but Michael had made it clear that sharing information with anyone would result in dire consequences. Any threats to the Committee's existence, members, or fortunes were quickly squelched.

CHAPTER 11

After visiting Joseph Wallace's office in Brookshire, Charles returned to his car and took a minute to reflect on what he'd just seen. The unkempt strip center office, the bank of video monitors, the old-fashioned receptionist, Ms. Swanson...it just didn't fit. The registered agent for a political action committee that had contributed as much money to as many candidates as AmFree had wouldn't operate from a location that was so dilapidated. They'd have a suite of offices in a high-rise complex downtown, near the Galleria, or in another upscale business district. The only explanation was that the rundown office was a front and Mr. Wallace's actual working location was somewhere else.

Charles looked around at the retail establishments adjacent to the strip mall so he could question some of the tenants. The nail salon and sandwich shop that anchored Wallace's office would be his first stops. Across the street there was a gas station with a convenience store, a fast food establishment, a laundromat, and a beauty supply store. They all appeared to have been there for years, looking similarly forlorn as the other surroundings. Nothing new had been built in that area of Brookshire for years. Somebody in one of those places had to know something about Wallace.

The owners of the nail salon and sandwich shop had only a limited grasp of the English language. As best Charles could surmise from their halting responses to his questions, neither had seen Wallace for the past several months. They weren't sure what type of car he drove or where he lived. Charles's questions to the proprietors of the other adjacent businesses didn't yield much information either. His last stop was the fast food establishment—a chicken joint. Charles noticed there was a security camera mounted above the chicken joint's awning, and fortuitously, it was pointed directly at Wallace's front entrance. Charles walked in to the restaurant and asked for the manager, who was behind the counter instructing one of the workers on how to sort the batch of newly fried chicken pieces into bins based on their spice levels.

She looked at him from the food preparation area. "What can I do for you, sir?"

"Ma'am, I'm Charles Scott, and I'm a reporter for the Houston *Ledger*. And your name is?

"Marjorie Woods. I'm the manager here."

"Ms. Woods, may I have a moment of your time?"

"I'm in the middle of preparing for the late afternoon rush, but how can I help you?"

"I'm writing a story about Texas small-town lawyers and was hoping to interview the attorney across the street, Joseph Wallace. Do you know anything about him?" Charles had developed an effective tactic when eliciting information from people who otherwise didn't talk to reporters. He gave them a general topic and tried to be as vague as possible. It was usually disarming.

"Not really. I hardly ever see him," she said as she picked up a chicken breast and placed it in the bin labeled "spicy."

"When was the last time you remember seeing him?"

"I really don't know. Maybe a month ago."

"Can you describe him? Is he tall or short? Thin, average, or heavy? What's his hair color and is his hair long or short?"

"I've only seen him at a glance the few times I've seen him, and he's usually wearing a hoodie. From a distance, he seems to be about six feet tall, but I've never seen his hair, so I can't tell you what color it is."

"Wearing a hoodie is unusual for an attorney, wouldn't you say?"

"Well, I thought it was a bit odd, but he may just be stopping by to pick up mail or paperwork on his way to the gym or somewhere else."

"What kind of car does he drive?"

"A dark-colored luxury car, possibly German, but I can't say for sure about the make or model."

"I see. May I ask you one more question? I saw your security camera outside. How long do you keep the footage?"

"We keep the footage for thirty days, but we don't normally let anyone view it except our security company or law enforcement. Mr. Scott, I really am busy," she said as she turned her attention to the employee operating the fryer.

"I've driven all the way from Houston, and it would really help me if I could view the film footage. I'd like to see how often Mr. Wallace stops by the office and what kind of car he drives. If I can establish a pattern in his routine, I may be able to return when he's expected to be at the office." What Charles really wanted to do was see Wallace's car and its license plate. He had some contacts at the Texas Department of Motor Vehicles, and he could potentially track down Wallace's home address.

"I suppose it wouldn't hurt to let you look at the footage in my office. But since I'm preparing for the next rush of customers, you'll have to either wait for about three hours or come back after eight o'clock."

"I'll come back after eight," he said as he left the restaurant and headed back to his car.

Charles knew the camera footage was a long shot, but he could sense there was a big story here. Americans for True Freedom had powerful players at its core.

Since Lloyd had authorized a small travel budget for this exploratory trip, Charles felt like he needed to show some results. He knew something was amiss. Call it reporter's intuition, if there was such a thing. He decided to grab a bite to eat then check into his motel. He'd come back to the restaurant after eight o'clock to view the security footage.

CHAPTER 12

Lloyd Palmer left his office at about six o'clock and was on his way home from the *Ledger* when his cell phone rang. The caller ID showed it was his best friend, Ron Singleton.

"Hey, Ron. How've you been?"

"Busy but good. Do you have any spare time this evening? I'd like to come by your house to talk to you about something. Are you at home or still at the office?"

"I'm in my car on my way home. I should be there in about fifteen minutes. What's up?"

"Like I said, I have something I'd like to talk to you about."

"Do you want to give me a hint now or keep me wondering?"

"It's somewhat complicated, so I'd rather wait and give you all the details when I get there. How does seven sound?"

"Sounds good. I should be home by then. Are you bringing Shirley with you?"

"Not this time. I'll be coming straight from work."

"Okay. I'll see you then."

Lloyd and Ron had been best friends since college. Five years earlier during the kidnapping and murder case Lloyd ultimately solved, Ron was caught up in a city dragnet to find the supposed kidnapper. When he was unfairly arrested and detained overnight, Lloyd was the one who posted his bond and picked him up from the city jail. Ron didn't want Shirley to go through the hassle that accompanied getting someone out of jail. The search and security procedures were much worse than what she'd experienced when traveling by air.

A day or so after Ron got out of jail, his profile was raised when he went on a local radio station and challenged city officials to make a public mea culpa. He also supported Lloyd's push to get the *Ledger* to run a full-page apology to Houston's Black citizens. His election to the Texas legislature was a direct result of his advocacy work on criminal justice reform.

Lloyd pulled into his driveway. His wife, Stephanie, was outside planting azalea bushes in the front yard of their two-story home. She took great pride in her yard work, especially since their daughter, Bria, had graduated from college and worked in Dallas as an accounting associate for one of the Big Four accounting firms.

Stephanie enjoyed teaching sixth grade in one of Houston metro's wealthiest school districts. With students that age, she felt like she was really making a difference and shaping the leaders of tomorrow. But since she and Lloyd now had an empty nest, Stephanie spent much of her spare time gardening. She was always competing with Mrs. Sherman, their neighbor in the next block, for their subdivision's Yard of the Month award. It was a friendly competition but fierce nonetheless.

"The flowers are beautiful," said Lloyd as he bent down and kissed Stephanie softly on her lips. "Think you'll win the award this month?" he asked with a chuckle. He found his wife's competitive spirit regarding her horticulture to be amusing.

"Laugh all you want," replied Stephanie with determination in her voice. "I'm giving Mrs. Sherman a run for her money. That Yard of the Month sign will be in our yard next time."

Lloyd remembered his call from Ron. "Ron called and said he was stopping by."

"On a weekday? That's unusual. Must be something important. Is Shirley coming with him?" asked Stephanie. Shirley, Ron's wife, often accompanied him when he came to the house. The Friday night card game competition between the two couples had been a monthly tradition for years. The game, spades, was played with partners, the ladies against the men. The ladies usually won.

"I don't think so. He seems like he wants to have a heart-to-heart talk with me."

The two men had been friends so long they could pick up each other's unspoken signals, even going so far as to complete the other's sentences. Their friendship had withstood college and the career years after, and they married women who turned out to be the best of friends.

"Sounds mysterious," Stephanie said. "I'm sure I'll find something to occupy my time while the two of you talk. Do you think he'll want to eat dinner?"

"I doubt it, but you normally cook enough so there are leftovers. Let's just play it by ear. He said he'd be here around seven, and it's almost that time now." Lloyd then reached his hand inside Stephanie's blouse and softly palmed her left breast, moving his hand in a circular motion.

"Lloyd," she whispered as she nudged him and leaned forward slightly, "the neighbors will see you."

"So what? They're all adults. Well, most of them are anyway. They know what goes on behind closed doors."

"Well, I'm almost done here," she replied as she gathered her tools together then removed her gardening gloves. "Let's go inside. We have just enough time for a quickie before Ron gets here."

CHAPTER 13

Ron left Lucille's Restaurant feeling both excited and perplexed. On the way back to his office, he reflected on his unusual lunch meeting with Michael Goldberg. He still didn't understand exactly why Michael had zeroed in on him as a potential Senate candidate. While he had gotten quite a bit of media exposure as a result of his public stance against police overreach in the faked Pauley kidnapping, he still was largely unknown outside the Houston metro area. A run for statewide office seemed premature.

But Ron had to admit he was excited about the possibility of running for such a high position and potentially winning the seat. If he won, he would be among one hundred of the most powerful political figures in the country—maybe even the world—and it could lead to even bigger things. In the modern era, two senators who looked like him had ended up as president and vice president. It was no longer considered to be impossible; that Rubicon had already been crossed. The prospect of winning was something he simply couldn't ignore.

But Ron had noticed Goldberg kept referring to "we" instead of "I" or "me." Clearly there were others involved, and Ron knew they had to be wealthy, influential, or both. He wondered if he should broach the subject at their next meeting because Ron wanted to know exactly who he'd be dealing with. Lloyd might have some insights about that since he'd been in the newspaper business for years. He knew something about the behind-the-scenes deals that were cut in the political arena.

He spent the afternoon fielding calls from community leaders and a couple of his fellow legislators. Ron decided to leave the office at six o'clock, and as soon as he got to his car heading for home, he called Lloyd on his cell phone. During their brief conversation, Lloyd indicated he was already close to home, and Ron headed that way. He decided to wait until after he spoke with Lloyd before sharing the news with Shirley. Lloyd might have a perspective that could alter Ron's decision whether or not to take Goldberg up on his offer. Or Lloyd could add to what Ron already believed so his conversation with Shirley would be better informed.

Once he arrived at Lloyd's house, he sat in his car for a few minutes. He wondered whether Lloyd would encourage him to pursue the Senate seat or whether he'd tell him he was nuts for even thinking about. Lloyd's tendency toward caution might help shed light on some factors Ron hadn't considered, and he wanted all of the pros and cons thoroughly thought through. It was easy to miss something important when you were emotionally invested in the outcome.

When he was ready to go in, he went to the Palmers' front door and rang the bell. Stephanie greeted him with a big grin.

"Hi, Ron. Lloyd told me you were coming by," she said as she gave him a big hug. "It's always good to see you."

"Same here, Steph. Lloyd told me he'd be home about this time."

"He's waiting for you in the study," she said as she headed toward the den to give them some privacy.

Lloyd was sitting at his desk working on his laptop when Ron walked in. He had been checking the *Ledger*'s story click board, and the leading stories were true to form: the murder of three family members followed by a suicide in Pasadena; a five-car pile-up on the Grand Parkway with three killed and several injured; and a Houston City Councilmember caught using meth in a hotel room—one, two, and three, in that order.

When Lloyd saw Ron, he stood up and gave him a hug. "How's it going, man? Glad to see you, but you sounded awfully mysterious on the phone. What's so important that it couldn't wait?"

They both sat down on the sofa Lloyd had placed in his study. "I had an interesting lunch meeting today. Have you ever heard of an attorney named Michael Goldberg?"

"Sure. He's one of the most successful lawyers in Houston."

"What else do you know about him?"

"He's pretty well connected politically, but he keeps a relatively low profile. I can do a search to see what we have on him in the newspaper's archives if that will help."

"That could be helpful. During lunch today, he presented an interesting proposition."

"Oh yeah, what's that?"

"He wants me to run for the U.S. Senate, and he says he can provide all of the financial backing and staff support I need."

Lloyd was stunned. "Whoa! The U.S. Senate? Talk about something coming out of left field." There was a pregnant pause then Lloyd asked the obvious question: "What was your answer?"

"I told him I had to think about it and discuss it with Shirley. But I'm giving it some serious thought. Can you imagine? I could be the first Black Senator from the state of Texas."

"That would definitely be an amazing feat. No other Black candidate has ever come close to winning." Lloyd's inquisitive nature as a journalist was kicking in. The *Ledger* had covered every Senate campaign since the paper was founded. During his tenure there, both as a reporter and as the editor, the paper had covered a couple of races where a Black candidate had tried running for the Senate. Whether running as a Democrat or a Republican, the candidate was basically a sacrificial lamb. The closest any candidate had come to winning was five points behind the victor.

"I can't think of anybody who could do a better job than you, but did Goldberg say why he selected you in particular for this privilege?"

"He said he'd been casually keeping track of my political activities since I got caught up in the Pauley kidnapping dragnet. He seemed to be impressed by what he's seen." Ron provided Lloyd with a recap of his lunch meeting with Goldberg.

"So are you leaning toward saying yes?"

"It depends on what Shirley says, but right now I'm over the halfway mark in terms of being in favor of the idea. Look at it this way: I couldn't do any worse than the two senators we already have in D.C.," Ron remarked sarcastically followed by the display of a wide grin.

Lloyd laughed. "You've got that right. That's a no-brainer, but I'd be very careful if I were you," offered Lloyd. "Remember the adage: Beware of strangers bearing gifts.

People who provide financial backing to political campaigns are always looking for something in return, either in the short term, the long term, or both."

"I've considered that, and I figure if Goldberg has some sort of dark ulterior motive, it will manifest itself during the campaign. And if it's truly alarming, I can always come up with a personal reason for dropping out of the race, like stress on my family, which happens in every campaign. When the stakes are higher, the stress level is higher too."

"That's a pretty good backup plan. You can pay attention to what's happening, but it's hard to be on the campaign trail and know what's taking place behind the scenes too. Goldberg has already said he'll supply your staff, and those will all be people that are loyal to him, not you. So who will you be able to trust? You need somebody to be your eyes and ears."

"I thought about that, and then a light bulb went off. There's something else I wanted to run by you because I have someone in mind."

Lloyd folded his hands together, interlocking his fingers, and leaned back on the sofa. "Don't keep me in suspense."

"I'd like Stephanie to be my campaign manager."

"*My* Stephanie?" asked Lloyd in disbelief. "What in God's name could you be thinking by putting Steph on your campaign staff, let alone running the show? Steph doesn't have any experience in politics whatsoever. Plus, she loathes it and always has. I'm not sure why, but it has something to do with adversity experienced in her family a long time ago. She votes during most elections, but that's the extent of her involvement in anything political."

"She may not seem like the ideal pick, but I trust her implicitly. She's smart, savvy, well organized, and intuitive—just the kind of person I need to be my eyes and ears during the campaign."

"When you rattle off a list of Steph's amazing qualities, you'll get no argument from me. But the campaign will last several months, maybe longer. She does have a full-time job, you know."

"I've already thought about that. The spring semester is almost over, which would be the perfect timing in terms of her getting started. She could take a leave of absence from teaching while the campaign is underway, and based on what Goldberg said, I'd be able to pay her at least double what she's making now. Plus, think of the civics lessons she'll learn about how our government actually works. She could use that to share with her students when she returns to the classroom."

The prospect of Stephanie doubling her salary in the short term was an attractive one to Lloyd. They had always wanted to purchase a summer home near Lake Jackson. This could be just the opportunity that would give them the substantial down payment they'd need to make the deal work.

But he wasn't going to be selfish. He also knew Stephanie and her disdain for politics was legendary...and visceral. He wasn't going to try to push her in either direction; it would have to be her decision alone.

"Have you discussed this with her?" probed Lloyd. "Knowing Steph and the way she absolutely despises politics, she'll probably respond to your request with a swift and emphatic 'hell no.'"

"I wanted to run it by you first to see what you thought. Maybe you can broach the subject with her so it won't be a complete shock when I ask her," said Ron, hoping Lloyd would help pave the way for a calm, measured discussion with Stephanie.

"Thanks for putting me in the hot seat," Lloyd replied sarcastically. "I can give her a heads up that you want to talk to her about something, but it will be up to you to convince her. I learned a long time ago not to try making Stephanie's decisions for her."

"I told Goldberg I'd give him an answer by Monday."

"In that case, you need to have your discussion with her right away," Lloyd advised. "Knowing Steph, she may not give you an immediate answer one way or the other. Since it's you who's asking, she may at least try to be open to it, but she'll need a day or two to mull it over. If her answer is no, you'll need to know that before your next conversation with Goldberg."

"Fair enough. Let me talk to Shirley about it first to make sure she's on board with the idea. If she gives me a green light, then I'll either come by or call over the weekend to talk to Stephanie."

"Okay, but make sure you call her by Friday because her weekend may be busy. Meanwhile, I'll find out what I can about Michael Goldberg."

CHAPTER 14

After Ron's talk with Lloyd, he spent his drive home trying to decompress from all that had happened. He had loads of nervous energy from the day's events. He thought listening to some old-school R&B would be relaxing, so he turned on his Luther Vandross playlist on Spotify. The lyrics to "Never Too Much" were a metaphor for what his wife, Shirley, had meant to him over their twenty-plus years together. He would need her full support to make this next push in his career work.

He continued to ponder the prospect of running for the Senate. The more Ron thought about Goldberg's offer to help him set up and finance his campaign, the more he leaned toward saying yes. He might never get a chance to wage a viable campaign for statewide office again, and he didn't want to spend the rest of his life with coulda—woulda—shoulda regrets. While listening to Luther's velvet tenor voice during his drive home, he contemplated the best approach to get Shirley's support.

He considered her most likely objections; the main one would be that their entire family would be exposed to public scrutiny. He really didn't have a response for that because that's what also raised his level of apprehension. But he believed they could get through it by being strong for each other. They didn't have anything to hide.

His races for city council and state representative had been relatively tame. Everybody already knew about the worst event of his life: being publicly and wrongfully handcuffed, arrested, and taken to jail. But because the entire city government had egg on its face from the colossal screw-up, he actually came out of that situation looking like a hero.

When Ron turned into his subdivision and arrived at home, he pulled his car into the driveway and took a deep breath before entering the front door. He could hear what sounded like Shirley in the midst of food preparation in the kitchen, and he walked in that direction.

"Hi, babe," he said and kissed Shirley on the cheek. "What's for dinner?"

Shirley placed a covered dish in the microwave and pushed the two-minute button. "I got home later than usual and decided to heat up the leftover lasagna and green beans we had last night. You're home later than usual too."

"I stopped by Lloyd's and Stephanie's on the way home because I wanted to talk to him about something," Ron said then paused. "I need to talk to you about it too."

"Did you know about this something when you left for work this morning?" The timer buzzed on the microwave, and Shirley removed the food she'd been warming. She turned and stirred it then placed it back in for one more minute.

"No. It's about something that transpired during the day."

"Well, don't keep me in suspense. It must be something big if you had to seek Lloyd's face-to-face advice."

"Calling it big would be an understatement."

The microwave timer buzzed. "Let's sit down, and you can tell me over dinner."

They both sat down at the kitchen table. "So are you going to tell me or make me guess?"

"I had lunch today with a lawyer named Michael Goldberg. Have you ever heard of him?"

"His name sounds somewhat familiar, but I can't place it," Shirley said as she reflected. "Who is he?"

"Well, he's a pretty well-connected guy...especially when it comes to politics."

"And?" asked Shirley, anxious to hear Ron's news.

"He wants to support me as a candidate for the U.S. Senate."

"The Senate? Really? Are you sure he's legit? He could be running a scam, pretending to be well connected to gain your confidence."

"I was skeptical too at first. But I asked Lloyd about him. Lloyd says he's heard about him but will also check the *Ledger* archives and let me know if he finds anything that would raise a red flag."

"But the Senate, babe? That takes a lot of money, millions of dollars—and a huge organization. You've just started to get your feet wet in politics in the Texas legislature. How in the world would you finance a Senate campaign?"

"Goldberg knows all the top-dollar political donors, so he says my campaign would be well financed. He told me money would be no problem."

"It sounds too good to be true, and you know what folks say about that."

"I realize that, but Goldberg seemed to be genuinely impressed by my track record since I've served in the Texas legislature. He said more people like me are needed in Washington."

"What about staffing the campaign? Do you know anyone with experience at that level?" Shirley asked with genuine concern. "During our last two campaigns, we had the whole family involved with fielding phone calls, distributing campaign literature, putting out yard signs, and knocking on doors. Those campaigns took every minute of our spare time. Running for the Senate is a whole different ballgame."

"He's got that covered too," Ron responded, sounding naïve even to himself. He'd never been especially ambitious, but since he'd entered politics, he'd started to believe that one person—strategically positioned and with the proper objectives—could make a difference. Ron told Shirley about the turnkey operation Goldberg said he could have up and running in short order.

"Really, babe?" she asked in disbelief. "You'd feel comfortable waging a campaign of this magnitude with a bunch of strangers at the helm? Sounds risky to me...and suspicious."

"I thought about that, and I may have a solution."

"What would that be? I'd love to hear it."

"I was going to ask Stephanie to be my campaign manager."

"*Our* Stephanie?"

"Now you sound like Lloyd."

"I'm glad I'm not the only one who is shocked by the suggestion. Did Lloyd give you a dose of reality?"

"He was skeptical, especially about Stephanie's involvement."

"As he should be. Have you asked her?"

"Not yet. I was trying to figure out the best approach."

"Good luck. You do realize that Stephanie hates politics, don't you?"

"Yes, but I don't know why. Do you?"

"I'm not sure. There seems to be something from her family's past that she hasn't felt like sharing. But she's made perfectly clear on more than one occasion that for her, any direct involvement in politics is completely out of the question."

"Even so, she's the best person I can think of for two reasons: One, I would be able to trust her to be my eyes and ears during the campaign. Two, the other staff members wouldn't consider her to be a threat. In fact, they might be more relaxed around her than they would a seasoned political operative."

"Babe, you know I'll support you whatever your decision, but I know you. You sound like your mind is already made up. I just hope you know what you're getting into. Politics is a sleazy business, and the higher you go, the sleazier it gets. When you lie down with dogs, you're going to get fleas."

"I can't argue with that, but the good that I may be able to do could outweigh the drawbacks of entering the race. Anyway, that's what I hope happens. But as long as we have each other, we'll weather whatever storms may come our way."

"That's the way it's always been, Babe, and that's the way it always will be," Shirley said as she smiled at Ron knowingly. "So…when do you plan to ask Stephanie about joining your campaign?"

"The sooner, the better. I told Goldberg I'd give him an answer by Monday, so that only gives me four days to convince Stephanie to join my campaign."

"Just know that the decision will be between you and her," Shirley added. "I don't want to get directly involved one way or the other. And if you two are going to be working together, now is the time to feel each other out. You'll be breaking new ground with Steph. Since we've known both her and Lloyd, it's been our personal relationship that we've relied on, and that's stayed strong over the years."

"We've never had any business or professional arrangements with either of them, and from what I've heard, mixing business with friendship can often irreparably damage both. I consider them to be like family, and I know you do too. I don't want to fracture our relationship by wading into unknown waters that may ultimately devour us all."

CHAPTER 15

Every member of the Committee was assigned a specific task; some were substantial, while others were small and inconsequential. Each member's task was designed to maximize their natural talents, and the media mogul was no different. His assignment was to manage the surveillance of potential and existing targets.

The media mogul was a peevish bald man, short in stature, with a face replete with pockmarks. He had an unsteady gait and wore ill-fitting clothes. With his round, barrel-shaped physique and at a height of just five feet four inches, those that encountered him said he resembled a penguin. His appearance didn't lend itself to romance as women found him to be universally repugnant. But his eye for what looked good on the big screen was nothing short of brilliant.

The resultant millions of dollars he'd accumulated since the eighties as a result of his cinematic skills gained him access to executive suites and board rooms around the world. That was how he met Michael, and the media mogul's considerable skills made him a natural as the Committee's video archivist.

His twenty-four-room, Tudor-style mansion included a theater room and a film collection that movie lovers would envy. He'd had a decades-long career as a successful filmmaker working with A-list actors and producing films that raked in billions of dollars. After his years in the industry, he had accumulated a massive library of classics, including Oscar-winning movies, global blockbusters, and even films that had never been released. But he had a special collection of bedroom scenes of potential Committee candidates and existing officeholders that he kept behind a hidden, recessed wall. The collection served as insurance in case any targets offered resistance to the Committee's commands. It was sort of like being a peeping Tom, which suited the media mogul just fine.

With his deeply unattractive appearance, his difficulty finding females that would be seen with him—in public or in private—was assuaged by the vast video library he'd amassed. There were millions of hours of porn produced by hidden cameras that he used to pleasure himself nightly until he climaxed.

But his Committee assignment also allowed him to satisfy his sexual urges vicariously by keeping tabs on the bedroom antics of his numerous targets, and he relished this task. Browsing pornography web sites was unnecessary when he had hours of camera footage of at least four dozen bedrooms from homes in gated communities.

When Michael gave him his marching orders about the Committee's targets, he was emphatic about what he wanted. "We need all the documentation you can find. Don't worry about the quality or the age of the images. We can piece some of them together to develop a narrative, or with your visual skills, we can create one from scratch."

"How far back do you want me to go? I mean, do we start with high school, the college years, or when?"

"Start with the childhood years if you're able to find some footage. That could give us some insight into their childhood traumas, motivations, perceived slights, and familial relationships. If they had a troubled or estranged relationship with one of their parents, we want to know about it." Michael wanted to be thorough.

"No problem. I'll get my researchers started, and I'll use only the best," the media mogul responded.

With the best data harvesters that money could buy, the media mogul amassed so much data about their targets that its storage required the Committee to lease a thirty thousand-square-foot facility to house the servers on which the data was stored. The information the Committee acquired was thorough, allowing them to choose top-tier candidates. And those candidates were not selected at random. They were surveilled for months to document their daily schedules as well as their habits, proclivities, vices, and deviations from the norm.

Before he became a member of the Committee, the media mogul managed surveillance work for a host of private clients. His clients ranged from wealthy VIPs that wanted to develop portfolios on their industry rivals to corporate tycoons in May December relationships that didn't trust their trophy wives to remain monogamous. Once he joined the Committee, he ended his work with private clients and devoted all his spare time to monitoring the Committee's targets. That was Michael's specific condition for him to accept his role within the organization.

In the early years of his work with the Committee, the media mogul's data collection efforts required hours upon hours of meticulous, painstaking work. It required him to hire dozens of private investigators to follow the targets' every move for months. But his surveillance work was made exponentially less tedious by the proliferation of social media.

The media mogul often marveled at how much personal information people were willing to divulge on social media platforms like Facebook, Instagram, Twitter, and TikTok. People shared where they dined, where they vacationed, where they worked, and where they played with the entire world. They would perform outlandish, dangerous, or freaky feats just to film themselves, share the videos, and pray they'd go viral. Nearly every detail of their private lives was released into cyberspace for public consumption, no matter how salacious. It was as if they didn't realize the global reach and the permanence of the images they shared. Decades later, the words and images posted to their accounts would surely come back to haunt them, ruining their careers and personal relationships.

If there was a dearth of incriminating social media photos within a politician's accounts, that didn't present a challenge. The media mogul could always gain access to the pol's cell phone photos that were stored in the cloud. In the 2020s, folks lived their lives via their cell phones; their vacations, their celebrations, and even their recriminations were all in the cloud.

The onset of artificial intelligence, the next new thing in technological advancement, presented a new weapon to add to the media mogul's arsenal. AI allowed the media mogul to create situations and events that had never actually taken place. This served the Committee well as their primary mission in creating the dossiers was not for the purpose of releasing the information to the media or the public. Rather, it was to keep the pols they had groomed under their control, in case they wanted to disobey directives. Or in case they wanted to take unauthorized actions on their own. Or in case they had the notion that the Committee was not in complete control. Or in case they thought their identities would be protected if they decided to play the whistleblower role.

The Committee could wield the most power by merely threatening to release the dossier's details. Releasing the information to the mainstream media was a last resort. The threat alone would usually immediately quell the pol's desire to bare their soul to anyone. This worked even with politicians that thought their reputations were squeaky clean. There was no such thing. An altered recording here, a photo-shopped image there, a tweaked document, or an edited video could do the trick. Once the pol was shown the imagery with the threat that it would go viral, the pol was practically begging the Committee to allow them to change their mind. The Committee always got what it wanted—always.

The media mogul spent hours at home in his indoor theater watching videos of the regular comings and goings of unsuspecting candidates. He took meticulous notes about their sexual impulses—the kinkier, the better. Once the candidates accepted the Committee's offer to be under their umbrella of influence, the scrutiny intensified. He hired out third parties to perform tasks that weren't routine and required special skill sets. And if it became necessary to set a trap for one of them, he had a high-level expert he engaged: Romulus.

CHAPTER 16

After Ron left the Palmer house and headed for home, Lloyd logged on to the *Ledger*'s website to search the paper's archives with regard to Michael Goldberg. He didn't know what he expected to find, but he was curious as to why Goldberg seemed to select Ron out of thin air as the recipient of his largesse. He thought a search of the archives might provide some clues.

If Lloyd had learned anything from his friend Hamisi, it was that things were rarely as they appeared to be on the surface. One had to dig deeper to find the truth, and the truth was seldom obvious. Lloyd knew that politics operated on quid pro quo arrangements. If Goldberg was handing Ron what appeared to be a gift, Lloyd was certain the lawyer would want something huge in return.

His query of Michael Goldberg's name yielded the usual news reports that would be expected with an attorney of Goldberg's caliber. Multimillion-dollar corporate settlements he'd negotiated, mergers and acquisitions he'd coordinated, new partners and associates that were added to his firm, and photos of Goldberg with Houston's wealthy elites at high-society social events.

As a career journalist, Lloyd knew digging into a subject's past life was the best way to discover the most intriguing information about them. Past events and connections that might appear to be trivial could take on increased significance in the context of the present. So Lloyd expanded his search to include news reports prior to the year 2000. Once he did, the listed news stories were scant in number but similar in nature. However, it was clear that the net worth of Goldberg's corporate clients had dramatically increased over time. Early in Goldberg's legal career, his clients were mostly million-dollar Houston-based companies. Now he was cutting deals representing multibillion-dollar, multinational behemoths around the world.

Then Lloyd noticed a college graduation photo from the mid-1990s among the image search listings. The photo was of Goldberg and one of his classmates, Joseph Wallace, who both hailed from Houston and graduated from Harvard the same year.

Goldberg went on to attend Harvard Law School, but Lloyd was unable to find any news articles about Wallace's law school matriculation. The absence of news meant the law school Wallace attended was probably second tier.

After a secondary search for Wallace's name, Lloyd noticed that Wallace and Goldberg didn't appear to have operated within the same social or professional circles in recent years. He found no more instances of news reports where Goldberg's and Wallace's names or photos appeared together.

Regarding Wallace, Lloyd discovered that he had been an associate at Beck, Miller & Beck for a few years, which explained why Wallace and Goldberg's paths didn't appear to cross in social circles. The field of personal injury law that dominated the Beck law firm's client list was worlds apart from the corporate clients Goldberg represented.

After leaving Beck, Wallace appeared to have moved his law practice to the town of Brookshire, opened an office there, and fallen off the grid. There were no recent photos of him, his family, or other legal associates. Lloyd checked the obits and there wasn't one for a Joseph T. Wallace of his age and location, so he must still be alive.

Lloyd conducted a Google Maps street view search of Wallace's law office, which was in a less than pristine area of the small bedroom community. The storefront property was in desperate need of a coat of paint, and the gold letters in the window that read "Joseph T. Wallace & Associates" were faded and peeling. Commercial establishments that were adjacent to the lawyer's storefront included a nail salon and a sandwich shop. Not exactly high society.

People that graduated from Harvard didn't usually end up practicing law in a tiny town like Brookshire. In a town that small, most of Wallace's legal work would center around handling divorces, writing last wills and testaments, and managing property probates. The fact that Wallace's career path had led him in this direction amounted to what Lloyd called a curious fact. Curious facts rarely occurred in isolation; they were always connected to something. Lloyd took a screenshot of the information he had found, created a folder on his computer named "Ron for Senate," and put the images in the folder so he could reference them easily later.

What he found could be nothing and have no bearing whatsoever on Ron's campaign. Or it could be substantial and lead to immense, damaging consequences. If Ron decided to run for the Senate—and he seemed to be leaning in that direction—Lloyd was going to make sure he wasn't blindsided by something he could have uncovered beforehand. One of the nuggets of wisdom Hamisi had once texted Lloyd was that he should always be on high alert and watch, fight, and pray. As Ron's best friend, Lloyd was going to be watching every single detail very carefully as this saga unfolded.

CHAPTER 17

Charles checked into his motel room while he waited the three hours the fast food manager required so he'd have access to the restaurant's security camera footage. He hoped she was still in a good mood and wasn't thoroughly exhausted after overseeing the evening's dinner crowd.

As he munched on the cheeseburger and French fries he'd purchased, he sat at his laptop and googled "Joseph Wallace" so he could find out more about his legal career. For someone who was the registered agent of an actively involved PAC, there was hardly any online information about him for the last ten years.

Before that, there were a few images of him with a group of attorneys from Beck, Miller & Beck. Everybody in the state of Texas knew about the law firm's "Annihilator" television advertisements that seemed to run every hour on the hour. Wallace's name was included in the firm's photo captions, but the articles never mentioned him directly.

Charles found the lack of online information about Wallace to be puzzling. Normally attorneys that represented well-financed PACs would be photographed, written about, and talked about even by smaller media outlets. But with Wallace, there was hardly anything.

Charles felt like he needed to have something tangible to report back to Lloyd within a day or so. Although he counted Lloyd among his closest friends, he took their professional relationship seriously. He knew Lloyd, as the *Ledger*'s editor, was under a lot of pressure to produce results. Lloyd had to keep the executives at bay in order to justify the news department's budget and keep them from exacting further budget cuts, all while trying to juggle staff utilization and salary allocations. It was a delicate balancing act. Charles was determined to make sure he left Brookshire with the foundation for a story or even a series of stories.

He set his cell phone alarm to beep at seven forty-five so he could get to the restaurant at precisely eight o'clock. Charles turned on the television to check out Brookshire's local evening news and reclined on the bed. He'd take a quick nap before heading back to the restaurant and was hoping the security footage would give him some clues about exactly who Joseph Wallace was.

CHAPTER 18

Stephanie Palmer came from a long line of teachers. Her mother, Audrey, retired after a forty-year career teaching elementary school students in Navasota, Texas. "Steph," her mother would affectionately say, using the shortened version of her name, "when you teach children, you're molding the next generation." Stephanie took those words to heart.

Stephanie's grandmother, Mamie, had passed away before she was born, but her mother frequently shared stories about Mamie's passion for reading with Stephanie and her two brothers, Craig and Jamal. Mamie, who was born in the early 1900s, washed, folded, and ironed laundry for some of the white folks that owned land where she lived in the tiny rural town of Washington, Texas. But Mamie wasn't deterred by her humble circumstances. She taught herself to read by lamp light after her husband, George, and seven children were asleep. She mastered reading well enough to teach George, her children, and some of the local sharecroppers' children how to read.

Later, some of the Black farmers in the area got together and hired a teacher from Paul Quinn College, a historically Black college based in Dallas, to run their community school. They used the First Baptist Church as their venue during the week, then held Spirit-filled church services on Sunday that started in the morning, broke for a potluck dinner, and continued until the early evening hours.

Stephanie loved being a teacher and believed it was her calling. As a child, during summer vacations from school, she would gather some of the neighborhood children together to play school. She would always designate herself to be the teacher, and none of the kids ever objected. On the rare occasions when the children in their neighborhood couldn't come out to play, Stephanie's younger brothers, Craig and Jamal, were willing pupils.

Her passion for teaching had only grown over the twenty years she'd been instructing middle schoolers. A lot of teachers sought administrative positions over spending eight hours a day with eleven- to thirteen-year-old kids, but Stephanie found the work exhilarating. The key was to present the students with assignments that were both challenging and engaging. Lazy teaching methods would not do.

On the evenings when Stephanie brought work home from school—papers to grade, lesson plans, memos from the principal or school district—Lloyd would sometimes bring his laptop in the den and they'd work silently, pausing occasionally to interject an update on the day's activities. So it wasn't out of the ordinary one evening when, as she was working, Lloyd tapped lightly on the door frame and asked if he could enter.

"Sure, babe. Are you planning to edit the stories for tomorrow's *Ledger*?" she posited since that was one of Lloyd's regular nighttime rituals as editor of the paper.

"Reviewing some, editing some, ordering rewrites for some...you know, the usual. But I wanted to give you a heads up about something."

Stephanie paused from the work she was doing on her laptop. “Okay. You’ve gotten my attention.”

“Ron’s going to be calling you soon to ask a favor. It could be today or tomorrow.”

“So are you going to tell me what it’s about or not?”

“He wanted to tell you himself.”

“Now you’ve really piqued my curiosity. Why are you being so cryptic?”

“Because anything I say could bias you, and I promised I wouldn’t do that.”

“Maybe I should call him myself rather than wait on pins and needles.”

“If you do that, he’ll think I broke my promise. Just wait until he calls, okay?”

“I could pretend like I’m calling for some other reason...to sort of throw him off the trail.”

“He’ll know something’s up. How often do you call him? Hardly ever. Shirley’s the one you’re chatty with on the phone. He’s going to call you—believe that. The only thing I’ll say about it is please keep an open mind when he talks to you.”

Stephanie paused. Her curiosity was going to kill her but she didn’t want to interfere with Lloyd and Ron’s long friendship. Keeping an open mind could mean anything. “All right,” she said reluctantly and went back to grading papers.

CHAPTER 19

Ron woke up Thursday morning filled with apprehension. As he got dressed for work, he contemplated the best time to call Stephanie to break the news and ask for her help. He realized there wasn't going to be a perfect time, so he might as well call her right away.

With Stephanie's revulsion of all things political, he needed to get this discussion over with…the sooner, the better. That way, if she said no, he'd have time to think of a Plan B. At the moment, he didn't have a Plan B and was putting all of his eggs in the Stephanie basket. He couldn't think of anyone else he'd rather have running his operation. Stephanie was a straightshooter and smart as a whip. He crossed his fingers and hoped that she would at least listen to his proposal and not immediately reject it.

When he got to the office, he took a few phone calls and did some busy work. He kept his eye on the clock, and the minutes seemed to slowly tick by. He knew that at the school where Stephanie taught, she usually took her mid-day break around eleven thirty, so he was simply biding his time until then.

At eleven thirty on the dot, he picked up his cell phone and dialed Stephanie's number. She answered almost immediately.

"Hi, Ron. What's going on? You don't usually call me in the middle of the day. Nothing's wrong, is there?" He could hear the sound of her chewing after that.

"No, nothing's wrong. I just wanted to talk to you about something. I realize I'm interrupting your lunch, but you'll probably spend more time listening than talking."

"Lloyd told me you might be calling, and it must be something out of the ordinary if you're calling me while we're both at work."

"I thought it was better to talk to you sooner rather than later."

"Well? I only get thirty minutes for lunch and I've just started eating my salad, so what's up?"

Ron took a deep breath. "Did Lloyd tell you I've been approached about running for the U.S. Senate?"

"No, he told me you had some major news but thought it was better if you told me yourself. Wow! That's an honor. Are you going to do it?"

"I'm not sure yet. I told the lawyer who approached me that I'd give him an answer by Monday."

"Was the person who approached you someone you already know?"

"Not exactly. He's someone I've heard of by way of reputation, but we had never met until yesterday."

"Well, if you have to give him an answer by Monday, that's only a few days from now. What does Shirley think?"

"You know Shirley. She's always had my back. She said she'll support whatever decision I make."

"That sounds like Shirley. So how can I help? Do you want us to put out yard signs? Host a fundraiser? You know the Palmer household will be all in to help you get elected."

"Actually, I was hoping you'd agree to be my campaign manager."

Shirley put her fork down and almost choked on her salad. She was speechless. "You've got to be kidding."

"No, I'm dead serious. I want you heading up my team. There's no one else I'd trust more to handle things and be my eyes and ears."

"Ron, I appreciate you thinking of me, but I would be more of a detriment than an asset. I have no experience in politics, plus I hate it with a passion."

"The lawyer said his crew will provide me with a campaign staff, but I'll be dealing with a bunch of strangers. They'll be more knowledgeable than I am about the inner workings of a political campaign. I don't want to be out there on an island all by myself with no one to watch my back."

"Ron, again, I'm honored that you'd think of me, but I don't think I have the skills or connections to be of any use. You need the best people on your team. To say I'm a political novice is an understatement."

"Stephanie, I think you're selling yourself short. I've seen you organize the neighborhood for all sorts of projects, and they're all successful. Remember when the residents wanted a traffic light installed at our subdivision entrance because traffic was always backed up? You organized a petition, got everyone to sign it, and presented it to the county office with a request that it be done within the next ninety days. Thanks to you, we now have a much safer neighborhood. People like you, listen to you, and trust you."

"Getting a petition signed is one thing. Running a statewide political operation requires skills I simply don't have."

"You have the exact skills I need. With your management style, you don't have any problem giving directives and expecting results."

"What about my job? I do love teaching, you know."

"I've thought about that. You wouldn't need to start until after the spring semester ends. And since it's my campaign, I plan to pay you a lot more than you're making now as a teacher. I'll be able to double or even triple your monthly salary."

There were a few seconds of silence as they both paused.

"The money is a very generous offer, but this really isn't about the money. I promised myself that I'd never get involved in politics."

"Just do me a favor and think about it," Ron nudged Stephanie further.

"You're not giving me much time if you need to give the attorney—I don't think you told me his name."

"He's Michael Goldberg, one of the most successful lawyers in the Houston metro area."

"Well, if Mr. Goldberg needs an answer by Monday, then you need me to give you an answer by Saturday at the latest."

"That's about right. Please give it serious consideration. I'd really like you on board."

"So Lloyd knew you were going to ask me this?"

"Yes, he did, but he said the decision was completely up to you."

"That may very well be, but I'll be talking his ear off for the next twenty-four hours until I give you my answer. I'm still leaning toward saying no, but this decision could affect our entire family. I'll call you Saturday morning with my answer, whatever it is."

"That's all I can ask for."

CHAPTER 20

Rudo Hamisi reclined into the soft leather of his first class seat on his British Airways flight from Zimbabwe to the United States. Following the crab salad he'd had for lunch, he'd asked the flight attendant for a cup of cranberry juice, and each sip he took had a refreshing effect. There were still eight hours remaining on the flight before the wheels touched down at JFK in New York City.

He was returning after eighteen months of living in his home country. As a griot from the Lemba tribe, Hamisi found that periodic immersion into his cultural roots kept him grounded and spiritually connected to his people and to humanity.

Hamisi had sold two hundred acres of the land that had been in his family for generations to developers that wanted to turn it into a wildlife preserve. As a tourist attraction for safari enthusiasts, it would rake in a sizable revenue for the corporation that had bought it. He had deposited the money from the sale in a bank account in Barbados, outside the watchful eye and jurisdiction of American authorities. The eight hundred acres he still retained were managed by his older brother, who ensured that the tradition of herding cows, goats, and sheep among his large extended family was maintained.

In contrast to his peaceful, quiet existence in Zimbabwe, Hamisi believed the Western world offered far too many distractions with its constant focus on fame and material wealth. Americans' obsession with money, fame, and social media gossip stunted the development of their spiritual senses and, he believed, would eventually lead to their undoing.

Americans had little discernment about the ulterior or sinister motives of others. They possessed little ability to anticipate the future by understanding the principle of cause and effect. They could see little other than what was directly in front of them, and some couldn't even see that. The more time he spent in the West, the more he could feel his spiritual powers waning, diminishing day by day. That's why he kept his visits relatively short.

Yet he didn't want to cut himself completely off from the modern world. In order to have an impact, he needed to understand what he was up against from spiritual forces that left destruction in their wake.

In addition to his tribal tongue, Hamisi spoke seven languages, including English, Spanish, Greek, Italian, and Polish. He had learned most of the European languages during his time in Zimbabwe spent working with one of the wealthy white landowners whose staff hailed from throughout Europe. He was also proficient with Russian, although he understood the language better than he spoke it. He served as a tutor to several of the landowners' children, which provided a relatively easy way for him to master the languages while serving in a position where others would not suspect his intellectual and spiritual prowess.

His tribe's genetic ties to the biblical Aaron, Moses' brother, rendered the innate ability of exceptional discernment and communication. On a previous three-month trip to America several years ago, use of his sixth and seventh senses had not only connected him to a new dear friend, Lloyd Palmer, but alerting members of the Lemba's enforcement squad of an imminent threat to Lloyd and his family had helped save their lives.

With Hamisi's guidance, Lloyd began his journey on his path to self-actualization. When he first met Lloyd, the frustrated news reporter was filled with self-doubt, lacking confidence in himself and his abilities as a journalist. He was going through a mid-life crisis, and his professional future was in doubt.

But after spending time with Hamisi as well as receiving his intuitive, timely text messages, Lloyd was transformed into a full-fledged, self-assured journalist who was now the editor at one of America's largest daily newspapers, the Houston *Ledger*. He still kept in touch with Lloyd occasionally through cryptic text messages—enough communication so Lloyd would know the two of them were still spiritually connected. The messages also helped give Lloyd guidance as he mastered the challenges of his new position.

There were more people Hamisi could help, he was sure of it. Staying under the radar—a requirement of being a Lemba griot—while raising the consciousness of others often presented a difficult balancing act. He had to keep his circle extremely small and stay off the digital grid.

That meant no American bank accounts, no landline use, no long-term phone number or address, and no social media footprint whatsoever. Hamisi had developed a routine for his visits to the States. Once he arrived, he purchased a large stock of disposable cell phones—burners—at different convenience stores. He'd use one phone for about a week, remove the phone's SIM card, and toss both the phone and SIM card in different waste baskets at different public transportation stops in different parts of whatever city he visited.

He had an email account via Yahoo, but he only accessed it at Internet cafés or coffee houses that had Wi-Fi access. He never went to the same location twice in a row. After sending or receiving an email, he deleted his account's history. He also used these locations to keep abreast of national and worldwide news, but he preferred print editions when they were available. He took every possible precaution to leave no digital footprint and to ensure that his movements in the United States could not be tracked or traced.

As was the custom of the Lemba people, he was independently wealthy. Wealth protected him from being controlled by foreign interlopers that used the poverty of indigenous people in third world nations as a means to dominate them. He periodically accessed the cash in his overseas bank accounts using pre-paid debit cards he loaded at the beginning of his trips.

Hamisi possessed a cadre of fake passports and identification cards to maintain his anonymity. Whenever he needed large sums of cash, he would email his bank contact in Barbados or one of the other island nations that offered discrete banking practices. He'd have them send the funds via MoneyGram to a twenty-four-hour check-cashing facility in whichever city he was in. He would have the funds wired incrementally in amounts small enough to avoid detection by federal authorities. The loosely worded Patriot Act was used by the feds as a control mechanism to keep tabs on

Americans' financial transactions, but Hamisi could work around the restrictions.

Hamisi was methodical. He utilized three different check-cashing facilities when he visited Houston, another added cautionary measure.

Hamisi was in his eighties but his ebony-hued skin showed minimal signs of aging. People often mistook him for a man in his sixties or even fifties. He was vibrant, enjoying his twilight years. His only wife had passed away years ago, and he had never remarried. He had two sons, John and Peter, both of whom were still in Zimbabwe. Several years ago they had been elevated to the positions of honored men, one of the highest designations among the Lemba people, and their futures were secure.

Once a year Hamisi traveled to the United States and always added a visit to Houston to his itinerary, usually traveling to Texas by bus or train after arriving in New York City by air. He felt no need to rush and could select a mode of transportation where he could travel at his leisure.

Once he arrived in a city where he'd remain for a few days, including Houston, he stayed off the grid by booking a room at an Airbnb instead of a hotel. In Houston, he always selected an Airbnb property in the area known as Midtown, which was accessible to public transportation, so he could avoid renting a car. He had one primary purpose for visiting H-town and that was to keep an eye on his good friend Lloyd Palmer.

He never alerted Lloyd that he'd be traveling to the United States or to Houston, but he kept a watchful eye. Sometimes he'd sit on the public bench across from the *Ledger*'s headquarters for hours, especially when the weather was nice, people-watching among the foot traffic of those that entered the building.

Sometimes he'd hire an Uber or Lyft driver to visit the subdivision where Lloyd and his family lived. He'd sit in the car and watch for thirty minutes or so—which was usually as long as most drivers allowed—making sure Lloyd wasn't being surveilled from a nearby parked vehicle. To his relief, no surveillance was ever observed during his visits. The hired assassin who had attempted to murder Lloyd several years ago had surveilled his home before setting his plan in motion—a plan that ultimately failed because of the Lemba's enforcement squad.

As for Hamisi's clothing, his appearance was always nondescript. He'd purchase a few items from a local thrift store to assume the role of a man down on his luck. Some passersby even presumed he was among the homeless men that sheltered in the doorways of vacant commercial buildings. He faded into the scenery so that even those monitoring the security cameras in the area would overlook his presence. Keeping his identity unknown had been easier during the height of the pandemic when everyone wore masks. He would still wear a mask from time to time if the situation warranted it.

Lloyd was already making a difference in his new position as editor of the *Ledger*, but Hamisi felt like there was much more in store for him. Hamisi believed his influence had made a significant impact in terms of Lloyd's self-confidence, and the pride he felt was similar to that he felt toward his two biological sons. The Lemba tribesman planned to be a part of Lloyd's future, both to inform and to protect. As the plane continued toward its final destination, Hamisi reclined his seat to take a nap for the remainder of the flight. As he drifted off to sleep, he dreamed of the Zambezi River and the magnificent Victoria Falls.

CHAPTER 21

Stephanie had hated politics all of her adult life and most of her formative years too. She'd made her disdain for what she called a "bottom-feeding profession" known to Lloyd but hadn't shared the reasons why. She loved Lloyd with all her heart, but some things were just too painful and personal to share with anyone, including one's spouse. But now that Ron had asked her to be his campaign manager, she could no longer keep the details about her family's harrowing brushes with the law from Lloyd, especially since politics was at the heart of it all.

She waited until later that evening to broach the subject. They were both in bed enjoying their usual nightly ritual: reading. For her, it was the latest novel by historical romance author Beverly Jenkins. Lloyd was on his laptop reading headlines and articles from the three daily newspapers he monitored most—the Dallas *Morning News*, the Atlanta *Journal-Constitution*, and the New York *Times*.

He kept track of the first two papers because their audiences most closely mirrored the *Ledger*'s. The latter, the *Times*, was widely considered to be the nation's newspaper of record among newspapers around the country, so whatever they printed was deemed to be important for the entire news industry. Monitoring other newspapers and their approach to reporting the news was his way of keeping up with and, hopefully, pulling ahead of the competition.

"Sweetie," Stephanie started, "you know I've always hated politics."

Lloyd looked up from the news story he was reading in the Atlanta *Journal-Constitution* about a hit-and-run accident in the suburbs. "That's exactly what I told Ron when he said he wanted to ask you to be his campaign manager. I cautioned him not to get his hopes up."

"Well," she sighed, "I'm ready to tell you the reasons why so you'll understand why I've been so adamantly against politics all these years."

"I'm all ears, and you know I'm here for you. I've wanted to know why you felt that way for years. I figured when you were ready to tell me, you would."

"This may take a while, but I need to get it all out there so you understand that my attitude about politics is rooted not only in anxiety but also in fear."

"Take all the time you need," Lloyd said as he closed his laptop and moved closer to her, hoping his physical contact would make her more at ease. He gave her a hug and planted an extended kiss on her cheek as she started.

"I've heard the stories about my grandfather as far back as I can remember. My father's father, Moses Campbell, was actively involved in voting rights efforts in the 1950s. In his small Georgia town, most of his Black friends were sharecroppers. They were constantly planting crops, chopping crops, and harvesting crops but never seemed to get ahead financially. At the end of the planting season, the sharecroppers were always in the hole and owed the landowner money. It was only a marginal step up from slavery. But Grandpa and his wife, Pearl, my grandmother, owned three acres of land and had built a four-room cabin on the property."

"I never got a chance to meet them, and you don't talk about your paternal grandparents very much," said Lloyd.

"I know. Both died when I was a child."

"That explains it. In all the years I've known you, since high school, you haven't said much about them."

"My father told me that my Grandpa Campbell was a proud man with an incredible work ethic. Being a landowner gave him a sense of confidence many of his friends didn't have.

"My grandfather had tried to get the local Black residents to register to vote," Stephanie continued. "Although voting was technically legal for Black folks, in actuality the town's Black adults didn't dare attempt to register for fear of retaliation by mobs of racist white people. The town's white folks, especially the men, did not hesitate to mete out a brutal beating—or worse—to anyone that went to the county courthouse to fill out a voter's registration card. Those that had tried to register in the past suffered fates that made them haunting examples for others."

Lloyd wanted to interrupt and ask a few questions, but Stephanie was transfixed with her eyes closed, as if she were reliving her grandparents' circumstances as they experienced them during the South's Jim Crow era.

"But Grandpa Campbell was stubborn. He'd fought for his country in World War II and believed he had earned his say-so about who governed the town, the county, and the state. My grandma, Miss Pearl as we called her, begged him not to go, but despite her pleas, he went to the county courthouse and registered to vote."

"He did?" Lloyd asked. "Even though he knew the potential consequences?"

"Like I said, he was stubborn…The next morning, Grandpa Campbell received a visit from a white man, Tom Moore, whose truck he sometimes repaired. Tom and Grandpa had formed a tenuous friendship since being friends with white folks in those days was tacitly forbidden. Tom didn't have a mean streak like most of the white men in the area; plus, he respected Grandpa's work ethic and ingenuity. Tom's unannounced visit that morning was unusual, and Grandpa wasn't sure what to think.

"The sequence of events that occurred the next day are part of our family history, passed down orally from one generation to the next, so I'll recount it as it was told to me," Stephanie said as she took a deep breath then sighed, as if reliving her grandparents' nightmare.

"Mr. Moore told my grandpa that he overheard some of the white men in the local tavern—they called it Nellie's Bar—the night before. They were having an animated discussion about Grandpa, saying that him being allowed to register to vote could not happen without a pointed response, one that would get the attention of all of the Negroes in the area."

"They all agreed that Grandpa needed to be taught a lesson, and they were planning to do something about it that night. Mr. Moore advised Grandpa and Grandma Pearl to pack a few of their things and get out of town until things settled down. Then Mr. Moore added this haunting caveat: 'It's possible that it may never blow over, but call me in a few days, and I'll let you know.'

"Grandpa shook Mr. Moore's left hand with a warm squeeze and said, 'I'm grateful for the warning, Mr. Tom. God bless you.'

"Grandpa told my father and his siblings that he would have stayed and faced the men with just him and his shotgun, but he couldn't live with himself if something happened to Grandma Pearl. So they packed their suitcase and grabbed some family photos and the family Bible left to them by Grandma Pearl's mother, Maude, just in case they were unable to return. That was their last time setting foot in Georgia."

"They never went back?" asked Lloyd.

"No, they never went back…It's a good thing Grandpa listened to what Tom Moore said because that night, their home—the one that Grandpa had built with his bare hands—was burned to the ground. The mob showed up with shotguns and torches and called for them to come outside. When the angry crowd that had gathered didn't get a response, they kicked the door in and searched from room to room. They were especially riled that they were unable to find either of my grandparents at home. Their adrenaline was in overdrive, and their outrage was revved up to a lynch mob's fever pitch. Anyone who had been at the Campbell home that night would have experienced a terrifying, gruesome death."

Stephanie teared up as she visualized her grandparents' horrific situation, and Lloyd pulled her to him and held her close until her tearful moment subsided. He rubbed her back and hoped some of his strength would transfer to her to help her continue telling him the rest of the story.

"My grandparents were thankful that Mr. Moore had warned them in advance. They fled to their cousin Alfred's home in Beaumont. Since it's only eighty miles east of here, Grandpa Campbell figured he'd be able to get a job somewhere in the Houston area, and he was right. Within a few weeks, he had found a job laying pipe for an oil and gas company, and the following year they were able to purchase a small, two-bedroom house just in time for the birth of their first born child, my father, Raymond."

"I'm amazed that you can recite all of the details about what happened to your grandparents," Lloyd said.

"It's really not that difficult. It's emblazoned in my brain. The saga of what happened to them has been passed along to extended family members and subsequent generations, including me. The elders repeat the story during family reunions. For me, it's evidence of the wickedness that often surrounds politics."

"I agree with you, but you have to admit that as horrible as your grandparents' situation was, that happened more than sixty years ago. Things aren't perfect now, but a lot has changed since then. Black people can vote now without being threatened, although sadly some choose not to.

"If you think about it," Lloyd continued, "back then there were no Black reporters at the *Ledger*. There were rarely any stories about Black people in the paper that didn't involve some sort of crime angle. And now I'm the editor, although sometimes I wish I wasn't. That's something your grandparents likely never envisioned in their wildest dreams."

"You're right. We've taken several steps forward, but there are also the occasional steps backward or even sideways that keep the system from being universally fair."

Stephanie wasn't finished. "I wish the evildoing ended with my grandparents' situation, but it didn't."

Lloyd was taken aback. "You mean, there's more that happened to your grandparents?"

"No, not to them. They ended up living the remainder of their days in safety among their friends and family in Beaumont. But one of my uncles, who lived in Shreveport, Louisiana, had his life ruined by politics. It wasn't a life-threatening situation like it was for my grandparents. This was much more recently and more directly tied to politics."

Lloyd had to be at the office at eight o'clock the next morning, and it was already well past midnight. But Stephanie had held these troubled feelings in for so long that he had no problem losing sleep to give her a chance to unload them.

CHAPTER 22

Stephanie took a deep breath and stretched her upper body by moving it from side to side at her waist. She had been sitting in one position for a while, and reciting the details of what happened to her grandparents had nearly exhausted her. But she had suppressed her family's history and held it back from Lloyd for so long that she was determined to tell him everything.

"My uncle, Frederick Reynolds, my father's oldest brother, was always active in his community and was involved in a lot of local causes in Shreveport. He decided to run for city council—This was in the late nineties. He had a lot of grassroots support and won his election by a landslide. After two terms in office, my uncle had spearheaded a number of initiatives that made a significant difference in the lives of his constituents. He had a lot to be proud of.

"One day while Uncle Frederick was working after hours at his office, a man who claimed to represent some of Shreveport's wealthy residents knocked on my uncle's door and asked if he could meet with him for a few minutes. My uncle's assistant had left for the day, so there was no gatekeeper for late evening visitors."

"According to my uncle, the man wore a very expensive suit and was well spoken, giving him instant credibility. It was about seven thirty, and my uncle had planned to leave the office for home at around eight o'clock."

"My uncle told the man that it would be better if he called his assistant the next day to make an appointment, but the man said he was an attorney, identified himself as Jonathan Gould, and said he wouldn't take more than ten minutes of my uncle's time. My uncle acquiesced, asked him to take a seat, and asked him why he was there. According to my uncle, this is how the conversation went."

"Mr. Reynolds, I'll get right to the point. I understand there is a non-profit for at-risk youth that you support."

"Yes, there is, the Jefferson-Mitchell Foundation. It's a grassroots organization started by community activists Aisha Jefferson and Sabrina Mitchell, and they are still getting their efforts off the ground. They've been hampered by slow fundraising results. Have you heard of it?"

"Yes, and that's my reason for being here. I may have a solution to their fundraising dilemma. I represent a couple of philanthropists who would like to make a donation to the Jefferson-Mitchell Foundation. The only stipulation is that they want to do so privately. As you can imagine, my clients get bombarded with donation requests and they simply can't support every entity...however worthwhile their cause."

Frederick was skeptical. "Who are these donors, and what brought the foundation to their attention?"

"They'd prefer to remain anonymous, although if I told you their names, you would recognize them immediately. One of them was once at-risk himself. He was raised by a single mother who became addicted to heroin and abandoned him when he was only eight years old. A non-profit mentoring organization with goals similar to the Jefferson-Mitchell Foundation helped him turn his life around. That organization no longer exists, but he believes in reaching

back and helping others like himself that may otherwise end up in the prison pipeline."

Stephanie interrupted her blow-by-blow account of her uncle's meeting to interject what her uncle had told her family he was thinking at the time. "Uncle Frederick told my dad that his internal antennae went up and he should have been more skeptical. But the guy seemed legit, and the Foundation really needed the lifeline to try to immediately save at least a few of the local at-risk youth that were headed in the wrong direction."

"How big of a donation are your donors considering?"

"They've already decided the amount they'd each like to donate, and you'll find it all here," Gould said as he placed a black leather carrying case on Frederick's desk. The case had leather handles and a zipper in the center. Frederick really hadn't noticed the case until then.

"Go ahead. Open it," said Gould.

Frederick unzipped the case and looked inside. He was stunned by what he saw, and he leaned back in his chair. At least two dozen neatly bound bundles of twenty-dollar bills with currency wrappers around each bundle were in the case. "How much is in here?" Frederick asked nervously and looked directly in Gould's eyes for an answer.

"Fifty thousand dollars."

"Fifty thousand dollars? Why are they giving the foundation cash instead of writing a check and going through the proper channels?"

"Besides the fact that they want to remain anonymous, they also want to help the foundation get things off the ground quickly and cut through some of the usual red tape. You've already mentioned that the foundation's fund raising

efforts have been stymied. My clients understand that these at-risk kids often get in trouble because their families are living hand to mouth and need money. This way the foundation can start helping kids immediately to get the resources they need without having to wait for an administrative process that could take weeks or even months. These kids need help now."

Gould placed emphasis on the word "now."

Frederick knew that the kids' needs were dire but was still hesitant. Gould sensed his reluctance and hoped to allay his anxiety.

"The cash is untraceable, and since anonymity is key in this situation, this will be between just the two of us."

Frederick felt himself breaking out in a cold sweat. If he said no, the Foundation could be on the ropes financially for an extended period of time. He felt somewhat responsible for their situation since he had boosted their optimism by telling them he'd help them secure sources of funding and very little had come through so far. And this guy was no flake. Gould was wearing an Armani suit and Cole Haan wingtip shoes and his hands were perfectly manicured. Clearly, he was the type of lawyer large companies and wealthy individuals hired.

Mr. Gould's offer seemed like a miracle, an answer to his prayers. He thought about how many kids could benefit right away from the fifty thousand-dollar donation and decided to accept the offer on behalf of the Foundation. He'd work out the financial reporting issue later.

"Mr. Gould, on behalf of the Jefferson-Mitchell Foundation, please give your donors our sincerest thanks for their generosity. Do you have a business card in case the

Foundation's founders want to thank you formally? Also, can you convey their appreciation to your clients?"

Frederick believed that the fact that he had Gould's contact information would at least provide a point of reference in case questions arose later on.

"I certainly will," Gould said as he stood and handed Frederick his business card. "Feel free to reach out to me should the need arise." They shook hands, and Gould left the office.

Frederick sat down and let the leather carrying case remain stationary on his desk for a few minutes. His palms were sweaty, and his heart was racing. At first he didn't touch the case, and he didn't look inside again. He stared at the case with a laser-like focus, mostly in disbelief. Then he put Mr. Gould's business card in his top drawer for safe keeping, just in case he needed to contact him.

A sudden thought occurred to him: What would happen if someone visited his office that night? It was well after business hours, but he didn't want to take any chances. He quickly got up and locked his office door. Now that the cash was in his possession, he hadn't thought about what he would do with the money overnight. He decided to lock it in his bottom desk drawer until the next day. He would call Aisha and Sabrina in the morning and find out the best way to transport the funds to them.

Frederick tossed and turned all night thinking about that leather case full of money locked in his desk drawer, but he dared not tell his wife, Angie, anything about it. The fewer people that knew about it, the better.

The next morning when he arrived at the office, he unlocked his desk drawer to make sure the case and the funds were still there, that he hadn't imagined the whole incident. To his relief, everything was as he had left it the night before.

Frederick initiated a conference call with Aisha and Sabrina, letting them know about the donation. He emphasized the necessity for absolute secrecy regarding the funds, and Aisha and Sabrina both agreed. They were elated, of course, and Frederick scheduled a meeting with them for the following day to deliver the funds to them. Among the three of them, they'd figure out how to best handle distributing the money to those in need. Later, they would decide if it would be feasible or prudent to consult with an accountant about the best procedure for dealing with anonymous cash donations. Or perhaps they would simply let sleeping dogs lie.

That same afternoon, two FBI agents arrived at his office and handed him a search warrant to inspect all drawers and closets in his office. The taller of the two had blond hair and a moustache. The shorter one wore glasses and did most of the talking. "Mr. Reynolds, we have a credible tip that you recently received a bribe in cash," he said and handed him the warrant.

Frederick experienced an oh-my-God moment; he was extremely nervous. The agents spent some cursory moments searching the bookshelves that were on the wall opposite his desk, but that appeared to be a formality as they zeroed in on Frederick's desk. They seemed to know exactly where to look for the leather carrying case and asked him to unlock his desk drawer.

Little did Frederick know that Gould had an electronic recording device hidden in the pin he wore on his Paul Smith necktie when he visited Frederick's office the night before.

The device filmed Frederick accepting the leather carrying case. Gould's image was nowhere to be seen, and worse, his voice was obscured before the video was anonymously emailed to the local FBI office.

"I can explain this," said Frederick when the agents pulled the carrying case from the drawer and looked inside. "This money has nothing to do with me or my position on the city council. It was a charitable contribution to a local non-profit foundation, and the donors wanted to remain anonymous."

"That's a convenient explanation, but it sounds pretty farfetched," replied the agent in charge, "especially since non-profit organizations are not supposed to receive cash donations unless the donor is clearly identified. Everything needs to be documented for tax purposes. What charity was the donation for?"

"I'd rather not get them involved since they haven't yet received the funds. I was going to deliver the package to them tomorrow."

"Do you have any proof regarding the identity of the alleged donors?"

"No, their attorney delivered the package to me last night. He said he was their representative and left me his business card," Frederick responded nervously as he opened his top desk drawer and handed the card to the agent.

"Hmm, the address on this card is a post office box. Wouldn't a legitimate lawyer have a physical location?" The agent handed the business card back to Frederick for his examination.

Frederick hadn't looked closely at the business card when Gould handed it to him and hadn't noticed the address.

He was so stunned by the case of thousands of dollars in cash that he put the card in his drawer without really looking at it. He also didn't notice that Gould's email address was a Hotmail account. Why would a successful lawyer dressed in what appeared to be at least a two thousand dollar suit not have an email address associated with his law firm?

"Sir, I assure you the gentleman appeared to be on the up and up. He said the donors wanted to avoid being bombarded with requests for funds, which was the reason for the anonymity. Let's call Mr. Gould's number and see if we can get him on the phone."

"Okay," said the agent, "dial the number, but put the phone on speaker." Frederick dialed the number and received the familiar message used by providers when they'd disconnected phone service: "This number is no longer in service." His heart sank as he realized that any proof that he thought he had of Gould's visit or even his existence had vanished into thin air.

"As a legislator, you should have known that accepting large sums of cash in exchange for any exercise of official discretion is illegal. The video that was emailed to our office anonymously recorded your voice accepting the cash for your vote on the upcoming bond initiative. We'll have to place you under arrest for accepting a bribe as a public official," said the FBI agent. "Please put your hands behind you so we can cuff you and recite your Miranda rights."

Humiliated, Frederick turned around. As the agents led him away in handcuffs, he at least had the presence of mind to ask his assistant to call his wife so she could meet him at the intake facility.

When Frederick got outside, there were TV cameras in front of his building from all of the local network affiliates. Clearly someone had alerted the press about the potential arrest, and, of course, media outlets thrive on all things sensational. By the time Frederick got to the federal intake facility, the entire city would know about his arrest. All of the years he had spent in community service and protecting his integrity were circling the drain and being flushed to oblivion.

His attorney told him he could spend up to fifteen years in a federal penitentiary, but because Frederick never actually spent any of the money or put it in one of his bank accounts, his lawyer was able to strike a plea bargain. He received five years' probation with no jail time, but his political career was essentially over. He would forever be remembered in the people's minds as the councilman who accepted a fifty thousand dollar bribe.

Stephanie described the motivations behind those who plotted to entrap her uncle. "The powers that be in Shreveport wanted Uncle Frederick jettisoned because he stood with the people when they needed him. He blocked some of the measures they wanted to implement that would have confiscated the long-time residents' land through eminent domain provisions in order to build a new highway.

"Although the offers to purchase the residents' property were at fair market value, the residents resisted. Many of them lived in homes that had been in their families for three or four generations. They didn't want to sell, and they didn't want to uproot their families when there was so much history in their neighborhood. Uncle Frederick had helped them find an attorney who would take their case pro bono to fight the powers that be.

"But the rich and powerful refused to take no for an answer. After my uncle's arrest, the residents had no public voice. Eventually the powers that be wore them down, and the residents sold their homes.

"My uncle had spent his entire adult life fighting for the less fortunate, and the indictment left him emotionally crushed. He also took a financial hit as he had trouble finding employment after that and has never fully recovered—emotionally or financially—from what happened. He's been existing, not living. He's in his late seventies now, full of regrets that his life was altered by one honest mistake. Worse still, when he passes on, his obituary will probably include the bribery charge."

Lloyd was stunned into silence as he digested all Stephanie had said. As a journalist, he was disappointed in how the media had handled things, but after years in the industry, he understood their default reaction was to lead with whatever would garner headlines and try cleaning up with the facts later. Sensationalism ruled the day.

"You would think that with everything your uncle had done for the community, they would stand by him," Lloyd said.

"That hurt him the most. He thought he could count on the support of so many he had helped in the past. He thought his integrity would stand on its own. But for whatever reason—jealousy, skepticism, the crab mentality—most chose to believe those first reports that he accepted a bribe. Bad news travels a lot faster than good news does.

"So now you know why I'm so adamantly opposed to participating in politics," said Stephanie, exhausted after over an hour of telling her family's story. "I consider it my civic duty to vote in elections, and I rarely miss doing so. Only an illness will generally keep me from the polls, and I try to vote early to avoid election day lines and mishaps. But that's the extent of my political involvement."

"So, Steph, what are you going to do about Ron? What are you going to tell him?"

"I honestly haven't decided yet, but I'm leaning in the direction of a hard no."

"Ron seems as though he wants to go forward with accepting Goldberg's offer and launching a Senate campaign whether you're involved or not. He's genuinely excited."

"That's what really worries me. Ron's excitement may blind him to obvious red flags that may pop up during the course of the campaign, let alone those that are not so obvious.

"Politics is unlike other professions. In sports, there are rules and referees that govern the games. There's an instant replay system so mistakes by the refs can be corrected. There's a governing body that makes adjustments when needed. In other industries, there's a code of conduct, and there are some actions that are deemed to be unacceptable. There are penalties if you break the rules. There's even a commissioner or a governing body that oversees things and keeps all the entities involved in check. And in sports, the players are on the field.

"But politics is entirely different. The real players are off the field, largely invisible to the public. In fact, the real power lies with folks that are unseen. It's a blood sport where anything goes as long as one can get away with it.

"Lying is their stock-in-trade and the bigger the lie, the more the public believes it. The victims have no real recourse once news of their misfortune goes viral. The narrative gets baked into the zeitgeist, part of urban legend, posted on Wikipedia, and, therefore, considered to be factual for all intents and purposes.

"You see what happened to my family: two generations of pain, life disruption, and unrealized dreams. I don't want to see that happen to Ron."

"You know Ron has been my best friend forever," Lloyd replied thoughtfully. "But if he's hellbent on running for this office, wouldn't it be a good idea for you to lead his campaign team? He may not see the pitfalls as they approach, but you will. He needs somebody to cover his back, and you'll always have his best interest at heart."

"That's the only reason I haven't already given him an emphatic no. I have to do some real soul-searching on this one. I wish I knew someone who knows the ins and outs of politics that I could meet with and pick their brain."

Lloyd thought for a moment. "You and your mom always talk about the power of prayer. I don't have the same kind of spiritual strength that the two of you possess, but I've seen your prayers move mountains. Well, now would be the time to put that into practice. Prayers are needed now more than ever."

"Thank you for reminding me of that, babe. Let's try to get some sleep since it's so late, but starting right now, I'll be asking God for wisdom and discernment in this situation and to cover Ron and Shirley with His arms of protection."

Hamisi had told Lloyd to watch, fight, and pray. Lloyd had been and would continue to keep watch. He wasn't sure when the actual fight would begin, but he'd be ready. And he was supporting Stephanie, the love of his life, to make sure there was no shortage of prayers for everyone involved.

CHAPTER 23

After Charles awoke from his one-hour nap at the motel in Brookshire, he headed back to the fast food restaurant in hopes the manager would let him view the surveillance footage of the front of Joseph Wallace's office. He waited until a little past eight o'clock to make sure the manager was available and that the evening dinner rush crowd had thinned out.

When he opened the restaurant door, Marjorie Woods, the manager, was behind the counter giving instructions to one of the cashiers. She nodded and beckoned him toward her. "I nearly forgot about you. You still want to see the videos?"

"Yes, Ms. Woods, if it wouldn't be too much trouble."

"I'm really tired and would like to go home as soon as possible. How long do you think it will take?"

"You said you only keep the footage for thirty days, so it shouldn't take very long. I can fast forward the video, and since Mr. Wallace doesn't visit his office very much, it should be fairly easy for me to see his routine in terms of arrival and departure."

"Okay, follow me," she said and led Charles to the rear of the restaurant to a door marked "Private." There was a bank of monitors mounted on one of the walls, and one screen showed a direct view of the front of Wallace's office.

"There. I'd like to see the footage from that one," Charles said and pointed to the monitor that would give him the answers he sought.

"Have a seat, Mr. Scott," she said and pointed to the chair to his right. There was a desk area that he could use to write down any information he found. Marjorie typed in a few commands to start the video. She showed him how to fast forward and slow down the footage. "It's all yours, but I want to leave here no later than nine thirty since I have to be back at the restaurant by eleven o'clock in the morning. Is that going to be a problem?"

"I'll keep that in mind and will make sure I'm done by then," Charles replied. "I appreciate you going out of your way to help me conduct my research."

Charles sat down and immediately began to play the film footage. He increased the speed of the frames that scrolled past and observed a steady stream of customers entering the nail salon and the sandwich shop that were adjacent to Wallace's office. For such a small town, those two businesses were clearly thriving.

After scrolling about halfway through the last thirty days of footage, the only person he had seen entering Wallace's office was his assistant, Ms. Swanson, and the mail carrier. Considering Marjorie's anxiousness to get home, Charles was facing a race against the clock, and he was becoming a little disheartened.

He continued scrolling and was about to give up hope when something finally caught his eye. A black late model Mercedes Benz pulled up in front of Wallace's office. A man wearing a hoodie exited the driver's side and, once he got out of the car, he hastily placed the hood over his head. Clearly, the driver didn't want to be seen and potentially recognized since, on that particular day, the weather was warm and it wasn't raining. He briskly walked toward the law office and entered using a key. Voila! This had to be Joseph Wallace.

Charles zoomed in on the license plate of the car and wrote down the numbers. The Mercedes bore Texas plates, and with his contacts at the Department of Motor Vehicles, he could obtain Wallace's home address. He wrote down the plate numbers and continued to watch until Wallace exited the office, which he did several minutes later. In his hands were a few pieces of mail and a couple of legal-sized file folders. The hood was in place, so he must have put it on before opening the door. Charles fast forwarded to the end of the footage. In a thirty-day span, Wallace had only visited his office once. No client meetings and no visitors. Charles could draw only one conclusion: Wallace's Brookshire office was strictly for show. Whatever legal work he did was handled elsewhere.

"Ms. Woods, thank you so much for your hospitality. I appreciate it very much."

"No problem. But please don't tell anyone I let you see this security footage or I could get in trouble with my boss."

"My lips are sealed."

Charles headed back to his motel. He'd await a reply text from his DMV contact, and after obtaining Wallace's home address, his next stop would be to show up at his doorstep to get his questions about AmFree answered.

CHAPTER 24

Stephanie got up the next morning and prepared for her day at school. Ron's request was at the front of her mind, but she also had to focus on the lesson she had planned that day for her students. She loved her students, even the difficult ones. The difficult ones tended to be experiencing some sort of trauma at home—hunger, abuse, being left alone for days on end because the one parent they lived with had disappeared—and her goal was to be a constant in their lives and provide at least a modicum of stability for a few hours a day.

It was a Friday, and her students were already distracted with their plans for the weekend. She liked to keep them engaged in what she was teaching them by making it relevant to their everyday lives.

Her morning classes proceeded uneventfully, and she decided to use her lunch break to do some deep thinking about whether or not to accept Ron's offer. She decided to eat lunch in her car and combined eating her meal with prayer time. Her faith was ingrained, and she needed some divine guidance. Her first instinct was to tell Ron no.

Summer break was approaching, and she was looking forward to relaxing, reading, and rejuvenating. Politics was the furthest thing from her mind. She and Lloyd had hoped to go on a road trip through the Tennessee mountains, assuming he could get the time off from work. Since he'd taken on the job of editor at the *Ledger*, he seemed to be working more hours than ever. Lloyd was paranoid about being away from the paper too long and for good reason. There was a constant tug of war between him and some of the veteran reporters who still had difficulty accepting the fact that he was their boss and undermined him at every turn. He was certain that given the opportunity, they would sabotage his efforts to raise the newspaper's standards or, worse, in his absence, publish one or more news stories for which sources hadn't been vetted and for which he would have to do some major cleanup upon his return.

But Stephanie felt like Ron needed her. The part of her that had been so close to him and Shirley for over twenty years was tugging at her heartstrings. If she didn't get involved and something terrible happened, would she be able to live with herself knowing she could have done something to prevent it? What about Lloyd? Would he forgive her?

Walking into an unknown situation that had such a potential for treachery was scary, but she couldn't abandon Ron to a bunch of strangers. If Michael Goldberg provided him with a ready-made team, their loyalty would be to him, not to Ron. She finished her sandwich and washed it down with a Coke.

During her time of reflection, albeit in her car over lunch, she'd made her decision. She'd sign on to Ron's campaign, but she'd insist on several non-negotiable conditions. She wasn't sure how flexible Goldberg would be, but she would soon find out.

CHAPTER 25

After sending Joseph Wallace's license plate number to his contact at the Texas DMV, Charles spent a quiet night at the motel and awaited a text response with the lawyer's home address. When he got up at seven the next morning, he checked his cell phone and had his answer from his DMV source. Wallace lived on Sheltering Pine Lane in Kingwood, Texas.

Kingwood was a 14,000-acre, master-planned community northeast of Houston and more than an hour's drive from Brookshire. Given Houston's notoriously heavy traffic, the commute during rush hour could easily be two hours. With such a long commute, Wallace's infrequent visits to his office were understandable.

Kingwood was known for its neighborhoods with palatial homes situated on lots spanning a half-acre or more. Charles decided that he'd make visiting Wallace's home his day's adventure. He needed answers to his curiosity about the disconnect between the lawyer's position with AmFree and the substandard office accommodations he leased. There was something fishy about the entire situation, and Charles was going to find out what it was.

He left the motel around nine o'clock so as not to drop in on the Wallace household too early. Plus, he wanted to miss most of the bumper-to-bumper, morning rush hour traffic between Brookshire and Kingwood. He arrived in Wallace's neighborhood at ten thirty, parked across the street from the

Wallace home, and sat in his car to survey the area and develop a game plan.

Wallace's home was impressive. The lawn was meticulously landscaped, and the property was well maintained. The house had to be close to five thousand square feet with a circular driveway and was backed by a secluded, wooded area. Charles thought there was probably an architecturally constructed pool area in the back. The property resembled the homes one saw featured in home and garden magazines.

Charles had conducted an online search of Harris County property records, and Wallace's house was valued at close to one million dollars. When researching Wallace's law practice, Charles couldn't find any evidence that he'd been hired by any major clients. That meant his job as registered agent for AmFree had to be paying him a boatload of money for him to be able to afford the mortgage on such a spacious dwelling.

Maybe Wallace was a penny-pincher where office space was concerned. But that would make no sense because a man who lived in a house like the one in Kingwood wouldn't be caught dead bringing clients to the eyesore in the Brookshire strip mall. That meant Wallace's law office in the strip center was merely a façade.

Charles decided to wait about thirty minutes to see if there was any outside activity at the house. No one opened the door or came outside, and there were no deliveries while he was parked. He got out of his car and walked across the street toward the Wallace's front door. As he approached, he noticed that one of the garage doors on the three-car garage was raised and Wallace's black Mercedes Benz was parked inside. Charles had his confirmation that he was at the right house.

Huge, wood-carved double doors greeted him as he approached the front of the house. He decided to ring the doorbell and see if he could talk to Wallace face to face. Wallace's initial reaction to a reporter showing up at his door unannounced would tell Charles a lot about whether or not he had something to hide. An attractive brunette woman in her late thirties or early forties answered the door. She was wearing a fuchsia-colored warm-up suit. He assumed it was Wallace's wife.

She looked at him warily. "Hello. May I help you?"

"Are you Mrs. Wallace?"

"Yes, and you are...?"

"I'm Charles Scott, a reporter for the Houston *Ledger*, and I'm here to speak with your husband, Joseph. Is he at home?"

"Yes, but he's busy right now working in his office."

"It's important that I speak with him. You see, I'm working on a feature story about small-town lawyers in Texas and became aware of your husband's law office in Brookshire. I thought he would be an excellent subject for my story, and I wanted to ask him about some of the challenges of practicing law in a town with a population of only five thousand people. I'm on deadline, so it would be helpful if I could speak with him. By the way, you have a beautiful home," Charles added, hoping to disarm her.

Hillary paused for a beat, contemplating if she should ask Joseph to come to the door or if she should just tell Charles to get lost. Joseph didn't like her to interrupt him when he was working, and he had made that perfectly clear on more than one occasion. But the fact that he was a reporter meant his visit could be important. She decided to err on the side of caution.

"Wait here a moment, and I'll see if Joseph is available," she said and closed the door. Charles hoped she wouldn't keep him outside for too long, because the Houston humidity could be brutal, even when the temperatures weren't extremely hot. At least the Wallaces' front porch had an extended overhang so he was shielded from the intensity of the morning sun.

Meanwhile, Hillary went upstairs to Joseph's office and rapped lightly on the door. She opened the door and stuck her head in. Joseph was on his cell phone, so she signaled that she needed to talk to him. He asked whoever was on the line to hold and put the call on mute.

"What is it, Hillary?" he said with a sharp tone. "I'm in the middle of an international call." Sometimes Joseph wished Hillary would get a job, even a part-time one, so she wouldn't be hovering around him all day.

"I know you don't like to be disturbed when you're working in the mornings, but there's a reporter at the front door from the Houston *Ledger* and he says he wants to speak with you."

Joseph immediately panicked on the inside but tried not to let his angst show on his face. He had spent the last ten years maintaining a low profile precisely so he could stay off the media's radar. Michael had been emphatic about that when they entered into their arrangement. But then he thought maybe he was overreacting. Maybe the reporter was inquiring about something that had nothing to do with his work with AmFree.

"A reporter? Did he give you his name or say what he wanted?"

"His name is Charles Scott, and he said he's writing a story about Texas's small-town lawyers. He wanted to interview you about the challenges of practicing law in a town like Brookshire."

Joseph breathed a temporary sigh of relief and thought he should at least feel the reporter out. He doubted a reporter would drive all the way to Brookshire from Houston for an interview he could easily complete over the phone. If he was fishing for information, Joseph needed to know what it was.

"Tell him to wait inside in the foyer, and I'll be down in a few minutes."

Hillary went downstairs to the front door and opened it. "Joseph said he will see you for a few minutes," she told Charles. "Please come in and wait in the foyer."

Charles was grateful to get out of the heat as he had started to break out in a light sweat on his forehead. "Thank you, Mrs. Wallace. I promise not to take up too much of his time," he replied as he went inside and waited.

The truth was that Charles planned to get as much information from Wallace as he could. He would pepper the lawyer with questions as long as possible—even if the Wallaces threw him out. As a reporter, he'd been asked to leave more places than he could count, and he was not going to leave empty-handed. When he called Lloyd that afternoon with an update, he wanted to be able to tell him something significant.

As he waited, Charles examined his surroundings. The house was even more impressive on the inside. The foyer had an octagonal shape and opened to a sprawling living and dining area. Tons of natural light streamed through the double-paned, beveled windows offering a picturesque view of the greenery in the wooded area in the rear of the house.

And he was right about there being a pool in the back, complete with a stone-stacked water fountain and a completely furnished patio. There was also a covered cabana draped with a sheer white overhang, perfect for daytime or nighttime social gatherings. Charles was momentarily transfixed.

"What can I do for you, Mr. Scott?" Wallace asked while descending the staircase, startling Charles in the process. When Wallace got to the bottom of the stairs, Charles extended his hand for a handshake.

"Nice to meet you, Mr. Wallace. As I told your wife, I'm working on a story and wanted to interview you for a few minutes."

"I never talk to reporters, Mr. Scott, but I'm curious…How did you get my home address?"

"I stopped by your law office yesterday and left a message with your assistant, Ms. Swanson. Didn't she tell you?"

"That doesn't answer my question. How did you get my home address?"

"Mr. Wallace, I've been a reporter for more than a decade, and it's really not that difficult to obtain anyone's home address these days. As you probably know, a Google search can provide a treasure trove of information."

"Be that as it may, no reporter has ever been here. But since you're here, I'm willing to give you five minutes to ask your questions. Let's have a seat in the living room."

Wallace extended his hand toward the open living area, and they sat on the teal button-tufted leather sofa. “Fire away, Mr. Scott.”

Charles saw no reason to vacillate and got straight to the point. “What I really wanted to know was how a small-town lawyer in Brookshire ends up as the registered agent for AmFree? Did you pursue the position, or was it offered to you by the people who formed the PAC?”

Joseph’s worst fears were realized, and his expression told Charles his opening question had hit home. Joseph was mortified as Charles had honed in on the unimaginable: having his role with AmFree made public. He had to shut this conversation down—now. He rose from his seated position on the sofa. “I’m afraid I’m going to have to ask you to leave, Mr. Scott,” Joseph said firmly.

“But you said you’d give me five minutes, and I was just getting started,” Charles objected. “I’m researching an article that will focus on political action committees, including the super PAC AmFree. Don’t you want your perspective to be included?” Charles was really toying with Wallace. He could see from the confounded expression on the attorney’s face that he had clearly struck a nerve.

“We are done. Now please leave, and if I have to ask again, it won’t be done nicely.”

Wallace walked toward the door; Charles rose to leave and headed that way. Wallace opened the door and turned to face Charles. “Don’t ever come back to my home again. Is that clear?”

“Crystal clear, Mr. Wallace, but I still plan to continue my research for my story. Don’t be surprised if your picture lands on the *Ledger*’s front page at some point in the future.”

Charles smiled at Wallace and walked outside in the direction of his car. During their brief interaction, he hadn't retrieved anything that was quotable, not even a "no comment" from Wallace. But his instincts were right: AmFree was a big deal.

Wallace closed the door and stood in his foyer momentarily. Having a reporter on his tail was one of the worst things that could happen. He had no choice but to place an urgent call to Michael and break the unpleasant news to him.

CHAPTER 26

Stephanie called Lloyd to break the news to him about her decision. "I'm really surprised, Steph, especially since you've been so adamantly opposed to getting involved in politics since I've known you. And after you told me about what happened to your family, I assumed your answer would be no. What made you change your mind?"

"Ron and Shirley are our best friends in the whole world. I didn't want to abandon him when it's clear he believes this could be a once-in-a-lifetime opportunity. If one of us asked for his help under the same circumstances, wouldn't we expect him to say yes?"

"Looking at it from that perspective, I agree with you completely. Have you told Ron yet?"

"I'm getting ready to call him right now."

"Well, let me know his reaction."

"Will do. Love you, and I'll see you when I get home." Stephanie ended the call with Lloyd and called Ron. He picked up on the first ring as if he were awaiting her call.

"Steph, I've been on pins and needles awaiting your call," Ron said anxiously. "I'm almost afraid to ask you what you've decided."

"I'll do it. I'll be your campaign manager."

Ron was so excited that he could barely contain himself. "I was hoping you would say yes, but I had prepared myself for the worst."

"You might not be so excited after you hear my two major conditions."

"Uh-oh. I should have known you'd be in deep thought about this before you arrived at a decision, but I'm sure whatever you're asking for is not unreasonable. You're probably proposing some necessary measures that I hadn't even considered."

"Well, here goes. First, I need to be the actual manager of the campaign, not simply in name only. This means I need to have complete authority over any major decisions, including personnel. I know Mr. Goldberg is providing you with a campaign team, but these will be people neither of us knows. I need to have an onboard interview with each one of them before they are added to the payroll. I can't watch your back if I'm a toothless tiger." Stephanie's last statement made them both smile.

"I completely agree with you," Ron responded. "I'll insist on you being my campaign manager, and that will be one of the conditions for me to accept Goldberg's offer. I want you running the show—period. What's the other condition?"

"I need to be in charge of the finances. The money is where the actual power lies in any organization, especially a political campaign. I remember when Al Gore ran for President in 2000. He appointed Donna Brazile to manage his campaign, but he put somebody else in charge of the finances. She was the first Black woman to run a major party presidential campaign, but without the power of the purse, she was all but neutered as head of the campaign. It was embarrassing to watch her squirm when she was asked about it during on-camera interviews. That is not going to be me."

Stephanie continued, "In order to control the finances, I need to have access to the campaign's account and approve all vendors and disbursements. A lot of campaigns are used as vehicles to funnel money to friends using over-priced no-bid contracts as the method of choice. We both know business owners who can provide some of the goods and services we need and the campaign's contracts should be open for all qualified vendors. We can't guarantee they will win contract bids, but at least they'll have a shot. Plus, by making the contracts competitive, our funds will go further. We'll need to be frugal if we plan to have the resources we'll need for the long haul."

"Those two conditions sound reasonable to me. With you at the helm of the campaign and keeping tabs on everything, I should be the odds-on favorite," Ron said confidently.

"You are forever the optimist, and that's good," Stephanie replied, "because we'll need that optimism down the stretch. I've already told Lloyd that I'm on board, so what's next?"

"Since I have to give Goldberg an answer by Monday, I'd like him to meet you at the same time I give him my answer. That will eliminate the need for us to set up a meeting later on and allow us to get started within a few weeks. Can you take off work a couple of hours on Monday?"

"The school district requires me to request time off two weeks in advance unless it's for sick leave. But why don't you set up the meeting at the end of the workday, and I'll be able to be get to your office by four o'clock. Will that work?"

"Sure. I'll tell Goldberg that I'd like to inform him of my decision in person at my office and schedule the meeting at four o'clock." Ron paused then pivoted. "If I were with you in person, I'd give you a hug, but I hope you can feel my appreciation over the phone. This means the world to me, and I'm sure Shirley will feel the same way once I tell her."

"I know you'd do the same for me under similar circumstances. Just know that we're all in this together…I have a suggestion," said Stephanie, already thinking ahead and in campaign manager mode.

"I'm all ears."

"The four of us need to get together in person before our meeting with Goldberg on Monday—what's known in corporate and large organization settings as the meeting before the meeting. We need to have a strategy for moving forward. That way, we'll have a game plan in place ahead of time. Goldberg will be expecting to deal with a political novice, which means he'll underestimate you. That gives us an advantage, and we need to use that time to strategize."

"You're already thinking like my campaign manager, and I love it!" said Ron excitedly. "Why don't you and Lloyd come to our house for Sunday dinner? We can talk about everything then."

"Okay, I'll ask Lloyd, but I'm sure if anything is on his schedule, he'll clear it for this powwow session, especially when it comes with one of Shirley's delicious meals," Stephanie said cheerfully. "Just let us know what time to be there."

CHAPTER 27

Charles left Joseph Wallace's home with a sense of triumph. Not only had he rattled Wallace's cage but he'd also confirmed what he suspected. Based on how Wallace had reacted to being asked about AmFree, Charles knew his hunch had merit. There was something nefarious about Americans for True Freedom, and Charles was going to get to the bottom of it.

He decided to call Lloyd to fill him in on what he'd found out so far. He was pretty sure Lloyd would be at his desk at the paper since it wasn't noon yet. When Lloyd answered, Charles didn't waste time with idle chitchat.

"Lloyd, I'm still in Brookshire, and I believe my hunch was right."

"Wait a minute…slow down. I was wondering when you would check in. I'd started to get worried."

"I didn't want to call you until I had something concrete."

"So what did you find out?"

"The registered agent for AmFree is Joseph Wallace. I visited his office and came up empty—"

Lloyd interrupted Charles in midsentence. "Wait a minute. Did you say you're in Brookshire and the registered agent for the PAC is Joseph Wallace?"

"Yes. Does any of this sound familiar?"

"It didn't until a couple of days ago. My friend, Ron, visited me and Stephanie at home on Wednesday and said he was approached by a lawyer named Michael Goldberg about running for the U.S. Senate. I did some background research on Goldberg and found an old photo online with him and Wallace as Harvard college buddies. It sounds like Goldberg may have been a reference so Wallace could get the assignment as AmFree's registered agent."

"You could be right. It seems to be a plum assignment. Wallace rarely goes to his office, but I was able to get his license plate number. The restaurant across the street allowed me to check their security footage, and during the month of footage they saved, he visited the office only once. I checked with my sources at the DMV, got his home address, and stopped by this morning unannounced. He was not pleased."

"Good work, Charles. Were you able to dig up anything else?" Lloyd asked, intrigued.

"Only that something's not adding up. His office is located in what can only be described as a hovel, but his house is practically a palace. AmFree must be paying him big bucks for him to be able to afford the mortgage on his house because I couldn't find his name connected to any other legal clients. He's almost a ghost as far as his legal career is concerned."

"Well, keep an eye on his house, and see if you can shadow his movements. He might meet with some of AmFree's donors or decision-makers. Stay out of sight, and don't let him know you're watching. If he senses he's being followed, he might change his patterns," Lloyd offered as a game plan.

"I didn't park in his driveway, so he doesn't know the type of car I'm driving."

"Good. Stay in the area a couple more days, and keep me posted if anything happens."

"Will do.

CHAPTER 28

After Charles left Joseph Wallace's home, the attorney was on the verge of a panic attack. He dreaded telling Michael about the reporter's visit, but he had no choice. He wasn't sure exactly how Michael would react, but he tried to prepare himself for his inevitable wrath. Joseph sent Michael a text message.

We need to talk. I'll call you in five minutes.

K. Use one of the burners.

Joseph opened his bottom desk drawer and retrieved one of the burners from the lockbox inside. He dialed Michael's number since no contacts had been entered, as Michael had instructed.

"Michael, it's Joseph."

Michael knew that unexpected incoming calls were almost never accompanied by good news. "Hi, Joseph. I'm sure you didn't call me for a casual chitchat. So what's going on?"

"A reporter from the Houston *Ledger* stopped by my house this morning. At first he said he was writing a story about small-town lawyers. I thought talking to him would be harmless, so I let him in for a few minutes."

"You did what?" Michael asked angrily. "I was explicit with my instructions when we entered into our arrangement. No media—period. Ever."

"It's not like I sought out media attention. He showed up at my door unannounced. But it gets worse. The first question he asked was about AmFree."

Michael was livid. He couldn't believe Joseph had been so careless. "And what was your response?"

"I told him absolutely nothing and shut down the interview immediately. I told him to leave and never come back. I gave him nothing that he could use to write about. Nothing at all. Not even 'No comment.'"

"It doesn't matter because it would appear that he already has the foundation for a story since he went to the trouble of tracking you down. He's got your office address and your home address and probably knows the car you drive. The fact that he's snooping around means he's likely to start putting pieces together."

"Well, if I don't talk to him, what can he write?"

"At this point, it doesn't matter whether you talk to him or not. Reporters will sometimes write a teaser article filled with innuendo and quotes from unnamed sources as a way to smoke out subjects of stories. Plus, you'd be surprised at what a reporter can find out, especially one that's willing to drive to Brookshire and do some leg work. What's the reporter's name?" Michael asked.

"Charles Scott. I've seen his byline several times in the paper. He's an experienced journalist and has been with the *Ledger* for at least ten years."

"This may just be one reporter at the paper who is trying to satisfy his curiosity and not a story the newspaper is planning to run anytime soon," Michael mused. "I'll call my contact at the *Ledger* and see what he knows. Until I have an answer, sit tight and lie low."

"Okay. Will you be calling me back soon?"

"My *Ledger* contact is paid to be accessible. I should have an answer by the end the day."

"No problem. I'll wait to hear from you." Joseph hoped he had dodged a bullet, but where Michael was concerned, things could go to a dark place very quickly.

CHAPTER 29

Michael had to expeditiously determine if Charles Scott's presence at Joseph's home was a fluke or part of a broader game plan for a feature story or exposé at the *Ledger*. He had worked painstakingly to keep AmFree out of the public's view, and he'd be damned if he allowed Joseph's sloppiness to expose the Committee's plans.

Any threats to the Committee had to be squelched without hesitation. They were so close to achieving their ultimate goal of controlling at least a quarter of the lawmakers in Washington, DC. With that level of control, they could easily overwhelm their fellow lawmakers and be able to build majorities for necessary appropriations votes. With that level of power at their disposal, within the next two to three years, the Committee's coffers would reach the trillion-dollar level.

Michael called Warren Blackstone, his contact at the *Ledger*.

Blackstone had the look of a typical old-school reporter: pale and badly in need of some sun, overweight by about fifty pounds, and balding with thin strands of hair combed over on the top of his head. He had been at the paper twenty-five years and had a successful career, but he was still carrying a grudge about being passed over for the editor's position after the *Ledger*'s executive vice president, Wilson Cox, had selected Lloyd Palmer for the job five years ago.

As far as Blackstone was concerned, the corporate executives on the top floor had appointed Lloyd strictly for political purposes—as cover for the paper's botched reporting of the Pauley kidnapping and the subsequent unlawful arrest of dozens of Houston's Black men. A Black man as the editor of the paper was a cover-your-ass move. Blackstone ignored the fact that Lloyd had single handedly solved the kidnapping caper. In his opinion, Lloyd was a diversity hire, pure and simple.

Based on Blackstone's long tenure as a reliable reporter at the paper, the former editor, Ed Jackson, had all but assured him that he was the next in line to be editor once Jackson retired. Jackson had been his mentor for years and had been grooming him for a promotion.

But Blackstone's dreams of career advancement at the *Ledger* had come to a screeching halt when Jackson was arrested and imprisoned for Palmer's attempted murder. That murder attempt had made Palmer a martyr, which meant that once he was promoted to editor, he was virtually untouchable.

The turn of events at the paper when Lloyd assumed the editor's post represented an opportunity for Michael and the Committee. Someone with an ax to grind could often be the best source of inside information in an organization. Michael periodically contacted Blackstone for updates about the inner rumblings at the *Ledger*. As an insider, Blackstone could be utilized in other ways. He'd boost positive press about the Committee's chosen candidates and plant negative stories about their opposition. The veteran reporter also let Michael know about stories that were brewing among other journalists at the paper that could directly affect the Committee before they hit the website or the front page.

Being the consummate professional that he was, Blackstone was genuinely conflicted about feeding Goldberg information. Although he was well paid for the information he provided, he felt like he was betraying his journalistic integrity to some degree, but he'd been in the trenches as a journalist for years and expected to have risen to the next level by now.

The transition in the news business from print to digital online reporting meant vacancies in higher positions were few and far between. The fact that Lloyd was standing in his way was stuck in his craw. That's how he rationalized his role as a de facto double agent. So as soon as he saw the incoming call was from Goldberg, he answered.

"Blackstone, it's Michael Goldberg. I need your help with something," Michael said matter-of-factly.

"At least you didn't pretend this was anything other than a fact-finding call by wasting time with pleasantries," Blackstone responded. "What can I do for you, Michael?"

"We both know the nature of our relationship, so there's no need to waste time with mindless chatter. I need to know what Charles Scott is working on. Have you heard about any background he's done for stories that he's planned for the short term?"

"Well, he's been out of the office for the past couple of days. I haven't heard about anything specific, but he wouldn't be likely to tell me what he was working on. He and Lloyd are bosom buddies, and they tend to keep whatever secrets they have strictly between the two of them.

If he's working on something new, Lloyd would likely be the only one who knows about it."

"Is it possible for you to find out, or would one of your colleagues know?"

"I'll check around, but I doubt it. Is there anything in particular you're curious about?"

There was, but there was no way Michael was going to reveal his true motives to Blackstone. "He contacted one of my corporate clients, who was concerned about negative press for his company. You know how paranoid these corporate types are," Michael said. Lying came naturally to him.

"I'm not sure when Charles will be back in the office. How soon do you need an answer?" Blackstone already knew what Michael would say. Michael only called him when the need for information was urgent.

"Let me know what you dig up between now and tomorrow, okay?"

"Okay. If you don't hear from me, that means I didn't find out anything."

Michael released the call. Blackstone may not have realized it, but he'd already given Michael an important detail. If Scott had been out of the office for a couple of days, that meant he was probably staying overnight in Brookshire. If he was staying overnight, that meant he believed he was on to something. If he believed he was on to something, he would keep digging until he unearthed enough to form the foundation of a story.

Michael couldn't take any chances. Joseph had become the weak link in their operation, and it was only a matter of time before Scott was able to wear him down. The reporter could be surveilling Joseph's house and keeping tabs on his activities at that very moment.

Scott had a reputation as being a go-getter among journalists. He could shadow Joseph's every move—showing up at his gym, the cleaners, and the grocery store. Joseph always was a Nervous Nellie and could be easily spooked. He'd been friends with Joseph for years, but this was where friendship and business diverged. Something had to be done.

CHAPTER 30

Michael called Joseph to tell him what he found out from Blackstone, but the meat of this conversation had to be delivered in person, not over the phone. "Joseph, I spoke with my contact at the *Ledger*. We need to talk. I'll be at your house this evening around six. When I get there, I'll text you, and you can meet me outside. We'll talk in the car so our conversation will be private."

Michael made sure his BMW 760i was swept for listening and tracking devices at least once a week. He was well aware that his political or professional enemies would have access to the same technology that he had at his disposal and wouldn't hesitate to use it to their advantage.

"Michael, you sound angry. I can hear it in your voice. Should I be worried?"

"No need to worry," Michael said in a more measured tone to set Joseph's mind at ease. "There are just some precautions we'll need to take. This Scott fellow sounds like he's a dog with a bone and won't let go until he's satisfied."

Joseph knew Michael would be there at six as he was always extremely prompt; he had an almost religious adherence to timeliness. He wasn't sure how far Michael would be willing to go to make sure Scott's research ended with what he'd already acquired. He just hoped Hillary and the kids wouldn't be impacted. Hillary knew nothing about his work, and it suited her just fine. She never asked about where all the money came from and preferred to be in the dark, as long as the limits on her credit cards remained high and she could go shopping whenever she wanted.

Meanwhile, Michael was at his office putting some finishing touches on the addition of a change of control provision to one of his client's contracts. It was four thirty, and he had to leave soon to be at Joseph's house by six. He had his meeting with the Committee at eight, so his conversation with Joseph needed to be brief.

He had already decided the steps that he'd need to take to protect the Committee from Joseph's slipup. His secretary interrupted his thoughts to inform him that Ron Singleton was on the line. Michael was hoping Ron would have some good news for him after what he'd been dealing with most of the day.

"Hi, Ron. Glad to hear from you, but I wasn't expecting you to call until Monday. Have you made your decision?"

"Yes, I have, but I'd like to meet with you on Monday at my office so I can fill you in on what I've decided."

Michael was dubious. He didn't like being strung along, although he'd used this tactic often on others. "If you know your decision, why not just tell me now?"

"I think the news would be best delivered in person," Ron said cheerfully. "Can you come by at four on Monday?"

Michael checked his calendar. He was available at that time on Monday but hated to give Ron the upper hand. Still, he'd all but settled on Ron as the Committee's Senate candidate and preferred not to have to start over by vetting new recruits. If the answer was no, he might have a better chance of changing Ron's mind with an in-person meeting rather than over the phone.

"I'll be at your office at four. Have a good weekend," Michael said before ending the call.

Now all Michael needed to do was wrap things up at the office so he could meet with Joseph at six. He'd be delivering some news Joseph might find overwhelming, but Joseph knew he would have to comply with whatever Michael instructed him to do.

CHAPTER 31

Michael arrived at Joseph's house at about five forty-five and parked in his driveway. He waited until exactly six o'clock to text Joseph about his arrival. Soon after, Joseph exited his home's front door, walked over to Michael's car, and got in on the passenger side.

"Okay, Michael, what did you find out?"

"Scott has been out of the office for a couple of days and is probably typing a draft of his feature article about AmFree as we speak."

"You think it's that bad?"

"He's approaching this like a carefully placed trail of bread crumbs just waiting for him to reach his final destination. An eager reporter like Scott will put things together piece by piece until he's found everything he needs. So there's only one move we can make."

"There is? What's that?"

"You'll need to leave the country until this blows over. Without you, there's really no evidence of AmFree's activities other than the monthly and quarterly documents you file with the Federal Election Commission. If he doesn't have access to you, the trail of bread crumbs ends."

"Leave the country? When?"

"As soon as possible. Tomorrow would be preferable but definitely by Sunday."

"That soon? For how long?"

"I'd say a month. That should be long enough for the trail to go cold, and Scott will likely abandon his story idea. After all, the news business has limited resources for stories that take weeks of leg work. That's why they rely so much on Twitter, YouTube, and TikTok."

"What country do I go to, and what do I tell Hillary?"

"Tell her you have to go out of the country for an extended business trip. Don't tell her any more than that. She'll have to accept it."

"You don't know Hillary. She won't like it, and she might ask a bunch of questions."

"I don't think you understand the gravity of the situation, Joseph. This is not a request. You must leave the country within the next forty-eight hours. We have some properties in Iceland and New Zealand that are quite nice, and those countries are not on the usual short-list of possibilities for tracking people down. Pick which of the two countries you prefer, and I'll make the necessary arrangements."

Michael looked at Joseph with the steely-eyed resolve Joseph had learned to fear. The decision had been made, and it was non-negotiable.

"I'd prefer New Zealand," replied Joseph, sounding defeated.

"Good choice. It's cold there this time of year, so take appropriate clothing. Or, better still, you can purchase some apparel once you get there."

"Can I at least tell Hillary where I'm going?"

"Absolutely not!" Michael roared in a tone that sent chills down Joseph's spine. "Charles Scott might stop by your house when you're gone and ask Hillary a bunch of questions. She might get flustered, slip up, and tell him where you are. If she doesn't know, she can't tell him anything, can she?"

Joseph was crushed, but what choice did he have? Michael was holding all the cards. "You have a point. I just hope she's still here when I get back."

"Hillary's been with you since college, and she's not going anywhere. She's not going to leave all these creature comforts behind. Besides, when you return, you can make it up to her by taking her for an exotic, romantic getaway and showering her with gifts."

Michael made it all sound so simple, but Joseph knew better. Smoothing things over with Hillary wasn't going to be that easy.

"It's not like you're going dark for the entire month. When you arrive, purchase a few prepaid cell phones with international call privileges. Use those phones when you call her so the location can't be traced. Do you understand?"

"Perfectly." Joseph would have to figure out a way to make things up to Hillary upon his return, assuming that Michael didn't extend his exodus beyond the one-month period he'd demanded.

"What about Ms. Swanson?" asked Joseph about the woman he'd hired years ago to manage the Brookshire office. She had been reliable and discrete, which were his two main requirements when he signed her on as his assistant.

"Ah, Ms. Swanson, your assistant. Tell her she has a month of paid vacation starting now. Her paychecks will be direct deposited as usual while you're away."

There was silence between them for a couple of minutes. Joseph was the first to break the silence. "I guess there's nothing left to be said, other than I'd better go back in and start packing," he said as he opened the car door and got out. "I'll take care of Ms. Swanson and will follow your instructions to the letter when I arrive in New Zealand."

"I knew I could count on you," Michael said with the confidence of a man in full command. Joseph went into his front door to break the news to Hillary. He'd start packing his suitcase in the morning and would pack fairly light. Michael's suggestion about buying clothes once he arrived in New Zealand meant one suitcase should suffice. Meanwhile, Michael pushed the start button for his BMW's engine and headed to the physician's home for the Committee's meeting.

CHAPTER 32

Michael called the Committee meeting to order at eight o'clock sharp. All of the members were in attendance except one of the Silicon Valley executives, who was overseas closing a billion dollar deal with the Chinese government. All members had to be present to cast a vote as meetings conducted via Zoom or other electronic means could be hacked by seasoned technology experts. Many of the hackers lived in their mothers' basements and spent their waking hours finding backdoors for entry to the world's most intricate computer networks.

Everyone knew the purpose of the meeting which was to select their chosen candidate for the upcoming U.S. Senate race. All of the vetting of Ron Singleton had been done. The only task remaining was for them all to be of one accord.

"This meeting shouldn't take very long as I've already picked out the perfect candidate for this race," Michael stated emphatically, in case there were any dissenting opinions among the other Committee members. As she was wont to do at these meetings, Sarah Reiner chimed in first, the sound of her voice reminding Michael of the agitating chime of a high-pitched doorbell.

"Shouldn't we all have the opportunity to present our prospects to make sure we put our best foot forward?" Sarah queried.

"Are you speaking for everyone at the table or just yourself, Sarah?" Michael's eyes were fixed on her as if he could see right through her. But Sarah was steadfast; neither Michael's words, tone, nor stare dissuaded her.

"I'm speaking for myself, but I'm sure other members of the Committee agree."

Everyone around the table was stone-faced and silent, some scrolling through the tablets in front of them or even looking under the table. No one wanted to cross Michael—ever. Michael looked around the table, satisfied that he had everyone's support or acquiescence.

"Well, speak up, Sarah, and make your point. This meeting doesn't have to be a long one unless you decide to make it that way."

"There is a highly qualified female attorney who would be perfect for this campaign," explained Sarah. "She's a Montgomery County Commissioner and has a natural talent for politics. Her name is Miriam Hardwick."

"Have you met her, Sarah?" Michael inquired, knowing that anyone Sarah suggested as a candidate would be a female.

"No, but I've thoroughly researched her background, and she's the exact type of person we look for."

"Thank you for your suggestion, but you know the member assigned to conduct background checks has to examine her history with a fine-tooth comb before we can present her to the Committee for a vote. Let's table your suggestion until the next meeting, okay?" Michael wanted to wrap things up quickly, not open the floor for debate.

"As long as we can put Miriam in the mix for next time..."

"We most certainly will," Michael said with little to no conviction. He redirected the Committee's attention to Ron

Singleton. "All of you are already familiar with Ron Singleton and his recent political activities since he's been in the news frequently over the past few years," Michael said. The members looked at their tablets, which were loaded with Singleton's curriculum vitae and a complete dossier of his life since age sixteen. "I've already met with him, and he's an ideal choice. He's all but given me the green light in terms of his running in the upcoming election. I'm meeting with him to finalize the arrangements on Monday, but him entering the race is a foregone conclusion."

The Committee members quickly closed ranks and nodded in agreement with Michael. "It's agreed then. Ron Singleton is our guy. We should be able to get his campaign up and running within the next thirty days."

CHAPTER 33

Miriam Hardwick had loved politics as far back as she could remember. She loved everything about it, including its unsavory aspects. Her first foray into politics was as an eleven-year-old girl running for sixth grade class president at Manor Middle School. She'd lost that race to Tommy Briggs, a red-haired, freckle-faced boy who wore braces and liked to skateboard.

But Miriam kept competing for student government positions until she finally became eighth grade vice president. She was later elected student body president of her high school senior class and had been running for office ever since. Presently, she was a county commissioner in Montgomery County, one of the fastest-growing counties in the Houston metropolitan area.

She was among the first in her family to go to college, and her parents were particularly proud of what she'd accomplished. They were always bragging to their neighbors and extended family members about their girl Miriam, who was a shy loner as a child but blossomed when she went off to college.

As an attorney and elected official, she was now at the top of her game professionally. Miriam was quite ambitious and had been exploring opportunities to advance politically. The junior senator from Texas had recently made some bone-headed moves, including taking his family on a vacation to

Aruba when millions of Texans had lost power and water due to a natural disaster.

Clearly politicians became tone-deaf and completely detached from the realities their constituents faced once they entered the city limits of Washington, D.C. He was vulnerable, and Miriam was thinking seriously about entering the race. She had been intentional about making all of the right connections and was just waiting to see if her financial backing would be sufficient to wage a competitive race. If her financing came through, she was all but declared as entering the race.

But there was a flip side to the public success she had achieved. Like millions of other middle-aged women with resumés filled with professional achievements, there was something missing in her personal life. Miriam lived a life of quiet desperation, devoid of romance or excitement.

She had been married for twenty-five years to a man who was consistent and committed but completely lacking in imagination. Her husband, Ralph, had run a successful small business as an electrician for years, but he recently retired and seemed to have given up on life. He spent most of his days watching television, playing solitaire on the computer, and taking extended naps. His best quality was his dependability, but that also morphed into predictability. His lack of interest in outside entertainment clashed with Miriam's zest for living. Whenever she tried to make plans to go out, he never showed any interest.

Their conversations usually went something like this:

Miriam: There's a theater production I'd like to go to next month. What do you think about us going together?

Ralph: No, I don't think so. If you've seen one play, you've seen them all. Why don't you go and you can tell me how it was?

Miriam: But, Ralph, I don't want to go by myself. Couples usually attend theater productions together.

Ralph: Ask one of your friends to go with you. Carolyn or Patsy usually accompany you to the theater, don't they?

Miriam: Yes, but I thought it would be a good idea for us to go together.

Ralph: Maybe next time.

But Miriam knew that the next time his answer would be the same. He'd claim to be busy but do absolutely nothing.

Miriam was eight years younger than Ralph and enjoyed an active social life. With her confident air, fashion sense, and well-maintained physique, she still commanded attention when she entered a room. Only her principles kept her from acting on the repeated overtures she received.

She would have preferred that her social life involve Ralph, but she wasn't going to try to drag him out of the house. At least she didn't have to worry about him being a philanderer, like some of her friends, who constantly checked their husbands' cell phones for new contacts, text messages, or other evidence of an affair. She almost wished Ralph had something on his mind other than being a hermit for life. Miriam continued to hope that he would be interested in something…anything. But he had few hobbies and even fewer friends. Years had gone by, and if anything, he had become more of a recluse.

The lack of romance was starting to gnaw away at her psyche and had burrowed into her subconscious. She occasionally had dreams about handsome, cultured men with manicured hands who took her dancing and showered her with passionate kisses. Her dreams were where the passion in her life resided.

The lovers in her dreams were faceless. She would awaken after orgasmic gyrations took control over the lower half of her body. The throbbing from the orgasms lasted several minutes, and she had to awaken fully to get her bearings on where she actually was. She'd look to her right, and there laid Ralph, snoring. Her movements as a result of her wet dreams didn't even make him stir. Miriam would lie there, staring at the ceiling until the throbbing subsided. She thought about the latter half of her life and didn't want it to be filled only with work and politics.

Against her better judgment, Miriam searched online for a male escort service. If Ralph didn't want to take her out, at least she could enjoy some male companionship that could remain largely anonymous. If one thing led to another and they ended up in bed, the men would never know her real identity. She scanned dozens of profile pictures and settled on a couple of men in their early forties who seemed fairly innocuous. Miriam created a fake dating profile and slid into their direct messages.

CHAPTER 34

Now that Charles knew where Joseph Wallace lived, he decided to surveil his house for a couple of days before taking further action. As he and Lloyd had discussed, following Wallace to some of his errands or meeting locations could lead Charles to more AmFree decision-makers. Since online information about the PAC was sketchy, he needed the people involved in order to develop a credible story.

Charles made sure he had ample food and drinks for two or three days. He bought several ready-made sandwiches, chips, pickles, and a few apples. He also purchased a case of bottled water; sodas and sweet drinks weren't a good idea during what was essentially a stakeout. The lack of balance to the solid foods in his stakeout diet required that he remain hydrated.

He decided to move to a motel closer to Kingwood to cut down on his travel time and gas expense. Lloyd had given him a very limited per diem budget, so he had to be prudent about every dollar he spent. The office in Brookshire had little to no activity since Wallace appeared to conduct his business from his Kingwood home, so changing motels made sense.

He got started with his surveillance on Saturday morning, parking across the street with a bird's eye view of Wallace's garage. If the attorney left the house, he would have to back out of his garage or leave through the front door. Charles could observe both access points without being seen.

On Saturday, there was no activity at the Wallace home whatsoever. Neither Wallace nor his wife went anywhere. Charles thought that was unusual because Saturdays were the days when most families ran errands and attended sporting events. But it was completely quiet in terms of outside activity.

He watched the house until about ten o'clock that night, and after spending all day in the cramped car, he needed to go back to the motel to get a good night's sleep. One might falsely consider sitting and watching the house as inaction, but the activities burned calories and required energy. When Charles got to his motel room, he turned on the TV, brushed his teeth, and took off the street clothes he'd been wearing all day in the car. He set his alarm for six o'clock so he could get an early start the next day. He laid down on the bed and was asleep within minutes.

CHAPTER 35

Six o'clock came quickly as the morning sunrise peeked through the curtains of Charles's motel room. Charles felt as though he had just fallen asleep, so it took him a while to orient himself. When he remembered where he was and what he had to do, he jumped out of bed, got dressed, and prepared himself for another day of checking out the Wallaces.

Lloyd had given him a couple of days to figure things out, and he would be expecting some results. Otherwise, it was back to the office, waiting for the next murder, car wreck, or school shooting to occur that would send him out on an on site reporting assignment. He knew in his gut there was something fishy about AmFree, but he needed some evidence to prove it.

After picking up some coffee, a couple of bacon and cheese omelet bites, and two blueberry scones from Starbucks, Charles headed back to Sheltering Pine Lane. He got there around seven o'clock and was hoping nothing had stirred at the Wallace household during his overnight absence. He was just finishing up his coffee and most of his breakfast when, at eight o'clock, a car bearing an Uber Black decal on its rear windshield pulled into the Wallaces' driveway. Apparently one or more members of the Wallace family had travel plans.

Charles kept his eyes fixed on the Wallaces' front door, and within a few minutes, Joseph Wallace exited the house with his briefcase and one medium-sized suitcase. The driver placed the suitcase in the trunk of the car and exited the driveway.

So Wallace was going out of town. Was it a planned trip, or was he leaving Kingwood as a result of Charles's investigation? Charles had no way of knowing for certain, but he was going to follow the Uber to its destination to find out.

As Charles tailed the Uber and followed it to the I-69 on-ramp, he made sure he stayed a couple of cars behind so the fact that he was following Wallace wouldn't be detected. The airport was only about thirteen miles away, so the trip wasn't very long. While driving, Charles thought about the timeframe and purpose of Wallace's trip. If it was a short trip for two or three days, wouldn't Wallace have driven himself to the airport and parked his car at the terminal? Catching an Uber could mean his stay might be extended.

Once the Uber driver turned onto John F Kennedy Boulevard, the street that vehicles used to enter Bush International Airport, Wallace's driver took the exit for Terminal E, where most international flights departed. Charles followed closely behind as Wallace's driver selected the lane for departing flights. The Uber driver parked and helped Wallace remove his suitcase from the trunk, after which Wallace entered the airport. Charles stayed in his car until the Uber driver got back in his own car. Charles then jumped out quickly and tapped on the driver's window.

"Do you need a ride?" the driver asked. "No, my friend just went into the airport, and I had something for him in my car," Charles said, referring to Wallace and hoping that posing as the lawyer's friend might make the driver more relaxed and willing to talk. "If he's coming back to Houston soon, then I'll just hang on to it until he returns."

"Well, you might be waiting a while because he's flying overseas."

"Really?" Charles paused as if he were reflecting on a previous conversation he'd had with Wallace. "Oh, that's right. He did say he was traveling internationally. I forgot which country he said he was visiting. Did he mention it?"

"No, he didn't say, just that he was going overseas."

The airport traffic police were motioning for them both to move their cars, so Charles thanked the Uber driver, returned to his car, and headed for the airport exit. At least he had part of his answer about Wallace's travel schedule. He was going overseas, and God only knew when he'd return. He was running scared, and evidently Charles was onto something with his investigative reporting.

Charles had few options to find out where Wallace was going and when he might be returning. He decided to circle back to the Wallace home to see if he could get anything out of Mrs. Wallace. Even a small clue would be helpful.

He headed back to Wallace's Kingwood neighborhood and pulled into the driveway. With Wallace gone, there was no need to stay out of sight. He rang the doorbell, and within a few seconds, Mrs. Wallace answered. She made no attempt to be cordial.

"What do you want, Mr. Scott? My husband told you to never come back here."

"I was just checking to make sure everything was okay. I saw your husband leaving this morning with a suitcase and was curious about when he would return. I have a few more questions to ask him."

"So my husband was right. You *have* been watching our house. And I have a sneaking suspicion that somehow your snooping around and showing up at our house unannounced has something to do with him leaving. Well, you won't get any information from me. I don't know anything anyway."

"So you don't know where your husband went or when he'll return?"

"I told you no, and I wouldn't tell you even if I knew."

Her tone became more forceful. "Now get away from my home, and don't ever come back. If you do, I will call the police and have you arrested for trespassing," she added as she closed the front door.

Charles had his answer. Wallace was in the wind, and who knew when he'd return. Since Wallace was his only real lead about AmFree, his story had essentially reached a dead end. Before calling Lloyd, he decided to take the one-hour drive back to Brookshire to visit Wallace's office. Even though it was a Sunday and it was unlikely that Ms. Swanson would be there, he thought some light might be shed on Wallace's whereabouts. When he arrived at the office, he was greeted by a printed sign on the door: *Office Closed Indefinitely. Hold All Mail at Post Office Until Further Notice.*

The dead end was absolutely dead. Since it was Sunday afternoon, Lloyd was likely at home or out somewhere spending time with Stephanie. Charles called him, and he answered almost immediately.

"Hi, Charles. Did you find out anything more on Wallace or AmFree?"

"Very little. Lloyd, I have some good news and some bad news."

Lloyd took a deep breath. "Give me the good news first."

"The good news is that I'm almost certain Wallace is being paid top dollar to be the agent and counsel for AmFree. His lifestyle far exceeds what he earned as an associate at Beck, Miller & Beck. That means AmFree has a tremendous amount of resources at its disposal."

"Well, that's something. It's more than we had when we started. Now what's the bad news?"

"Wallace has left the country for parts unknown, and he's closed his office indefinitely, which means he may not return for weeks or even months. I visited his home and spoke with Mrs. Wallace. I don't think even she knows where he is, but, if she does, I'm the last person she'd tell."

"That's a shame that you weren't able to get more information. It really sounded like a promising story. With Wallace gone, you have no other leads, correct?"

"No other leads. I'll check out of my motel, and I'll be in the office tomorrow. Thanks, Lloyd, for at least allowing me to investigate this."

"No problem. The cost to the *Ledger* was minimal, and who knows, something might turn up later."

"I hope so. I really do."

"I'm having dinner with my friend, Ron, today to discuss his campaign. He's planning to run for the Senate, and I have a hunch that Michael Goldberg and AmFree are somehow connected. We just have to figure out what that connection is and how Ron might be affected by it."

CHAPTER 36

Sunday dinners were a mainstay for the Palmers and the Singletons. Lloyd and Ron were like brothers; the only thing missing was the matching DNA.

Shirley was an excellent cook, and the atmosphere was always relaxing. Lloyd and Stephanie brought a bouquet of mixed flowers and presented them to Ron when he opened the door.

"To the future Senator from Texas," Lloyd said and gave Ron a big smile as he and Stephanie entered the Singletons' home.

"From your lips to God's ears," Ron responded, giving both Lloyd and Stephanie hugs. "Come on in. You might as well sit at the dining room table since dinner is almost ready. I'll find a vase for these flowers."

Shortly thereafter, Shirley entered the dining room carrying a bowl of one of her signature dishes: her tuna and corn pasta salad. "Hi, you two. So glad to see you. Ron and I can't wait to talk about how we're going to approach this campaign," she said as she placed the red serving bowl on the table.

"When he first told me, I was hesitant about him running. I didn't want to discourage him, but I was hoping he'd change his mind. But the idea is starting to grow on me. I think he will be an excellent senator." Shirley beamed as she blew Ron a kiss.

"I think we all agree on that," replied Lloyd, "and Stephanie is going to be his secret weapon to make sure his campaign runs smoothly as she steers him toward victory."

"Do you need any help in the kitchen, Shirley?" Stephanie piped in and walked in that direction, not waiting for a response. She didn't want to draw more attention to herself with additional accolades. The whole idea of taking on the task of being Ron's campaign manager was humbling…and scary.

Stephanie treasured Lloyd's full support, but she was still wary about her capabilities. What little she knew about politics made her want to run into a bunker and hide. She'd been continually praying for strength and wisdom, and she knew she would need an unending supply of both.

Stephanie and Shirley brought all of the serving dishes in from the kitchen and placed them on the table. In addition to the pasta, the scrumptious meal included roast beef smothered in onions and gravy, sautéed mixed vegetables, dinner rolls, and iced tea.

"Since this is a special occasion, I bought some red cabernet sauvignon to go with Shirley's roast beef," Ron said as he held up the bottle and then uncorked it. He poured wine in each of their wine glasses.

After they were all seated, Lloyd offered to bless the table. "Prayer isn't my strong suit, but I'd like to offer prayers for this situation. Let's join hands." They did and also bowed their heads.

"Lord, we're all gathered here this evening to ask your blessings over Ron's candidacy for the Senate. We're all entering an arena that's new to us, but we know that if you are for us, it's more than the whole world against us. Cover

Ron and Stephanie with your hedge of protection, and give me and Shirley the courage and energy to support them whenever they need us. In Jesus' name we pray."

Everyone around the table said, "Amen."

"Now, let's eat, and then we can talk about a game plan for tomorrow's meeting and for moving forward during the campaign," said Ron enthusiastically, passing the first of the dishes around the table. After everyone had spooned their portions onto their plates, they all started their meals in silence for the first few minutes.

"Shirley, everything is delicious, as usual," said Stephanie. "Your seasoning for your dishes is always perfect."

"Thanks, Steph. Cooking for my loved ones always brings out the best in me."

Lloyd opened the discussion. "While we're all finishing our meal, let's get down to business. Goldberg says you'll have all of the staff and financing you'll need right, Ron?"

"He said there would be no problem with either. Apparently there's a turnkey operation that can hit the ground running as soon as I accept his offer," said Ron.

"It's clear that he's approached others in the past and set up their campaigns as well," Lloyd speculated.

"That would make sense."

"If Goldberg already has a ready-made staff, how would Stephanie fit into all this?"

"He doesn't know it yet, but we plan to break the news to him tomorrow. He's going to meet me at my office at four o'clock so I can tell him my decision. What he doesn't know is that Stephanie will be at the meeting and her being my campaign manager is non-negotiable."

Lloyd looked at Stephanie inquisitively. “Lloyd, with everything that’s happened, I didn’t have a chance to tell you about tomorrow’s meeting. I had Ron schedule it late in the day so I could be there.”

“How do you think Goldberg will react to this ultimatum?” Lloyd asked, addressing both Ron and Stephanie. “From the way you’ve described him, he seems to be wound pretty tight and likes to call the shots—at least the important ones.”

“If he wants me to accept the offer to run for the U.S. Senate, he’ll have to.”

“What does he want in return? You know there’s got to be a quid pro quo.”

“During our conversations, he’s always alluding to wanting to get good, honest people in office that have their constituents’ best interests at heart.”

“That’s sounds like he’s trying to butter you up…but for what?”

“I realize there’s a lot that can happen. That’s why I want Stephanie handling the campaign and watching my back.”

“If you want my advice, I’d say that you and Stephanie have to be an unshakable team in the midst of all of the people Goldberg may insert into the mix. You have to be in agreement on everything publicly. If you have a difference of opinion, be sure to discuss it in private and work everything out before you have interactions with any staff he may bring along. Divide and conquer is one of the most common tactics used in these types of situations.”

“That makes perfect sense. Any other advice?”

"No, but I'll continue to do background research on Goldberg and his law practice. I may find something that gives us some leverage that we may need in the future."

"Great. I think we're ready for tomorrow's meeting. Here's a toast to being bold, fearless, and two steps ahead." Ron held up his glass, and the others followed suit.

"To being bold, fearless, and two steps ahead," they said in unison and clinked their glasses.

CHAPTER 37

Part of the reason Michael had formed the Committee and acted as its leader was because he enjoyed the predictable nature of dealing with politicians. He had several theories regarding politicians, the primary one being that they possessed much more ego than intelligence. Few of them ever suspected his motives when he approached them. They were too busy congratulating themselves on achieving their lifelong dream of moving up the political ladder.

Some of the more naïve ones were actually under the illusion that the higher they went up the proverbial legislative rung, the more they could achieve. Although they had accomplished little when they held seats on their local city council, became mayors of their cities or towns, or were elected to the state legislature or even statewide office, they still believed they had more power than they actually possessed. And that belief kept them in the political arena. Politics was driven by a specific skill set: superior acting skills, effectively communicating sound bites, and strategically playing the blame game. All one had to do was find a scapegoat for why nothing ever actually got done.

But the wellspring of hope never ran dry among politicians. Those hopes continued to spring eternal. The ultimate prize was being elected to the U.S. Congress or Senate—for some, even President of the United States. Once there, the pols deluded themselves into thinking they were among the most powerful political figures in the country.

Little did they know they were all under the thumb of groups like the Committee, or other clandestine operators, that were pulling all of the strings. They were so malleable, so easy to manipulate, that sometimes Michael wished his job was a bit harder. But not really.

These thoughts were running through Michael's head as the classical music he played wafted through the Rockford Fosgate sound system in his BMW on his way to Ron Singleton's office. Today was the day when he'd hear Ron's decision about running for the Senate, but for Michael, the decision was already made. Ron showed all of the signs of being eager to hit the campaign trail.

He pulled into the parking lot and caught the elevator to the fifth floor, where Ron's office was located. The receptionist announced his arrival, guided him to Ron's office door, and tapped it lightly. "Mr. Singleton, Mr. Goldberg has arrived," Ron's assistant, Lisa, said and motioned for Goldberg to go ahead and enter.

There was a broad smile on Goldberg's face when Ron greeted him and shook his hand, but the sight of Stephanie Palmer seated in one of the chair's facing Ron's desk made Michael stop in his tracks. "I assumed this meeting was just between the two of us," said Michael cautiously.

"That's what I wanted to talk to you about, Michael. Please have a seat," said Ron, and he directed him to the other seat that faced his desk. Ron then took his seat behind his desk.

"First, I'd like to introduce you to Stephanie Palmer. I'm sure you're familiar with her husband, Lloyd Palmer, editor of the *Ledger*."

"I've never met him, but I certainly know him by reputation and have great respect for him. Nice to meet you, Ms. Palmer."

"Same here, Mr. Goldberg. Please call me Stephanie."

"Of course, Stephanie, and I believe we'll be on a first-name basis all around."

"Okay," responded Stephanie, "then Michael it is."

"I've asked Stephanie to attend this meeting since she will be an integral part of my campaign. Michael, I accept your offer to run for the U.S. Senate seat and appreciate your confidence in supporting my candidacy."

"That's great news, Ron. You'll make an excellent campaigner, and the voters will love you. You're already well respected in the Houston community," said Michael, pleased that his assessment about Ron accepting the Committee's offer was correct.

"So will Stephanie be your assistant during the campaign?" he asked.

"No, Michael, that's what I wanted to talk to you about. I want Stephanie to be my campaign manager. I accept your offer, but her position as campaign manager is non-negotiable. If you want me to run, Stephanie is part of the package and will be heading my team." Ron stared directly at Michael when he spoke.

Michael was thrown for a loop. This development was completely unexpected.

"I hope you don't mind me asking this question, but does Stephanie have any experience running a political campaign?"

"Not directly, but she has been very effective executing some of our neighborhood initiatives. She's also very organized, she is an excellent judge of character, and I trust her implicitly."

"What aspect of the campaign will she be managing?" inquired Michael, hoping to dissuade Ron from what he saw as a reckless decision.

"All of it—hiring decisions, the day-to-day management, and the finances."

"But I had told you we had a staff ready to go and that this is a turnkey operation. We already have someone on our team who has management experience."

"I'm sure you do, but that person will report to Stephanie," Ron said as he leaned back in his chair and crossed his arms. "Also, she will have an onboard interview with each staff member we hire to make sure they are compatible with her management style and vision for the campaign. Some of them might not make the cut."

Michael could see that Ron wasn't going to budge. For now, he'd appear to acquiesce. The counter response would come later. "Well, Stephanie, welcome to Ron's campaign," he said and shook her hand. "My role is to be a facilitator in getting the campaign off the ground as I work largely behind the scenes. I'll put you in touch with the manager—I mean, the assistant manager, who will be helping you get things off the ground. His name is Joel Radner."

Until that point, Stephanie had let Ron do all the talking as she observed Michael's reaction to what had transpired so far. "I look forward to meeting Joel and the other team members," Stephanie replied. "I'd also like to put out some feelers among some of the political operatives I know to hire some people who understand working at the grassroots."

"Of course," said Michael through gritted teeth. He rose from his chair to leave and headed for Ron's door. "I'll be talking with both of you soon."

Michael headed for the elevator, seething.

CHAPTER 38

Michael needed some time to decompress from the shocker of a meeting he'd had with Ron and his so-called campaign manager, Stephanie Palmer. Apparently he had misjudged Ron in terms of his level of compliance with the established hierarchy. The idea that Ron thought he could present an ultimatum to him and actually succeed was laughable. But the problem was that Michael had invested too many resources, as well as his reputation, on Ron Singleton's candidacy. It was too late for him to go back to the drawing board and select someone else. The vetting process simply took too long.

Ron wasn't the first among the Committee's selected candidates to try to make his own moves, but he *was* the first that Michael didn't see coming. It wasn't something he'd anticipated could ever happen. After leaving Ron's office, Michael decided to go to one of his favorite places to unwind, the Four Seasons Hotel. The Bayou & Bottle, the chic bourbon bar inside the hotel, had just the right ambiance. The head waiter, Raphael Morton, always had his favorite corner table available, where he could meet or think in private. He'd eat dinner, but first he'd have one of their special whiskys on the rocks.

He texted Heather to let her know he'd be home late. Then he texted Joel Radner, his point man for the Singleton campaign.

Michael: Joel, meet me at the Bayou & Bottle, and be here within the next thirty minutes.

Joel: Okay. Be there shortly.

Joel, as were all the operatives in Michael's universe, was at his beck and call and had been expecting to hear from Michael after his meeting with Ron. The arrangement was that Joel would be Michael's point man within Ron's campaign organization, having control over all the finances and steering Ron in the political, social, and legislative directions that Michael required. That would still happen, but it would be a bit trickier.

Joel walked into the bar in less than the time allotted, went over to Michael's table, and sat down. "How'd everything go at Singleton's office?"

"He accepted our offer to run for the Senate like we knew he would, but there's been a slight wrinkle in our plan."

"A wrinkle? What kind of wrinkle?"

"Ron picked his own campaign manager and insisted she run things. He said it was non-negotiable. On top of that, she's the wife of the editor of the Houston *Ledger*, so I couldn't simply ignore the request. Her name is Stephanie Palmer."

"But you told me I'd be the campaign manager. I've been waiting a couple of years for this chance."

Michael hated whiners. "I know that, and eventually you will. For starters, though, we'll have to make sure she's comfortably in charge, at least as far as she knows. Stephanie has no experience with political campaigns and will soon be in over her head. Just bide your time, and you'll be running the show in no time."

"How can you be so sure?"

"For starters, I'm giving you control over a ten million-dollar campaign account where you can hire the contractors of your choice for various assignments. It's an account Stephanie won't know anything about. I'll provide her with another account with a much smaller deposit, and she'll believe that all of the campaign funds are in that one."

Michael's revelation made Joel immediately cheer up, but he still wanted the public pronouncement that he was actually in charge as campaign manager.

"What if Stephanie manages to gain enough control where Ron is satisfied with the results and she refuses to step down?"

"If she doesn't relinquish the reins willingly, we'll have to make it obvious that she's incompetent. That won't be a problem. Your assignment for the time being is to act as though you're totally on board with her being in charge and that you fully support her. Are you comfortable doing that, Joel? Because if you're not, I can easily appoint one of the other operatives to this position."

Joel quickly responded, "I can do that as long as I don't have to be number two for too long."

"You'll have to do that for as long as it takes, but I predict that within ninety days, she'll throw in the towel. Meanwhile, don't give her any reason to be suspicious. Is that clear?"

Joel was disappointed but also hopeful. Michael had always been a man of his word. Joel had seen him do the impossible. He could wait a few months to take on the biggest assignment of his professional career.

"Stephanie won't suspect a thing, I assure you."

CHAPTER 39

Two weeks after Ron's meeting with Michael, the Ron Singleton for Senate campaign headquarters opened to great fanfare. More than two hundred people attended the morning event—elected officials, community leaders, and Ron's family and friends. Local, statewide, and national media outlets all covered the grand opening. Utilizing her connections at the grassroots and her incredible organizational skills, Stephanie had found a recently vacated office space in an ideal location in the heart of downtown Houston and had it furnished and communications installed in nearly record time.

"Today I'm announcing my candidacy for the U.S. Senate," Ron said in his opening remarks, "and I want to represent the citizens of Texas with integrity, wisdom, and compassion. These qualities have been missing in Washington for years, and I hope to help bring some civility back to our nation's capital."

Ron was flanked by Shirley and Stephanie, who were both all smiles. He continued with his speech and then gave closing remarks. "I want to give special thanks to my wife, Shirley, who has been with me through thick and thin. Our daughter, Destiny, couldn't be here today, but she'll be representing our campaign in several parts of the state." He smiled at Shirley, and she mouthed the words "I love you."

"I also want to thank Stephanie Palmer, my campaign manager, for her hard work, dedication, and loyalty. There is no one I'd trust more to lead our team." Stephanie gave a quick curtsy.

The photographers took lots of pictures, and there were a few questions from reporters. After that, things settled down, and Ron and Stephanie met in his office to map out the rest of the day and the coming week.

"The main thing on today's agenda is meeting with the team Michael put together," she said as she accessed Ron's schedule on her tablet. "I'll need to interview them individually and sign off on each one."

"When are they scheduled to arrive?"

"Starting at one o'clock. I scheduled them at thirty-minute intervals and should be done with the interviews by the end of the day. I placed their interviews in order of importance in terms of responsibility. The first one is Joel Radner. He was supposed to be the campaign manager, and since that's now my job, he'll be the assistant. I want to get a feel for whether or not he accepts being number two. The news couldn't have made him happy."

"Happy or not, he'll be the number two or nothing at all," Ron responded decisively. "I'll be out of the office for most of the afternoon meeting with potential donors. It's one of my least favorite things about campaigning, but it comes with the territory."

"Okay, check in and let me know how things are going."

Stephanie went into her office and checked her laptop for the media coverage of the grand opening. All four local television affiliates had featured it on their websites. One had sent a camera crew and interviewed a couple of the supporters that had attended.

Lloyd had sent a reporter from the *Ledger,* and the story was featured as one of the top four items on their home page. She checked the comments on each of the websites because comments could often be a valuable source of feedback. She loathed the negative ones, but sometimes critical comments could reveal problems before they festered and got out of control.

There were a few volunteers on hand in the main office area who were manning the phones and greeting those that had questions or wanted to volunteer. Stephanie wanted to utilize volunteers as much as possible to keep their personnel costs down. Political campaigns had been known to burn through millions of dollars in only a matter of months, also known as the burn rate. That's why she wanted control over the finances since Ron planned to be in the race for the long haul.

One of the volunteers informed her that Joel Radner had arrived for his onboard interview. Stephanie hadn't met him yet, but as he walked into her office, her first impression of him was that he seemed shy and bookish. He had dark, frizzy hair; wore round, gold-metal glasses; and was below average in height.

"Hi, Joel. Have a seat."

"It's great to meet you, Stephanie, and I look forward to working with you. Getting Ron elected is my primary objective, and I'm all in," he said eagerly.

"I would expect nothing less," replied Stephanie. Joel's over exuberance was a red flag as far as Stephanie was concerned, and she paid attention to all red flags. He should have been less energetic, especially in light of his demotion on the team.

"I'll be meeting with the rest of the team this afternoon. I assume you've worked with them before." Her statement was understood to be a question.

"Yes, but not all on the same team before. That will be new. I've worked with them individually on different campaigns."

"Well, things may be run in a manner that's different than you're used to. They are not all sure hires until I meet with them and evaluate their attitudes and skill sets. There may be some disappointments today, so you should be prepared for that."

"Of course. I'm here to assist you in whatever way I can," Joel said. He'd been prepped by Michael to be as affable as possible, although it was killing him inside to ingratiate himself to a woman who had zero political experience.

"I've taken the initial step of identifying some of the key locations for Ron's campaign offices across the state," Joel said and handed Stephanie a laminated copy of a printed map of the state of Texas. "The cities where I think offices will be essential are marked in red."

Stephanie examined the map carefully. "Hmm, I see you've targeted the suburban areas surrounding the big cities and the wealthy zip codes in the urban areas but don't have much coverage in the areas with significant numbers of Black voters."

"Well, there is a reason for that..." Joel started, but Stephanie interrupted him.

"The way we are going to win this statewide campaign is to cover the suburbs as well as the urban areas. We need strong support in the Black community, and a grassroots campaign is what's going to get us over the top. We also need to have a large presence on college campuses. I've been studying Barack Obama's presidential campaign of 2008, and that's how he was able to win during both the primaries and the general election."

Joel didn't like the pushback. He was already being rebuffed regarding a task he'd performed a dozen times before.

"Please revise this map, and provide me with a copy when it's done," Stephanie directed.

"Of course. I'll take care of this, and you'll have a new map tomorrow. Anything else?"

"That's all for now. I'll let you know what else I need after I've interviewed the other campaign staff members."

Joel sulked out of Stephanie's office but tried not to let her see it. In his mind, he kept repeating what Michael had told him: All he had to do was bide his time. Stephanie would be gone soon.

CHAPTER 40

Immediately after Stephanie interviewed Joel, he showed her how to access the financial records and bank account that had been set up for Ron's campaign. True to his word, Michael had set up the campaign's bank account with an initial deposit of two million dollars, and Stephanie and Ron were the only two authorized signers on the account. Michael was also a signer, but any checks he wrote had to be co-signed by either Stephanie or Ron.

The initial funds were meant to finance the first six months of the campaign, including staff, office space, and contractors, but Stephanie planned to let the funds go much further than six months by scrutinizing every expense. Two million dollars was a lot of money, and she would be watching every penny that was expended.

Stephanie spent the rest of the afternoon interviewing the remaining staffers one by one. They all seemed qualified and personable, except one. The team member who was assigned to be in charge of the volunteers had little to no personality.

Stephanie had worked with volunteers before during her many neighborhood initiatives. Volunteers needed to be treated with respect to know their contributions mattered. Having the attitude that they were peons—which was essentially the stance of Claudia Simmons, the person who was supposed to manage that portion of the campaign—was a recipe for disaster. After finances, the lifeblood of any political campaign was a team of committed volunteers.

During the interview, Stephanie told Claudia that she wouldn't be hired as volunteer coordinator because she didn't embrace the Singleton campaign's team philosophy of respecting everyone regardless of their station in life or their position within the campaign. "Perhaps you'll find a home within another campaign, but it won't be this one," Stephanie told her bluntly.

Mentally exhausted after her afternoon of interviews, Stephanie made plans to go home. She felt that her day had been productive and she'd gotten something significant done: She'd assembled the core of the campaign team.

As she gathered her laptop and the files she planned to review at home, Joel tapped on her open office door.

"How did things go today?" he asked.

"They went well for the most part. I decided we'd hire all but one of the people who were on the list of team members."

"Which one didn't make the cut?"

"Claudia Simmons. Do you know her?"

"Yes, I've worked with her before. I'm surprised she didn't work out." In fact, Claudia was Joel's long-time friend; he'd even dated her a few years ago, but things didn't work out. He'd expected to have her on the campaign to help him manage things.

"It was obvious she held volunteers in general and our volunteers specifically in contempt. That was simply unacceptable."

"I certainly understand that."

At that moment, Stephanie noticed a file folder in Joel's hand. "Is that for me?"

"Yes, I thought you might want to see the list of declared candidates who will be running against Ron in the primary,"

Joel said and handed Stephanie the file. He'd already emailed the list to Michael using the private email address they used to communicate.

"That's definitely a list I'd like to see. How many candidates are there?"

"So far, there are only four who have the resources to mount an effective campaign: Miriam Hardwick, Marty Price, Timothy McPherson, and Bishop Samuel Rutherford Jones III. I've included a bit of opposition research on each. There are a few other declared candidates, but they are either perennial ones or are mounting symbolic campaigns. It doesn't hurt to know our competitors' strengths and weaknesses."

"I agree. Ron wants to run a clean campaign with no dirty political tricks, but knowing the backgrounds of other candidates running in the primary will bolster our chances. I'll review everything at home as my bedtime reading," she said and smiled.

Joel smiled back and bid her goodnight.

CHAPTER 41

"I'm sick of being your booty call, Marty. This isn't how you said things would be. You lied to me," said Melanie Lancaster. "It's been five years, and you keep telling me you're going to leave your wife soon. But *soon* never seems to mean *now*, and I'm tired of waiting."

Marty and Melanie had just finished a round of their usual vigorous lovemaking. He lay in bed completely sated but irritated by Melanie's constant nagging. He was starting to weigh whether her incredible sexual skills were worth the myriad problems she caused.

Marty Price had lived a political life for two decades, starting at the school board level and working his way up to the U.S. Congress. He had met Melanie at a political fundraiser five years earlier. They first made eye contact while perusing the wine and assorted hors d'oeuvres on the lavish buffet table. As Melanie placed a stuffed shrimp in her mouth, Marty's eyes took in her well-formed curves in the Oscar de la Renta cocktail dress she was wearing. She looked him dead in his eyes and slowly wet her lips with her tongue.

Later, as they sat at adjacent round tables and listened to the speaker's monotone presentation, she smiled at him mischievously and winked. Melanie slowly put her index finger in her mouth then parted her legs slightly, revealing the obvious absence of underwear.

Before the event ended, Melanie rose from her chair as if to leave the venue. Instead, Melanie went to the bellman's stand and tipped the valet parking attendant to tell her which limo was Marty's. She was quite resourceful.

Melanie met him at his car as he was leaving the event, and Marty offered her a ride home. She accepted and joined him in the back seat of his limo. The tinted glass barrier was raised so the driver couldn't see or hear what they were doing.

Within a few moments, she unzipped his pants, groped his throbbing member, then gave him the most incredible blow job he'd ever had. For weeks after, he visited her apartment at least three times a week, and the sex was amazing. Three months later, she announced she was pregnant and that she was keeping the baby.

Marty was careful to keep this affair under wraps so his wife, Erin, wouldn't find out. Erin had been dutiful and took excellent care of their two boys, John and Timothy. After spending hours at her part-time job and transporting the boys to and from their sporting events and extracurricular activities, Erin was usually too tired or disinterested to have sex, and after all, a man had needs.

Now Marty wished he'd never met Melanie. Other than her sexual prowess, she served no real purpose. She was constantly nagging him about making their relationship permanent and public, in other words, divorcing his wife and marrying her. That was never going to happen.

But she had upped the ante by threatening to tell his wife or, worse, expose him to the media. He could kick himself for not ending the relationship soon after it started, but Melanie was like an addiction he couldn't shake. He couldn't help himself; the sex was just too good. The result, though, was the birth of two children—three-year-old Jeremy and eighteen-month-old Patricia—that neither Erin nor the public knew anything about.

Marty had his eye on an upcoming open Senate seat and was considering running. So far he'd been able to keep his relationship with Melanie under wraps, but he knew that couldn't last forever. He had even contemplated making arrangements for Melanie to meet an untimely death. One well-placed phone call and it could all be taken care of with no connection to him whatsoever. The only thing holding him back was the thought of what would become of Jeremy and Patricia if Melanie wasn't around.

"I told you the timing just isn't right" Marty sighed, hoping this would calm Melanie down. "I'm just trying to put all of my ducks in a row."

Melanie was bitter. "That's the answer you always give me when I ask you for a commitment," she responded and cocked her head to the side. "Well, you'd better arrange those ducks soon. I've learned a thing or two being hooked up with you all of these years, especially about how to manipulate the media.

"Who knows? I might call one of the TV networks and hold a press conference with Jeremy and Patricia by my side. I think the voters would notice the resemblance when I tell them these are your two love children. And I'll be sure to offer a paternity test as proof."

"Why do you feel like you have to keep up the threats, Melanie? Haven't I provided for you and the kids financially all these years? I'm paying your rent and all your expenses. Plus, I just bought you a new Cadillac. Doesn't that mean anything?"

“Sure, I’m grateful, but material things can’t keep me warm at night. I need you to be here—with us.”

“I’m here as often as I can be,” sighed Marty while contemplating how he could break things off before she made good on her threats. Maybe he could move them all to another city or even another state. He had to do something before everything he’d worked for fell apart.

CHAPTER 42

Timothy McPherson was a high-functioning alcoholic, although he'd never admit that to himself or anyone else. Last week, when he traipsed completely naked to his next door neighbor's house and rang the doorbell, he had been on one of his drunken binges and didn't even remember it. His neighbor's wife, Susan, answered the door, gasped and placed her hand over her mouth, and said, "Timothy, are you crazy? Go home, or I'm calling the police." She slammed the door, looked through the peephole and waited for him to leave.

He was fortunate that her reaction was only a threat and she didn't follow through with her 911 call. Timothy was also fortunate that he lived in an exclusive, gated community where the lots were at least a half-acre and the houses were spaced apart. Otherwise, his political career would be over, and a continuous climb up the political ladder was his life-long passion.

Like most alcoholics, Timothy was convinced he could stop drinking whenever he wanted to, and since he didn't have a drink every day, he didn't see it as a problem. He drank mostly at home, away from the prying eyes of the media and local busybodies. At home he could savor every drop and didn't have to worry about driving home and being pulled over for driving under the influence. He mostly drank on weekends, but his drunken stupors sometimes caused blackouts. He'd wake up twenty-four hours later not remembering exactly what had happened.

Meanwhile, his wife, Natalie, lived in constant fear, hoping that Tim's next drinking binge would occur in the distant future. He wasn't a particularly mean drunk, but he could be unpredictable. He sometimes suffered from hallucinations, heard voices, and had paranoid ideations. It was the not knowing that kept her on pins and needles.

Tim had set his sights on the open seat for the U.S. Senate, but Natalie secretly hoped his Senate campaign would fizzle out before it got off the ground. Otherwise, their lives would be on national television, scrutinized and ridiculed by the public, and they might never recover, financially or otherwise. She thought she would crumble under the weight of the humiliation. She'd thought about packing her bags and leaving him and was getting close to her breaking point.

CHAPTER 43

Bishop Samuel Rutherford Jones III was one of the most renowned Black pastors in the state of Texas. In addition to its central headquarters in Houston, his church, the House of the Living God Cathedral of Love, had multiple satellite locations in the state—Katy, a Houston suburb; Waller, which was close to the Prairie View A&M University campus, an historically Black college; and San Antonio. The location in San Antonio was by far the largest, boasting two thousand attendees every Sunday. It also was the location that produced the largest financial windfall for Jones and the members of the Cathedral's first family.

Jones made sure the offerings at each site were secure. He had a finance chair designated at each location whose highest priority was to transport the Sunday offerings directly to the main Cathedral headquarters offices. The funds were dropped directly into the bank bag from the offering buckets and the bag was immediately padlocked. The chairperson was instructed not to look in the bank bag nor did he know the amount being transported. The funds were then to be transported without delay, ensuring that the bag arrived within three hours after each church service ended. If the funds arrived even one minute late, the finance chair was relieved of his duties.

Bishop Jones exerted total control over his ministerial enterprise, including the satellite locations, even though he had a minister assigned to each who preached the Sunday sermons and taught the Wednesday Bible study classes. Each minister was given strict guidelines and was expected to follow them to the letter so that the indoctrination at all locations was complete. But there was another reason for the bishop's nearly maniacal control: It kept each of the ministers from developing their own small faction of followers, thus siphoning off sources of the weekly cash flow the Cathedral sorely needed.

The monetary donations contributed by the Cathedral's members had catapulted Bishop Jones and his family to a level of opulence far beyond his humble beginnings in Houston's Fifth Ward. Jones had grown up in a blighted area that hadn't seen any redevelopment investment dollars in decades. He had vowed never to return to that hand-to-mouth existence again, and he'd do whatever it took to make sure that didn't happen. He stretched his parishioners' pocketbooks as far as he reasonably could to keep them believing for a financial breakthrough without abandoning their commitment and church membership.

The bishop wasn't pious; to the contrary, he was practical to a fault. He knew that most of the people who attended his Sunday and Wednesday services would defer to what they perceived as his godly authority and follow his edicts. Jones had craftily cobbled together enough relevant scriptures to support his assertion that if his parishioners pledged enough of their income to the Cathedral, a boomerang blessing was just around the corner.

But the pledges were only the first step. Step two involved constant reinforcement through carefully crafted scripture references. If steps one and two didn't reap the desired financial rewards for church coffers, he could always depend on one or two testimonials from those that had recently received a salary increase or a job bonus and attributed the financial windfall to their Cathedral contributions.

Less than two weeks before, Deacon Thaddeus McDonald did that very thing. During the Wednesday night Bible study session when attendees had the opportunity to announce good news, or "praise reports," Deacon McDonald stood up and raised his clasped hands above his head. "I've been praying for a financial breakthrough," he said, his voice breaking with emotion, "and I paid a special offering last month in hopes that it would come to pass."

"I've been working at my city government job for ten years and have never been promoted," he continued. "My supervisor recently got transferred to another department, and he recommended me to fill his place. I start my new job next week with a ten thousand dollar raise in salary. My special offering was my pathway to increase. Praise the Lord!" he declared, eliciting a standing ovation and a rhapsodic chorus of "hallelujahs," "amens," and "praise Gods."

After one of these types of public pronouncements of perceived newfound prosperity, the Cathedral's coffers always received a substantial boost. Even though most of these instances of job promotions and raises would have occurred through the natural course of time, Jones knew members of his flock would draw a different conclusion.

Jones knew he was preying on their gullibility, but he also knew the desire to believe was a strong human emotion. He knew that manipulating the vulnerable was wrong in God's eyes, but he believed his numerous acts of benevolence would outweigh his occasional sinful motives.

Over the years, Jones had developed what he called an internal sin-ometer; he could get close enough to the line of committing the outright sin of idolatry—worshipping his own possessions and lifestyle—without actually crossing it. He'd get around to donating some of his riches to charity…eventually.

But the control he wielded at the Cathedral only satisfied a portion of Jones's lust for power and wealth. He also had political ambitions. Political power would expand his reach far beyond his congregation and give him potential authority over billions of dollars from the Texas treasury as well as the ability to pass state laws. Maybe he could even set his sights higher and run for the U.S. Congress or Senate!

CHAPTER 44

Joel handed off the list of Ron's four best-financed primary opponents to Stephanie so she could become familiar with the opposition. He then went into his office, which was on the opposite side of the building from hers, and settled in at his desk. The initial steps in Michael's overarching plan were already in motion. In the coming weeks, each of Ron's opponents would be vanquished one by one through a variety of means.

Joel didn't know the behind-the-scenes operations when it came to Michael's strategic plans. All he knew was that Michael was never wrong. If he said something was going to happen, it happened.

Once the opponents were out of the way, Ron's campaign would receive a large influx of campaign contributions, which would be used to purchase advertising slots on all the major television networks, cable stations, and talk radio shows. With the four opponents sidelined, the campaign would have to spend next to nothing on advertising during the primary and could save its financial war chest for the general election.

Social media outlets had instituted rules to limit the amount of direct political advertising that appeared on their platforms, but there were ways to get around that. Joel would get one of his covert social media influencers to share negative information about Ron's general election opponent, and in a matter of days, the posts would be shared hundreds of thousands of times. He paid the influencers under the table, which was one of the reasons why he had separate bank accounts from the one Stephanie used.

The campaign funds she oversaw were peanuts compared to the much larger account Michael had set up for Joel's use. That made it easier for Joel to stomach being the number two man on the campaign, at least in the short term. He still had control of the bulk of the finances, and as Michael reminded him on numerous occasions, he who has the gold rules.

Meanwhile, Michael instructed the media mogul to create dossiers on all four of Ron's primary opponents. In his usual fashion, the mogul assigned three of the candidates to his most reliable operative—Romulus—for handling. The media mogul decided to try a different tack with the other. Too many tips emanating from Blackstone's desk at the *Ledger* might raise suspicions from the editor and his fellow reporters. There was a newcomer in the *Ledger*'s news room, and the mogul thought he'd use her inexperience to his advantage. Her name was Chelsea Bannon.

CHAPTER 45

Romulus leaned back in the rocking chair on the porch of his Catskills Mountains cabin, enjoying the brilliance of the yellow-hued sunset. He had purchased the cabin with the proceeds from his last two assignments, using one of his shell corporations to complete the real estate transaction. He enjoyed his solitude in the New York mountain range immensely. But the Catskills' hiking trails and ski resorts—located just a few miles west of the cabin—also provided just the right amount of entertainment when he brought a female companion to his hideaway for an occasional fun-filled weekend.

Of course, Romulus wasn't his real name. He had many aliases and chose each name carefully based on the type of job he was assigned by one of his well-heeled clients. He used the moniker Romulus for his political clients, a name he selected because Romulus was the first king of Rome. As a problem fixer, Romulus considered himself to be set apart from the clueless masses that were only slightly more insightful than sheep.

His work required complete secrecy and near complete anonymity. The only thing his clients knew about him was that he was highly skilled, highly proficient, and very expensive. He did a thorough background check on each of his potential clients before agreeing to accept their assignments. It was a clear case of role reversal, but that was part of what made him special. He also required a monthly retainer of at least six figures from his clients. The payments his clients provided were transferred through a minimum of three or four different countries' financial institutions before landing in his offshore account. The Committee had him on retainer at the insistence of Michael Goldberg, which meant Romulus was at the Committee's beck and call.

Some of his best clients were political operatives that were the puppet masters behind most elected officials. Romulus's role was part detective, part intermediary, part problem-solver, and, when necessary, part assassin. With his thin, muscular physique; steely eyes; emotionless expression and understated attire, he tended to blend into the scenery wherever he traveled. In the rare event that his profile was flagged on surveillance footage, he fit the description of thousands of adult men traveling with a single carry-on bag.

Most of the jobs assigned to him by the Committee involved placing political candidates in compromising positions and then leaking photos and videos of them to the media at the opportune time. One negative news story that went viral on the cable news channels and social media platforms was enough to make all but the most resilient or committed candidates drop out of the race.

And recent technological advances had made his surveillance work much easier. He rarely had to enter his targets' homes to plant video and audio bugs anymore. Now all he had to do was tap into their many home-based devices that operated using cameras or sound. Siri, Alexa, Ring, iRobot, and laptop cameras were among his best techy friends. These devices usually gave Romulus access to every room in his target's home. People had no idea how vulnerable they were to being tracked by any recluse working out of his mother's basement.

He used a disposable cell phone that could be neither tracked nor traced that he assigned to each client for communication. Just to be on the safe side, he removed the SIM card from each phone immediately after speaking with whomever was on the other end.

Romulus had been working with the Committee for about five years, and all of his communications were with one man. His last contact with the Committee occurred a few days before and had been a simple text exchange.

Committee: Need mother and children relocated to another state. Will provide funding for their travel and relocation.

Romulus: Any particular region?

Committee: No, but make sure she knows her children will disappear if she doesn't comply, doesn't stay hidden, or confides in anyone.

Romulus: Got it.

The Committee left the creativity up to Romulus to solve problems as he saw fit.

Romulus also cleaned up messes for the Committee's chosen candidates. When one of the candidates had a lover, friend, or family member that posed a problem the media could pounce on, he dealt with those situations in different ways. Sometimes there was a payoff. Sometimes there was a relocation. Sometimes the distraction—and the person—simply disappeared.

The Committee, as did most of his clients, had rules. Unless there was no other option, harming children was strictly off limits. Threats were okay as long as no harm actually occurred. Also, there could be absolutely no trail of evidence leading authorities to the Committee. If Romulus was arrested or questioned by the police, he was on his own.

That's why Romulus maintained a multimillion-dollar offshore account specifically for legal fees. He hired a lawyer in Miami to whom he provided full power of attorney to post bond in the event of an arrest. He had all of his bases covered in terms of contingencies.

Romulus built a digital dossier on all his targets before taking action, studying their habits, patterns, and comings and goings. He also used social media platforms to great effect, creating a number of fake Facebook, Instagram, Twitter, and TikTok accounts. When a compromising photo of a subject needed to be quickly circulated, he would post the photo utilizing a provocative caption and tag all the appropriate media outlets and reporters.

There was no video footage of Timothy McPherson knocking on his neighbor's door wearing only his birthday suit, but his neighbor had reported the incident to the local sheriff's office. About an hour after her call, they came to investigate, but everything had blown over. McPherson was in his home passed out in a drunken stupor, but the official report stayed in the system.

That's how Romulus found out about McPherson's dark secret. Part of his process for finding skeletons of potential candidates was to hack the law enforcement databases for arrest records. Most of the reports never saw the light of day in terms of ever making news headlines, but by law, the arrest records had to remain in the system.

McPherson's neighbor hadn't installed a Ring video system at her door, so there was no video evidence of the sordid incident. But Romulus used AI to recreate the scene, including the stunned look on McPherson's neighbor's face when she stood behind her screen door warning McPherson to leave or she'd call the authorities.

Getting an image of the front of the neighbor's house was easy enough using Google's street view feature. Romulus googled images of nude white males' backsides that matched McPherson's general description: six feet tall with brown hair cut just above the nape of his neck. A simple drop-and-drag of the image using artful positioning of the remaining background did the trick.

Romulus had also accessed McPherson's insurance records and found a medical report for the biopsy of a mole on McPherson's left butt cheek. The report described the mole's positioning and exact diameter. That was easy enough to recreate on the photo so even McPherson wouldn't be able to tell the difference. At heart, Romulus considered himself to be an artist of sorts, creating new images, sounds, and thoughts where they hadn't existed before.

On the day McPherson had shocked his neighbor by showing up naked at her front door, his back had been turned, so using another man's backside would allow the viewers' collective minds to do the rest. Romulus texted the manipulated image to McPherson from one of his many burner cell phones. Since McPherson was drunk and wearing no clothes whatsoever when he stumbled onto his neighbor's porch, he'd believe the fabricated photo and would be ashamed enough to drop out of the race.

After completing his work discrediting McPherson, he turned his attention to Miriam Hardwick. He'd been monitoring the social media page she'd created under the assumed name, Misty Hunt, where she set up dates with male escorts. Romulus noticed she used her same initials, a common mistake made by novices trying to hide their identities. He slid into her DMs and started a conversation using one of his dummy accounts, accompanied by a fake photo and a fake name, Greg.

G: Hey, Misty. I'm Greg. I've been following your profile and I'd like to take you out.

M: Hi, Greg. I had to do a double take because you are so handsome. What do you like to do in your spare time?

G: I like to go to movies, concerts, and the theater. How about you?

M: Same for me, but I haven't been to one with a man in years. Is there a particular one occurring soon where we can meet and get to know each other?

G: There's a club in the Montrose area that plays live music. Can we meet there Friday night?

M: Sure, what time?

G: How does eight o'clock sound?

M: It's perfect. How will I know you?

G: I'll be wearing a University of Texas polo shirt. That's my alma mater. And I'll sit close to the front door.

M: I'll be there on time. I can't wait to meet you.

G: Misty, one more thing.

M: What's that?

G: You're so pretty in your pictures. Would you send me a photo of you wearing lingerie? I'd like something to look at until we meet.

Miriam—or Misty—thought that was odd, but what the hell. She'd send him a photo and wear a costume mask to hide her identity.

M: Okay. It will take me a couple of hours to change and take the photo, but I'll send it soon.

G: I can't wait. See you Friday.

Romulus would await the arrival of the provocative photo. Then he'd put together the screenshots of their DMs with the photos and send it to one of his social media pals on the dark web. The files would be uploaded to all the social media platforms with #miriamhardwick. Within a day or two, they'd be seen by millions, and Miriam would be forced to drop out of the race.

Among the assignments given to him by the Committee, this was one of Romulus's easier ones. But easy or difficult made no difference as long as the funds were transferred to his overseas account on the agreed upon date. When necessary, he occasionally used the services of international subcontractors, especially when he was juggling multiple jobs. He considered himself to be a one-man cottage industry.

CHAPTER 46

As the weeks went by, Stephanie settled into a consistent routine at Ron's campaign headquarters. One of her primary objectives was to ensure Ron received some sort of positive media coverage at least three times a week. The negative coverage would occur on its own from opponents and media operatives hungry to make a name for themselves. Positive coverage had to be intentional.

So far, she had succeeded. Ron had visited several youth facilities that focused on tutoring middle school students or preparing high schoolers for the college experience. He'd persuaded several large, Texas-based companies to expand their scholarship programs, and he'd visited a homeless shelter to distribute meals to the less fortunate. Stephanie made sure all of these activities received media coverage.

The media manager she'd hired—the one who was part of the team that arrived with Joel—didn't seem to understand the importance of Ron reaching out to diverse communities. She'd called Joel into her office to discuss the manager's deficiencies.

"I thought you said Angela had top-notch media credentials. So far, most of the news coverage Ron's received has been initiated by me," Stephanie said emphatically, "and she seems to be intentionally avoiding reaching out to urban media outlets."

Joel swallowed before he spoke and mentally counted to three. "Since I've worked with her, she's always been among the best there is in that role."

"Well, if she doesn't shape up soon, *I'll* need to replace her," she said, emphasizing that the decision would be hers.

"I'll speak to her about your concerns. I'm sure she's up to the job."

"I'm not pleased at all, so you may need to reassess your impressions of her skill level."

"I support any decision you make, Stephanie," he replied disingenuously. "We all want what's best for Ron's campaign." Joel paused. "Is that all?"

"At the moment, but the so-called experienced team that you brought on board seems to be dropping like flies one by one due to incompetence."

Joel slowly counted to three again under his breath, incensed that Stephanie would question his political skills. After all, he'd been doing this for over a decade, and she was merely a novice who'd bitten off more than she could chew. He'd continue to bide his time, but it was getting harder and harder.

CHAPTER 47

When Joel arrived at the office one morning a few days later, he checked his email alerts as well as the local, statewide, and national news sites. As he scrolled, one story near the top of the list caught his attention since it involved one of Ron's major opponents in the Senate race.

Apparently Timothy McPherson had been hiding an addiction to alcohol for years. No one on his staff knew, and even his close friends were unaware of this vice. The secret was revealed when he was caught naked on his neighbor's porch in a drunken stupor. Camera footage from an outdoor camera in the area caught McPherson in the nude, banging on his next-door neighbor's door. The video had already been uploaded to YouTube. Joel checked the number of views, which had already surpassed two hundred thousand. By tomorrow, McPherson's campaign would be on life support.

Joel continued to check his other sources. One of his favorite online destinations was a site called Politricks that featured political gossip. He searched the site's home page to see if there was any recent buzz, and lo and behold, there was a link with the header, "Attorney and Senate Candidate Miriam Hardwick Trolls for Escorts."

Hardwick, whose public persona was as a strait-laced, all-business lawyer, was leading a secret double life. Even her husband didn't know about it because when the Politricks reporter called him for a response, he gasped and then froze in stunned silence. There was no way Hardwick could stay in the race once this news went viral. Within the next few hours, the ravenous wolves in the media would broadcast both stories with wall-to-wall coverage.

Joel knew Michael could perform magic when it came to opposition research, but the way these two opponents were so deftly dispatched, with no fingerprints from the Singleton campaign whatsoever, had him awestruck. He decided to let Stephanie in on the good news. He needed to get back in her good graces after the two staffers he had brought on board had flamed out. He crafted an email to Stephanie and included the links to the stories before going to her office.

Stephanie's office door was open. She was at her desk focusing on her laptop screen when Joel tapped on her door.

"Good morning, Stephanie. I'm sorry to interrupt you, but I just sent you an email that I knew you'd want to see."

"Let me take a look," she said, opening the email and quickly reading its contents. "Both McPherson and Hardwick experienced scandals almost simultaneously? That's an amazing coincidence, wouldn't you say?" She looked at Joel for a response.

"Sometimes coincidences happen like this in politics. At least it's in our favor."

"I find it hard to believe that something this fortuitous could happen in a few short weeks after we launched our campaign. Do you know anything about what happened? I'd like an honest answer," she said as she crossed her arms and waited for his answer.

"Of course not. How could I?" Joel was being truthful since he really didn't know how any of this had occurred.

"Ron insists on running a clean campaign with none of the political shenanigans that most candidates engage in.

He's out campaigning in Dallas and Fort Worth today, meeting with community leaders and some of the Chambers of Commerce. It could potentially be good news for us, although I don't take pleasure in anyone's downfall."

"Nor do I, but let's not look a gift horse in the mouth. If it helps get Ron elected, it's got to be positive, right?"

"That remains to be seen. Let's proceed with caution. If someone from the media asks about this, our response is 'No comment.'"

"I agree with you, and I'll let the other members of the team know as well," Joel replied. "I'll go back to my desk now and work on tomorrow's schedule." He felt like he'd made a bit of progress with setting Stephanie's mind at ease. He wanted her to be completely unaware that a future change to the campaign was imminent.

CHAPTER 48

Lloyd sat at his desk and checked the newspaper's click board every hour on the hour. Presently, the top three stories were last night's Houston Astros versus the San Diego Padres baseball game, which ended with the Astros being the victors; Texas Public Service officers who caught and arrested a human trafficker; and Senate candidate Timothy McPherson being caught naked on his neighbor's porch. McPherson was wasted on alcohol at the time and claimed he didn't recall the incident. Unfortunately for him, the entire incident was caught on his neighbor's security camera, so there was no denying it had taken place.

Warren Blackstone, the reporter who had often been a thorn in Lloyd's side, was the first to break the McPherson story. He submitted a draft to Lloyd that was not only factually correct but also included quotes from residents in McPherson's subdivision. Since Lloyd was Ron's best friend, any stories that impacted the Texas Senate race represented a minor conflict of interest for Lloyd, so he had to tread lightly. He had to make sure the *Ledger* fully covered the Senate race without appearing to weigh heavily on one side or the other.

He and Stephanie had decided that they wouldn't talk on the phone during the day while she was working at Ron's campaign office. Someone might overhear the conversation, and that could lead to problems later on. If there were any developments during the day that were of concern, they would discuss them at home after work.

When he got home that evening, Stephanie had already arrived. She often worked late at the campaign headquarters but not today. He unlocked the front door and let her know he'd arrived.

"Hey, Steph," he called out to determine where she was in the house by the sound of her voice. "I see you got home early. Was everything okay at work?"

Stephanie was in the kitchen unpacking some takeout meals she'd picked up from an area soul food restaurant. "I haven't been home long. It was a normal day, but some information came to my attention, and I was anxious to discuss it with you," she said as she looked up from her unpacking.

"Is it about Timothy McPherson?"

"I wondered if you knew about that. So you heard?"

"Sure did. We ran an article in today's *Ledger,* and it's getting a lot of traction. Based on what we're reporting, his situation is somewhat bizarre, but politicians often have skeletons in their closets. I'll admit, his was more colorful than most," Lloyd said with a chuckle.

"Is that the only one of Ron's opponents that you covered in the *Ledger*?"

"Yes," Lloyd paused, pondering the intent behind Stephanie's question. "Did you hear about something else?"

"Joel made me aware of a news item on one of the political gossip websites he frequents. It detailed a story about Miriam Hardwick."

"Miriam Hardwick? Another one of Ron's opponents?"

"She seems to have a habit of meeting male escorts via social media then hooking up with them in person."

"What? She seems so strait-laced."

"Those that appear to be buttoned-up and quiet are often the ones that have something wild going on in their spare time."

"How accurate is the information?"

"The article included some back-and-forth between her and one of her escorts. I'm not sure how the gossip site got access to it, but her DMs are all over social media. I'm surprised one of the reporters at the *Ledger* didn't pick up on it yet."

"Wow, two of Ron's opponents will be out of the race in a matter of days. How lucky is that?" Lloyd asked rhetorically.

"Too lucky if you ask me. I'm getting an eerie feeling that some machinations are going on behind the scenes. By whom, I'm not sure. But coincidences like this don't usually happen—not this fast anyway."

Lloyd thought that Stephanie had a point. "Have you discussed this with Ron?"

"Not yet. I wanted to talk to you first. How do you think we should handle it?"

"Ron definitely needs to be made aware of the status of his competition. It could be good news, you know."

"I'm hoping that's the extent of it. I just have a funny feeling..." Stephanie grimaced.

"Let's give Ron a call and see what he thinks about it," Lloyd said as he took out his cell phone and called. Ron picked up right away.

"Hi, Lloyd. How's it going?"

Lloyd put the call on speaker. "Everything's good on our end. I'm standing here with Stephanie, and she has some news."

"Hope it's good news, but I have a feeling that's not a guarantee."

Stephanie spoke next. "Ron, two of your opponents will likely be dropping out of the race soon."

"Really? That's good news, right? What happened?"

"They were both involved in scandalous activities that they won't be able to explain away. The media will have a feeding frenzy, and they'll have no choice but to drop out."

"Well, the fewer competitors, the better, right?" Ron was an eternal optimist.

"Don't you think it's strange that both of them have to drop out so soon?"

"It's strange but not unprecedented. Let's count our blessings and keep the campaign rolling. Have you prepared any sort of statement from the campaign?"

Stephanie decided to take Ron's cue and get back to business. "Not yet. I was going to issue a blanket 'no comment' press release once the news breaks everywhere. It's best to steer clear of both sordid affairs."

"See, that's why I made you my campaign manager. You're handling things beautifully. Is there anything else? I'm about to go into a fundraising event at one of the donors' mansions in Austin."

Stephanie shrugged and looked at Lloyd. "No, that's it. Enjoy yourself, and let me know how it goes," she said, ending the call.

"Ron's so focused on his campaign that he may not see some red flags that pop up here and there. That's why he has us—to watch his back," said Lloyd. "We'll both keep an eye out for anything else that appears to be out of the ordinary."

Stephanie nodded. "I agree, although I'm still not fully convinced this is nothing. I just have a funny feeling..."

CHAPTER 49

Charles had been back in the office for weeks and had been following his usual reporting routine. But he was still in a funk, disappointed about reaching a dead-end on the AmFree story. He hoped some news about the super PAC would eventually resurface. He was reviewing his incoming email when he saw Chelsea walking in his direction. She was a welcome distraction from the humdrum leads in his email inbox.

"Morning, Chelsea. Have you gotten used to the routine at the *Ledger* yet?"

"Sort of. I wonder if you could help me with something. I received a tip on a news story and wondered how I can know whether or not it's legitimate."

"The most important thing is that you consider the source. Who'd the tip come from, and what's it about?"

"That's just it. I'm not sure where it came from because the email address doesn't have a name attached to it. It's from concernedcitizen911@aol.com."

"Well, there's your first clue. AOL is nearly defunct. The only people who still use it are over the age of fifty. What was the tip?"

"It was about Marty Price, who's running in the Senate race. There's some video footage of him with a young woman, Melanie Lancaster, who's clearly not his wife. The email said he has two love children with this woman, but apparently, she and her children have disappeared. You know what they say: The first suspect is the husband or lover when someone seemingly vanishes into thin air."

"Hmmm…could be something to it. Let me take a look at what the *concerned citizen* sent you. If I think there's something there, we can work on the story together and share the byline, okay?" Charles had been hoping for some one-on-one time with Chelsea and couldn't believe the good fortune that had come his way.

Charles opened the video first and was astonished by what he saw. Price and his mistress, Melanie, were engaged in vigorous sexual activity. Their faces were both clearly visible. After they had satisfied their carnal urges, their conversation focused on the—not one but two—children they shared. She was putting pressure on him to make their relationship public…or else. He was not pleased.

Now Melanie and her two children were missing. The neighbors hadn't seen them in several days, and her family members were anxious and fearful about what had happened. Price would be in the media's crosshairs, if he wasn't already. But the fact that Price was one of Ron Singleton's opponents raised his journalistic antenna. He went to Chelsea's desk to give her his informed opinion.

"Chelsea, I believe you have the makings of a news story, one that could be in the *Ledger* for several days with continuous coverage. Let's go talk to Lloyd about it," he said and nodded toward Lloyd's office. Chelsea followed Charles in that direction. Lloyd's door was open, and he was at his desk, as usual.

"Lloyd, Chelsea received a tip about a story that you'll want to see. If we can verify some of the facts, the *Ledger* would be the first to break the story. It's about the Texas Senate race."

That really caught Lloyd's attention. Ron's race had another twist to it. "Is it about one of Ron Singleton's opponents?" Lloyd asked.

"Yes, Marty Price."

"That makes three out of four."

"What do you mean?"

"Two of his opponents were already involved in scandals that will force them out of the race. Is Marty Price also involved in a scandal?"

"You could definitely call it that. Someone sent Chelsea video footage of Price and his side chick in bed. But now his side chick and her two children are missing. Price is the children's father."

"Who's the source?"

"The sender of the video is anonymous, but the footage is clear."

"I wonder why whoever acquired the footage sent it to Chelsea." Lloyd looked in Chelsea's direction. "No offense, Chelsea, but new reporters are rarely the recipients of this kind of explosive news."

"Maybe they thought the information wouldn't be scrutinized as much," Charles offered.

"Well, that's not going to be the case. Since Chelsea received the email, the two of you can work on confirming some of the details. Talk to the woman's neighbors and family members to confirm the affair. Find out exactly when she and the kids went missing. Then write a draft of the story and send it to me for final editing and approval."

"Thanks, Mr. Palmer, for allowing me to work on the story. It will be my first major byline," Chelsea said cheerfully.

"You're welcome. The two of you need to get busy because I'd like to have the draft by five o'clock tomorrow," Lloyd replied as Charles and Chelsea nodded and left his office.

Lloyd wanted to call Stephanie immediately, but he couldn't. He'd have to wait until he got home to add to the anxiety she was already experiencing with two of Ron's opponents caught up in scandals almost simultaneously. Stephanie would be skeptical that an unfortunate mishap involving a third opponent of Ron's could be a mere coincidence.

CHAPTER 50

Bishop Samuel Rutherford Jones III was elated after hearing the news that two of his opponents in the Senate race would soon be dropping out. When he had decided to file his statement of candidacy for the Senate race five weeks earlier, he estimated his chances were less than thirty percent. There were five declared candidates including him, but the one who presented the greatest challenge was Ron Singleton, who was well financed and well regarded. Now that there were only three remaining candidates, he might have a real chance to win.

He'd presented the idea of his running for office to his congregation a couple of months earlier right after his Sunday morning message. The members of the House of the Living God Cathedral of Love gave him a standing ovation and thunderous applause. They were behind him one hundred percent!

Several dozen of them had volunteered to work on his campaign, which allowed him to keep his expenses to a minimum. He realized mixing politics and piety could be perceived as unethical, but he made sure there was separation of church and state. He kept their work at his campaign office separate from his ministry to their spiritual needs.

He had spent Saturday night perfecting his Sunday morning message and was prepared to deliver a powerful exhortation on the benefits of supporting their spiritual leader—him. Jones made sure the ministers at the three satellite locations were all singing from the same hymn book. That Sunday morning, his delivery was powerful and passionate. He stayed afterward to shake the hands of the parishioners as they left the sanctuary.

Meanwhile, the finance chair of the San Antonio location had left the building a tad late. Maintaining his position as chair was one of the most important assignments he'd ever had. He didn't want to be ousted and replaced by one of his assistant chairs who was eagerly waiting in the wings. Traveling on I-10 at well over the speed limit so he could arrive at the Cathedral headquarters on time, the finance chair lost control of his vehicle and hit the guardrail. His SUV rolled over multiple times and landed on the median. The car burst into flames, along with the driver and Bishop Jones's political aspirations.

CHAPTER 51

Michael could scarcely believe the Committee's good fortune. All four of Ron Singleton's opponents were vanquished in a matter of weeks, with the most recent one's campaign imploding without any interference whatsoever from the Committee. He couldn't believe one poor guy had lost his life trying to rush a bag of money to a church! Not only was Bishop Jones's political career in shambles, but his days as a viable church leader were probably also numbered.

Now the pathway was clear for Ron's victory in the fall. The fact that Ron was the last man standing and had raised more than twenty million dollars since launching his candidacy would discourage others from entering the race.

Michael was also pleasantly surprised at how adept Ron was at campaigning, especially after his initial hesitation to accept the Committee's offer. He was having fun out on the campaign trail and was so busy glad-handing with potential voters he could care less about the details behind the scenes. He'd left all that to Stephanie's discretion, who, surprisingly from Michael's perspective, was running a fairly tight ship. She had a keen attention to detail and didn't suffer fools. Joel had found that out in a hurry when he tried to add two of his inexperienced—and incompetent—friends to the campaign payroll. Stephanie had handed them their walking papers without hesitation.

Stephanie's apparent proficiency as campaign manager could present a problem down the road. The crux of

Michael's scheme depended on her being so overwhelmed she would quit. He might have to think of another way to get her to resign so Joel could take her place. With Ron's opponents on the sidelines, Michael had more time to consider other options. Like Joel, he, too, was biding his time.

CHAPTER 52

"Lloyd, all four of Ron's competitors in the Senate race have dropped out due to scandals within six weeks of the start of the campaign," Stephanie posited a few nights later as they shared their nightly reading time before going to sleep. She'd been keeping late hours at the campaign office, and bedtime was often the only opportunity for them to discuss the day's developments. "I know I'm an amateur when it comes to politics, but this seems unprecedented. Is it?"

Lloyd was on his laptop and had been checking the *Ledger*'s click board. The top three stories were Bishop Jones's finance chair's untimely death, Marty Price's missing side chick and children, and Timothy McPherson's nude backside, in that order. It was unusual for all of the top three stories to be political in nature, but all three were salacious, which the readers loved. The kinds of stories that caused them to gawk, click, and share.

"I agree that it's highly unusual, but you don't really think all of these incidents were related and engineered by someone, do you? Especially the car accident involving the member of Bishop Jones's church...Who could possibly manipulate all of these different incidents? It would require a tremendous amount of coordination and resources." Lloyd's question was largely rhetorical. He didn't expect Stephanie to have an answer that would satisfy either of them.

Then Lloyd remembered the pattern Charles had discovered months ago involving another political campaign.

"You know, Charles noticed something similar with another campaign where the opponents seemed to flame out one by one akin to what's happening with Ron's campaign. He found that the winning candidates all received large sums from a political action committee called AmFree."

"Was he able to track down the funding source for AmFree or any of the decision makers?" Stephanie asked warily.

"He thought he had a lead, but his source left the country for God only knows where and for how long. The trail ended with him, so Charles stopped the background reporting he was doing. He was out of the office for almost a week, and with my budget being so limited, I couldn't spare him any longer than that.

"I'm violating all kinds of conflicts of interest by even talking about this, but there's no way I'd keep anything from you if I thought it would make a difference. We just have to continue to be careful and only discuss this when we're at home."

Stephanie's anxiety was palpable. "You don't think Ron is in any kind of danger, do you?"

"I don't know why he would be. His background is as clean as a whistle—no scandals or skeletons that I know of, and I've known Ron since college. He didn't even smoke weed back in the day." Lloyd chuckled thinking about how strait-laced Ron had been even in his early twenties. He had been all about engineering and getting his degree. His family had been counting on him being the first to graduate from college.

"I sure hope you're right. I told you I have a really funny feeling, especially based on how things have transpired."

Lloyd gave her a hug. "Everything will be fine," he said to reassure her and himself as he turned off the light so they could go to sleep. They held each other close as they slept, knowing that they were together as one regardless of any challenges that might be right around the corner.

As the days went by, Stephanie continued to work long hours as Ron's campaign manager. Everything was falling into place. His campaign coffers continued to grow from the donations he was receiving from around the country. Small donations of fewer than fifty dollars were the lifeblood of his campaign. Many of his donors were contributing small amounts every month or every pay period.

The following week, Stephanie was working late at the campaign headquarters and went into Joel's office to check the daily media report he had generated. Joel kept track of every mention of Ron in the media, whether the coverage emanated from one of the larger television networks or a feature story was written on him in a small community newspaper.

While she was at Joel's desk, she noticed his computer was still logged on and the password had already been entered, so she decided to take a look at some of his campaign files. She noticed a folder marked "Campaign Account," opened it, and saw a completely different bank account and financial statements than the ones she was privy to. The account balance was more than twenty million dollars.

This was what she had feared all along. The same thing that had happened to Donna Brazile—the Black woman who had managed Al Gore's presidential campaign more than twenty years ago—was happening to her. She wasn't in charge of the finances after all—it was all an illusion—and this was a circumstance that, for her, was totally unacceptable. She wasn't going to be undermined by Joel, Michael, or anyone else. But she wouldn't confront Joel about it just yet, not until after she discussed it with Lloyd. Lloyd would know what to do.

CHAPTER 53

The next morning Joel arrived at the office earlier than usual, at seven o'clock. Volunteers would be arriving at eight o'clock to call registered voters and ask for their support for the Singleton campaign. The support could be contributing monetarily, posting a yard sign, telling their friends and neighbors, or simply voting. In an era where everyone had cell phones and blocked or didn't answer unrecognized phone numbers, cold calling was getting a bit tricky. But the mother lode was reaching older Texans over the age of sixty. They had a tendency to answer their phones and were more reliable voters than were those voters labeled Gen Z, Gen X, or Millennials.

Joel walked into his office, sat down at his laptop, and immediately knew something was amiss. He thought he had logged off of his computer so no one could access it in his absence. Then he remembered: He'd been on a phone call when he left the office and had forgotten to log off. When he'd left, the only one still at the office was Stephanie. Stephanie…if she had accessed his hard drive, there was no telling what she had seen.

He soon had his answer. The secret file on his laptop that contained the information for the bank account Michael had assigned him was still open in the background. Stephanie had seen the file and, apparently, didn't mind if he found out about it since she had kept it open. How could he have been so careless? Michael would not be pleased, and that was an understatement. Their plan of complete secrecy was about to unravel.

Joel hesitated to deliver the bad news to Michael for fear of being demoted or jettisoned entirely from Michael's vast web of influence. Joel had already mapped out his future, and the sky was the limit. Piggybacking off Michael's connections, Joel expected to be running a national campaign soon, maybe even a presidential campaign. That's where the big bucks rolled in, and he could be making fifty thousand dollars a month in consulting fees.

He weighed his options and concluded that it was better to tell Michael sooner rather than later. If the pill was going to be bitter, he might as well swallow it now. Joel called Michael using one of his burner phones.

"Good morning, Joel. If you're calling me this early, it can't be good news," Michael said, always cutting to the chase.

"It's not, but I thought you should know right away." Joel paused then exhaled. "Stephanie accessed the secret campaign bank account information that is on my computer."

There was complete silence on the phone for a full thirty seconds. Michael's response was pointed. It was clear that he was furious. "You didn't word your statement correctly."

"I don't know what you mean," Joel replied sheepishly.

"You should have said you left the account file exposed, which is a gross dereliction of your duties."

Joel was quick to correct himself, hoping that placating Michael would work to his benefit. "You're right of course. I left the file exposed. I have no excuse. I just wanted to let you know so you could...you know...tell me how to handle it."

"Say nothing for now to Stephanie or anyone else. Then check with your computer guy and tell him to encrypt the file so no one can access it without multiple layers of security."

"I'll take care of having the file encrypted right away, and my lips are sealed. But what if Stephanie asks me about it?"

"I don't think she will. If she was going to confront you, she would have done so immediately. But if she does, tell her the bank account was set up to replenish the funds for the account she uses to be sure money is always available. That's a plausible explanation and should satisfy her."

"Remember what I told you about politics," Michael added. "Politics isn't about the truth. It's about telling the story you want people to believe."

"But what if my explanation *doesn't* satisfy her?" Joel asked in a pleading tone.

"Don't worry about that. Just leave it to me, and it will be handled."

"Okay, I'll leave it in your hands." Joel had the assurance of knowing that Michael always solved whatever problems occurred. In the seven years Joel had been part of his team, Michael's track record had been flawless.

Michael ended the call and contemplated his next move. He should have followed his instincts and insisted that Stephanie not be a part of Ron's campaign—certainly not as manager. His instincts never failed him, and not following them was a miscalculation on his part. That wouldn't happen again.

Now he would have to take other measures because clearly this problem was not going to solve itself. Stephanie was not a shrinking violet; her devotion to Ron had provided her with an unflappable disposition. Michael gave specific instructions to the media mogul, who passed the assignment on to Romulus.

CHAPTER 54

Romulus had received his marching orders from the Committee. Stephanie Palmer was a problem that needed to be handled. His instructions were to create a life-threatening situation, ensuring that although she would be harmed, the injuries would be relatively minor and not result in death. The media mogul was explicit about the care that should be taken in carrying out the assignment.

Romulus had the perfect pair in mind for this project and decided to assign this task to two Russian operatives, Ivan and Konstantin, he had contracted for jobs that involved explosives. They were actually twin brothers and two of his best fixers. Their expertise lay in their precision.

Anyone with limited intelligence could murder someone using explosives, but it took special skills and training to inflict just the right amount of damage without exceeding the overall objective. The twins' fees were a bit on the high side but well worth the cost. The Russians would plant an explosive at the Singleton campaign headquarters in the area farthest away from Stephanie's office and set the timer to go off at nine o'clock at night. The other campaign staffers and volunteers left the office by seven thirty, so she'd be all alone.

Romulus gave them a week to complete the task. The twins had already surveilled the campaign office for three consecutive nights to verify the approximate times each staffer left for the evening. Once Romulus passed the ball to the Russians, there would be no further communication between them. They'd receive half the funds as a down payment and the other half when the job was done. Romulus used one of his many offshore accounts to wire the Russians the funds for the job. As was their usual practice, they'd go to a check cashing facility to pick up the down payment for their initial out-of-pocket expenses.

CHAPTER 55

Rudo Hamisi was experiencing the final days of his summer trip to Houston. He'd been there for several months, and it was almost time to visit one of the other cities he frequented. The weather in Zimbabwe was the opposite of that in the United States. The coldest month in his homeland, which was in the southern part of Africa, was July; the hottest was November. It was August, one of Houston's hottest months, and since Hamisi preferred warm climates, he was considering either Memphis or Charleston as his next destination.

Hamisi had transferred some of his funds from one of his overseas accounts to Houston for his travel expenses. He went to one of his many designated twenty-four-hour check cashing facilities to retrieve the money. He usually went in the evening, when there were fewer people inside and the lines were shorter. When he entered, he was third in line behind two other customers.

The elderly African wasn't in the habit of listening to other people's conversations, but he noticed the two men in line ahead of him were speaking in Russian. It had been a few years since he'd spoken or heard the language, and his Russian was a bit rusty. He understood Russian better than he spoke it, but he had retained some of his proficiency since his days as a tutor.

He noticed that the men were identical twins, and their banter included something about a job they were doing. Then he overheard them mention the name Stephanie Palmer. He listened more intently as they continued in Russian, “The job is supposed to be quick, using untraceable explosives. We get paid half now, and the other half will be wired after there’s proof that the job was done. We’ll plant the device during the wee hours after midnight tonight, when no prying eyes are in the area. He’ll have his proof tomorrow night when the device is detonated.”

Being careful not to react, Hamisi continued to listen as they discussed their plans, assuming no one in the vicinity had a grasp of the Russian language. Hamisi had heard several news stories about Stephanie Palmer being the manager for Lloyd’s friend Ron’s campaign. The Russians were discussing a plan to bomb the office while Stephanie was working there late at night. He had to warn Lloyd.

After he’d conducted his business and received his funds from the wire transfer, Hamisi sent Lloyd a text message: *Make sure Stephanie is not at the headquarters tomorrow evening after seven o’clock. Danger.*

CHAPTER 56

It was after nine o'clock when Lloyd received Hamisi's text message. He was in his wind-down mode, attempting to read articles on his laptop and nearly falling asleep, but the text message was jarring. The sleepiness he had felt quickly vanished. Most of the time Hamisi's text messages were general in nature, often cryptic and usually not specific. This message about Stephanie suggested—no, more than suggested, asserted—that her life was in danger. He was quiet, nearly holding his breath, and Stephanie noticed.

"Lloyd, is something wrong?"

"Yes, you could say that. Something is very wrong."

She had heard the chime of his text message notification. "Does it have to do with the text message you just received?"

"Yes. It's from Hamisi, and he says for you not to work late at the office tomorrow. He then used the simple word *danger*."

Stephanie still didn't understand the relationship Lloyd and Hamisi had. It was almost like a father son connection. If Hamisi said something, Lloyd took it almost as gospel.

"Babe, how would Hamisi know anything about my working at the office? I don't understand this relationship you two have. Does he have a crystal ball?" Stephanie asked. She was puzzled and wanted answers.

"I don't know how Hamisi knows things, but he's always right—one hundred percent of the time. If he says there'll be danger tomorrow, I guarantee you there will be."

"What am I supposed to do about work tomorrow? What am I supposed to tell the staffers? Ron has a full schedule of activities."

"According to Hamisi, it's just the evening you have to be worried about. You don't have to tell the staff anything. After all, you're the boss."

"Do you think this has something to do with the secret file I found on Joel's computer?" Stephanie had told Lloyd about the file the same night she saw it. They both had agreed to take a wait-and-see approach. "I haven't confronted him about it, and for all I know, he doesn't even know I saw it."

"Possibly. All I know is that Hamisi wasn't ambiguous. His statements were very specific. You being in the office tomorrow night is out of the question."

"Lloyd, I wish I had the same confidence in Hamisi that you do. It just sounds too incredible. But I do have confidence in you, and I know that you'd move heaven and earth to make sure I was safe," Stephanie said, pausing briefly as she thought of a compromise.

"So this is what I'm going to do. I will go to work tomorrow and act as though nothing is wrong. I'll take the staff out for happy hour as a reward for their hard work, and we'll all go to one of the bars in the area. We'll leave at six o'clock, and I'll lock the office for the night. After happy hour, I'll come home. Will that satisfy you?"

"It will set my mind at ease. After all, by six o'clock, most offices are closed anyway. You and the staff deserve a night off and a little bit of enjoyment to go with it."

"What about Ron? Should we tell him?" Stephanie asked.

"Not until we have something more definitive," Lloyd responded. "He's been traveling across the state for the past couple of weeks and won't be back at the campaign headquarters until next week. Of course, if something does happen tomorrow night, he'll be among the first to know."

CHAPTER 57

Stephanie arrived at the office early the next morning ahead of most of the staffers. During the course of the day, she tried not to be distracted by the prospect of imminent danger at the headquarters. It wasn't easy to act as though nothing out of the ordinary had occurred behind the scenes. As she sat at her desk trying to focus on the campaign issues before her, she found herself sleepwalking through the day, hoping and praying Hamisi's intentions were good but he was simply wrong about his assertions.

She waited until the lunch hour to announce to the staff that their reward for their hard work was a visit to Butler's Bar & Grill for happy hour and that the campaign was picking up the tab. This unexpected group outing put the staffers in a joyful mood for the remainder of the day.

The staff and volunteers were very dedicated, a group of mostly twenty-somethings that were driven largely by their idealism. The volunteers were, of course, using their personal time, but sometimes Stephanie felt like the staffers would work for free if that's what it took to get Ron elected. They were that committed to his campaign and what he stood for. They all deserved some rest and relaxation, but Stephanie wished it hadn't taken the prospect of a potential catastrophe for her to give them an after-work outing. They had earned it.

They all left the office at around six o'clock and walked the three short blocks to Butler's. In addition to a wide selection of beer, wine, and cocktails, Butler's also had a delectable selection of appetizers. Stephanie had given instructions that they could eat as much as they wanted and they could each order three drinks on the house. No need to create a media event leading to a headline: *Singleton Campaign Staffers Caught Drunk After Work.*

They all stayed at Butler's until well after eight thirty—all except for Joel.

Joel left the bar a few minutes before nine o'clock and returned to the headquarters. He had forgotten some files he planned to review at home and wanted to retrieve them before leaving the area.

While he was in his office looking through the file drawer at his desk, he was knocked off his feet by a riveting explosion. He lay on the floor, dazed and disoriented, for a few minutes. There was a massive hole in the wall adjacent to him and plenty of sheetrock and debris on the floor. His leg was wounded and he had difficulty standing, yet he felt lucky to be alive. But the area around him was unstable. An antique floor lamp that had been positioned in the corner of the room then fell on his head, knocking him unconscious. The blow to his head caused a severe brain hemorrhage, and within minutes, Joel was dead.

CHAPTER 58

Stephanie was having a great time laughing it up with the staffers when they heard a series of firetruck and ambulance sirens whizzing by. "Must be a bad car accident," she said to Courtney, who was in charge of the campaign phone banks.

"Must be," said Courtney as she looked out Butler's front window. "It looks like they're going in the direction of the headquarters."

Stephanie had just taken another sip of her apple margarita when she saw a Houston Police Department SUV speed by, its lights whirring. Her heart sank as she went out of the bar's front door and looked down the street. There was a billow of smoke visible at the spot where the Ron Singleton Campaign Office stood. Other staffers came outside and gathered together, giving each other support.

"You all stay here," Stephanie directed, "and I'll go see what's going on." She ran toward the office, and as she got closer, she saw that there was damage to one side of the building and smoke emanating from the rooftop. The first responders were already on the scene, and the fire department had hosed down the flames, which were limited. There was mostly smoke, but the building had suffered a great deal of damage. She spoke to the police officer who had placed yellow crime scene tape around the building.

"Officer, I'm Stephanie Palmer, and I'm the manager of this office. Do you know what happened?"

"We won't know the full details until the investigation is complete, but it looks like some explosives were planted and detonated."

"Oh my God," Stephanie said shakily, realizing that without Hamisi's text message, she would probably have been inside. Just then she saw the EMTs bringing out a gurney with what appeared to be a body on it under a white sheet.

"Is that one of the first responders?" Stephanie asked. "None of our staffers were inside. We all went to Butler's Bar & Grill after work."

"He appears to be one of yours," the officer replied. "Maybe you can identify him. It looks like he may have survived the explosion but something fell on his head."

The EMT stopped the gurney in front of Stephanie, and she took a deep breath as they removed the sheet. It was Joel. "Oh my God," said Stephanie as she burst into tears.

CHAPTER 59

While Stephanie was at the happy hour with her staff, Lloyd decided to work late at the Houston *Ledger*'s office, where he heard the message come across the police scanner that he kept there so he could quickly assign reporters to crime and accident scenes. *Explosion downtown on Travis Street at the Singleton campaign headquarters.*

Lloyd had been hoping against hope that Hamisi had somehow gotten the wrong information or perhaps misunderstood whatever he had overheard or was told. To Lloyd's dismay, Hamisi's text message had been spot on. He immediately picked up his cell phone and called Stephanie. She picked up on the first ring, and it was clear she had been crying.

"Steph, are you okay? I just heard about the explosion on the police scanner."

"I'm fine, but I feel lucky to be alive," she replied between sniffles. "Joel wasn't so fortunate."

"What are you saying?"

"Joel's dead, Lloyd. The police officers said he seemed to survive the blast, but the lamp in his office fell on his head and caused swelling of the brain. That's what actually killed him."

"Babe, I am so, so sorry, but you don't know how relieved I am that you're all right."

Lloyd paused. “Hamisi has never been wrong about anything. I told you that, but I was actually hoping that the message he sent me was some sort of mistake.”

“We’ll need to call Ron right away and break the news to him,” Lloyd said. “I’ll call him myself. Do you think you’re okay to drive home?”

“I am. First I need to go back to Butler’s and break the sad news to the staff.”

“Okay, but then please go home. I’ll feel a lot better knowing you’re safe and sound.”

“I promise that I will.”

Lloyd located Ron’s phone number among his contacts and initiated the call. This was going to be tough. Ron answered after two rings, sounding incredibly cheerful.

“Hey, Lloyd, how’ve you been? I’ve been meaning to reach out to you, but the campaign has kept me really busy.”

“I’m fine, but I have some bad news to deliver. Are you somewhere you can talk?”

“Right now I’m in my car on my way to my hotel. Nothing’s happened to Shirley, has it?”

“No, but something almost happened to Stephanie. Ron, your campaign office was bombed tonight.”

“Bombed? What do you mean?”

“Someone planted an explosive, and the blast happened around nine o’clock.”

“Was Stephanie there?” Ron asked apprehensively. “She normally works late and is the last one to leave.”

“No, she decided to take the staffers to happy hour after work. But Joel, the assistant manager, is dead.”

“Joel? I can’t believe it. He didn’t go to the happy hour event?”

"Yes, he was there, but apparently he returned to the office. Shortly thereafter, the explosion occurred."

"I can't believe this has happened. I was planning to stay overnight here in San Antonio, but I'm going to drive back home tonight. I need to be there."

"There's not much you can do now, but I understand you wanting to be here. Just be careful since it's already late and you won't get back to Houston until after midnight."

"I need to call Stephanie."

"I've already spoken to her. She's a bit shaken up, but she's okay and will be headed for home. You can talk to her in the morning. It's best that you're not distracted and are able to focus on driving home."

Just then, Ron received an incoming call from Shirley. "Okay, Lloyd. I'll see you both tomorrow. Shirley's calling, so I guess she heard the news."

CHAPTER 60

Ron had plenty of time to think during his drive from San Antonio to Houston. His office being bombed jolted him back in time to the 1960s, when African-American churches, homes, and other institutions were often bombed. That sort of thing had rarely happened in recent decades, and he'd experienced no racial incidents while on the campaign trail. Was the bombing racial in nature? Was it political? Was it personal? He had no answers, only questions.

But one thing was certain: The campaign was simply too dangerous to proceed. He would not endanger the lives of his long-time friends, family or campaign workers for his personal political advancement. He simply wouldn't expose them to such unimaginable treachery. He'd call Michael in the morning and tell him he was withdrawing from the race and shutting down his campaign.

He arrived at home at about one in the morning and drove his car into the garage. Shirley greeted him as he entered the house and gave him a bear hug. "I'm so glad you're here and unharmed. Is Stephanie okay?"

"She's fine, but one of the campaign staffers was killed. Shirley, I'm dropping out of the race. I wasn't expecting my running for office to be a life-threatening exercise. There was so much good I wanted to do, but I won't put any of you in danger."

"I was gung-ho when you told me you were running, and things seemed to be going so well. But you can still make a difference in the Texas legislature, where you've been all along. Michael Goldberg offered you a chance to run, and you took it. I agree with you that now it's time to move on."

"You mean so much to me, Shirley. You've always been my cheerleader, counselor, and lover all rolled into one," he said as he kissed her passionately on her lips.

"Now let's go to bed. We'll deal with all of this in the morning."

CHAPTER 61

When Ron woke up the next morning, his first task was to call Michael and tell him he was shutting down the campaign. Ron was surprised he hadn't received a call from Michael, if for no other reason than to check on his well-being and that of his staffers. Joel was part of the team Michael had recommended so he had to have heard the news of Joel's death by now.

Michael answered right away. "Good morning, Ron. I was planning to call you, but you beat me to it. I heard about the explosion at your campaign office on the early morning news. Poor Joel. I've known him for years, and I'll break the news to his family. Do the authorities have any leads? Was it caused by a gas leak or faulty wiring?"

Michael had given specific instructions to the media mogul to hire someone who would get the job just right. Now it was all a mess. Good help was increasingly hard to find.

"The fire marshal says it was caused by an explosive device someone planted. In other words, someone intentionally tried to kill me or my staffers. This is serious, Michael."

"It certainly is. Once we move the campaign office to a different location, we'll hire twenty-four-hour security to ensure everyone's safety."

"There's not going to be another campaign office."

"What do you mean?"

"I'm withdrawing from the race, Michael. I'm not going to put anyone's life in danger for the sake of political ambition."

"But I just told you we would hire a security firm to make sure everyone is safe."

"That's not good enough. I'm withdrawing and will be calling a press conference and making an announcement this afternoon."

This wasn't going at all the way Michael had planned. His specially selected candidates didn't quit on him. It just didn't happen. He wasn't going to let it happen.

"Ron, I don't think you understand. We've invested a considerable sum in your campaign with the caveat that you would be in it for the long haul. The millions of dollars we've spent would need to be repaid if you drop out of the race."

"What do you mean the money would have to be repaid?"

"That was part of the contract you signed with us when we hired your staff and bankrolled your expenses. At least five million dollars has been spent so far by your campaign. How do you plan to pay it back?"

Ron was speechless. He remembered signing some papers, but he had thought they were just leases and employment contracts for the staff.

Michael knew he had Ron on the ropes. "Once you've had a chance to think about this more clearly, I'm sure you'll see things my way. Otherwise, your future could include bankruptcy and the seizure of all your assets. Talk it over with your wife, and get back to me tomorrow," he said and hung up.

Ron stood in his den for a moment and stared at his phone. Did Michael just threaten him with financial ruin if he withdrew from the race? It sure sounded like it.

He and Shirley would have to rethink their plans. But first he'd talk to Lloyd and see if he had any ideas about how to move forward.

CHAPTER 62

Ron called Lloyd and informed him about the ultimatum he had received from Michael. "Lloyd, is there anything I can do? I should have known Michael's offer was too good to be true. Now he thinks he owns me—or at least owns my political career."

"We're not going to let that happen. As the editor of the *Ledger*, I can't get too directly involved with this any more than I have already. But Michael may not know that, which gives us leverage."

"At the *Ledger*, we've been working on some background about a political action committee, and Michael is involved. I'm sure of it. But the bits and pieces have been hard to put together. Whoever is behind the PAC has gone to a lot of trouble to keep it out of the public eye. Let's get Michael back on the phone on a three-way call, and let me do most of the talking."

Ron rang Michael's phone number and Michael picked up immediately. "So, Ron, have you had a chance to reconsider?"

"Actually, Mr. Goldberg, you're speaking with Lloyd Palmer, editor at the *Ledger*. I have some information that may be of interest to you."

"Mr. Palmer, it's a pleasure meeting you by phone since I don't believe we've ever met in person."

"You might not think it's such a pleasure after you hear what I have to say."

"I'm all ears," Michael responded wanly.

"One of my reporters has been doing some background research on a group calling itself AmFree. They finance dozens of political campaigns, and their candidates have a surprisingly high rate of success. It seems their opponents drop out under mysterious circumstances."

"Really? What does that have to do with me?"

"Well, it seems your old college buddy, Joseph Wallace, is the registered agent for the PAC. My reporter tracked him down but lost the trail. But I'm sure if we put more resources behind our investigative reporting, we'll peel back the layers of the onion and get to the crux of what the organization does as well as its funding sources."

Lloyd was bluffing because the *Ledger* didn't have the budget for a full-scale investigation. He was counting on the fact that Michael didn't know that.

"What do you want?" Michael asked, his anger bubbling up to a level where it could explode.

"Ron will drop out of the race, and you will take no action against him. Otherwise, I'll put my reporter back on the AmFree story this afternoon. So do we have an understanding or not?"

Michael hesitated. "We have an understanding," he said and abruptly ended the call.

Lloyd knew that backing off an explosive story like this one was a conflict of interest, but he wouldn't put his family or his friends in jeopardy over a potential news story.

EPILOGUE

Michael decided to back off…for now. The media mogul assured him that the team that planted the explosive was long gone, so any investigative measures taken by the authorities would lead nowhere.

He couldn't believe he'd been bested by a former civil servant and a newspaper editor. Men at that level never operated in his world—he was on another, much higher plane. There would be other Ron Singletons out there for the Committee to manage. He simply couldn't afford for AmFree to be under a large media microscope and would live to fight another day.

Ron decided he was satisfied being a Texas legislator. He'd dipped his toe in the well-spring of national politics, and the unknown factors were simply too risky.

Stephanie returned to school in the fall, educating a classroom full of sixth graders. During her stint as a campaign manager, she had learned some valuable lessons she could use in the classroom and as the administrator of her homeowners' association.

Lloyd sent Hamisi a text message thanking him for saving his and Stephanie's lives once again. He still believed he could do some good as editor at the *Ledger*, the click board be damned.

Hamisi left Houston for parts unknown, but was determined to keep Lloyd Palmer safe. He'd always be watching.

AUTHOR'S NOTE

At age thirty, while living in Houston, I received a call from a prominent, politically connected real estate developer who invited me to lunch. For the two years prior to this phone call, I had been writing political opinion pieces for the local daily paper, and several of them had been prominently placed and published in their Sunday editions. As a result, I had been invited to be a commentator on local public affairs television and radio shows and to participate in community forums.

The call from the real estate developer came out of the blue, and I did not know him or his reputation. I told him I would call him back and let him know. After I made some inquiries, a close friend of mine said the developer was well connected and someone who was worth meeting. So I accepted his invitation to lunch, not knowing what our conversation would be about.

When I met him, I noticed he was several years older than I and very well dressed. We sat down at the table, and a few minutes after the initial small talk, he began his pitch. He said he had read my columns and was very impressed with my ability to analyze social and political issues. Then he stated the real reason for the meeting: "We want to make you a leader," he stated matter-of-factly. He specifically used the word *we*.

I was young and had little political experience, but I wasn't entirely naive. As a young entrepreneur, I had no interest in being under anyone's thumb, and the prospect of what he was offering held no interest for me whatsoever.

My response was: "Leaders come from the people; they work among the people, and the people decide who leads them. So, no, I would have no interest in anyone making me a leader."

He didn't press further, and there was little lunchtime conversation after that. I never heard from him again directly, although our paths did cross a few times at informal settings. But that encounter left an indelible impression on me about the nature of American politics and the power behind the throne with regard to our elected officials. I've never forgotten it.

When I decided to write the sequel to *The Genesis Files*, I thought of the "what ifs" with regard to that lunch meeting. What if I had said yes to his offer to groom me for leadership? What if I had run for office? What if I had gotten elected? What would my future have looked like? *Exodus From Treachery* is a fictional depiction of the suspenseful events that I imagine could have occurred had I accepted his offer.

If you enjoyed *Exodus From Treachery*, please post a review on Amazon, Goodreads, or wherever you provide your book reviews. As you can imagine, reviews are very important for future book sales. If you're a member of a book club, I'd love to have a Zoom discussion with your group. To schedule a Zoom meeting or to provide feedback about the book, please contact me via email at gwenrichardson123@gmail.com.

Made in the USA
Middletown, DE
07 November 2023

42134388R00166